THE MATCH
THE LEBLANC BROTHERS
LAYLA HAGEN

CW01431406

Copyright © 2025 by Layla Hagen

All rights reserved.

No portion of this book may be reproduced in any form without written permission from the publisher or author, except as permitted by U.S. copyright law.

CONTENTS

CHAPTER ONE
ZACHARY

"Uncle Zachary," my niece, Bella, said in a conspiratorial tone, "we need to talk."

I sat back in my chair, glancing at the rest of the family out of the corner of my eye. Everyone was chatting. I knew Bella had chosen this moment specifically, which meant she wanted to talk to me alone.

"Sure."

She glanced at the family too. Even though she was only ten years old, she already seemed so much more mature. These days, every time she said, "We need to talk," I braced myself, as I never knew what I'd be in for.

"Cricket, do you need anything?" my brother Chad asked.

"No, Daddy, I'm good." Bella sighed, giving me an exasperated look. "Thank you." Then she added in a whisper, "Maybe we should talk another time."

"Sure." I gave her a wink. "I promise I'll call."

Bella nodded and went back to her seat.

There were six of us LeBlanc brothers, and Bella went to each uncle for specific advice. She typically came to me when she needed advice on "fixing" a problem—usually something related to her friends. She went straight to Julian when she wanted something her dad wouldn't approve of—like more sweets. Chad had been a single dad for a long time, so we'd all been very involved in her upbringing.

"All right, everyone, food's here," Chad exclaimed as the waiters arrived with the huge pots of gumbo and put them on the table.

The perks of owning LeBlanc & Broussard, one of the most famous restaurants on Royal Street in New Orleans, was that we often came here to eat. Today, the entire family had gathered. It wasn't a special occasion—we simply liked getting together.

"You know, I still think the gumbo was better in our time," Isabeau said.

Celine sighed. "Oh, give it a rest, Isabeau. Scarlett is an excellent chef."

"Oh, I know. I was just saying." But she didn't press the point.

My grandmothers, Isabeau and Celine, had long been the chefs at LeBlanc & Broussard. They still took pride in their work even though they'd been retired for years. Currently, Chad's fiancée, Scarlett, was the chef. In my opinion, she was amazing. But Isabeau always felt the need to compete with other chefs. After so many years, it was ingrained in her. Or maybe it was just a chef thing.

My grandfathers were sitting next to their wives. Both of them snickered but didn't comment on Isabeau's remark.

As the waiter served everyone, I decided it was the right time to bring up a topic that had been at the back of my mind for a while. Since all of us brothers were currently running the Orleans Conglomerate, we often asked one another for advice about business. Our father had run it before us, and our grandparents before that. I wanted to hear everyone's opinion on this even though it wasn't, strictly speaking, a business decision.

"By the way," I said, "an opportunity came up."

"For business?" Xander asked, perking up.

I nodded. "It's what I already told you, Anthony, and Beckett at the confectionery. But I want to hear everyone else's opinion." That got the family's attention, and I continued. "So, there's a ranch by the bayou that specializes in therapy horses. They're looking for someone to partner with, as they need capital to renovate and so on. It appears to be a really good cause that helps a lot of people, and I'm interested in investing."

"What a wonderful idea," Isabeau said, clapping her hands in praise.

Xander frowned. "Wait, you actually want to spend time managing that? I figured you'd simply donate money. Why not just give them some bank and stay out of it?"

Out of all of us, Xander was the one who was most efficient. I admired that about him, but I also thought he was missing out on things. Although, he'd changed a lot since he'd met his fiancée, Bailey.

"So... a ranch with horses used for therapy purposes. That's so interesting," Mom said.

"I found out back when I volunteered as an EMT that using animals in therapy is a pretty common thing."

"You know, we always thought you might end up being a doctor," Isabeau said.

That didn't surprise me. As a teenager, I'd taken an EMT course and worked with the fire department's squad voluntarily all through college and even after I started interning in the family business. I'd enjoyed helping people and was very good at it. But running the shipping side of the business was no small feat, and I ultimately had to make a decision. Being a CEO didn't leave much time for extracurriculars. This ranch, though—the project simply beckoned to me.

"Is Grace Deveraux still interested in the ranch?" Anthony asked.

I nodded. "Yes."

The name Deveraux grated on my nerves.

Her brothers, Kyle and Beau, had swindled half the businesses they worked with. They weren't well thought of around town. Last year, Xander exposed them and their antics, and the two hadn't been heard from since.

"Do you know anything about Grace?" I asked, looking pointedly at my grandmothers. I'd asked around in my business circles but didn't get anything reliable. Everyone assumed she was like her brothers: arrogant, lacking integrity, and dismissive. I didn't like to assume, though. I wanted facts.

Isabeau narrowed her eyes. "She was Grace Cointreau until her divorce. She used to work in her family's company, but now I don't know what she does."

"I think she took a break from that," Celine added.

"You know her personally?" I asked. They were both social butterflies. If there was an event in New Orleans, chances were they either attended or knew someone who had.

Isabeau shook her head. "No, not at all. But the Deveraux name is well known."

"Grace didn't go to school with us, did she?" Anthony asked Beckett.

I remembered Kyle and Beau from school, but not Grace. Then again, if she was a few years younger, that was no surprise.

"She went to an all-girls school." That came from Celine. "It came up at a party years ago."

"You know a lot about her for someone who hasn't actually met her."

Celine smiled. "What can I say? My mind retains gossip."

But I didn't want to know gossip. I wanted to know what her business was—if she was the same as her brothers and why she was interested in the ranch. Apparently, I wasn't going to get that information from my family.

"Well, let's just all focus on food," Chad said as if reading my thoughts, just as the waiters came to serve everyone.

Having our offices above LeBlanc & Broussard was hands down the best idea we'd ever had. Chad, Anthony, Beckett, and I all worked here. Julian mostly stayed in the office he had behind his bar on Dumaine. Xander was in the business district. I, for one, had chosen this location simply because it was convenient. I often had food sent up for lunch—sometimes even dinner if we stayed late. I liked being in the French Quarter. In my opinion, it was the heartbeat of New Orleans.

After my family and I finished dinner, we all dispersed. I decided to pay Julian a visit at his bar rather than go straight home. On the way, I called my go-to person when I wanted a potential business partner vetted.

"Hi, Marcel," I said when he answered.

"Zachary LeBlanc. What an honor. What can I do for you?"

"I'm interested in a business opportunity, but someone else is too. Grace Deveraux."

"Of *that* Deveraux family?" Marcel asked.

"Yes. I want to invest in a ranch, and so does she."

"Right. You want a scoop on the competition."

His tone was already judgmental, which I didn't appreciate. I knew Kyle and Beau were swindlers, but as far as we knew, the rest of the family hadn't been involved.

"Text me the details of the ranch, and I'll get back to you soon," he said. "What exactly do you want to know?"

"What type of business she's doing and if she's legit."

He scoffed. "That'll be hard to find out if she's as good at hiding things as her brothers."

"Assume she has a clean slate and go from there."

"You always assume the best of people."

It was the way I did things, and it had never really failed me. I didn't understand why anyone would go through life assuming the worst of people. It had to be exhausting.

No matter what, I was looking forward to finding out more about this Grace Deveraux.

CHAPTER TWO
GRACE

"All right, everyone. This was productive," I told Alice and Keisha. They were my two right hands, and I couldn't function without them.

"I've got so many new ideas, Grace," Keisha said.

My skincare business was booming, and I couldn't be happier. I grinned. "I'm so excited!"

Alice nodded. "So are we. Your enthusiasm is contagious. But if it's okay with you, we're going to leave. It's pretty late."

I glanced at the clock and gasped. "Oh, I'm so sorry. I didn't want to keep you this long."

"No problem," Alice replied. "We got a lot accomplished, so it was worth the extra time."

Both of them were married and had kids, so they liked to be home for dinner. *Crap.* Ever since my divorce, I'd thrown all my effort and all my time into the business, which included working at odd hours. Sometimes I forgot other people needed to adhere to a schedule.

"Shoo, shoo, you two. Get out of here. I'm going to leave soon as well."

After we said our goodbyes and they left my office, I rose to my feet, tilting my neck from one side to the other, smiling at the view out of my floor-to-ceiling window. I loved being in the business district. It had such fresh energy. When I'd been looking for offices, I first considered the Quarter—it was one of my most beloved areas in the city—but I wanted something more modern. There were a lot of start-ups in this area. Granted, they focused on tech software, but I still enjoyed being around people who were creating something. Sometimes I couldn't believe I'd only started this business a year ago. It seemed much longer than that.

It was the fresh start I'd *so* needed.

My ex would hate seeing me so content. The day of the wedding, I had stars in my eyes and felt hopeful about the future. But it became harder and harder to keep my optimism as my marriage progressed. I'd been working in my family's company back then, in the marketing department. I'd been very good at my job, but my husband convinced me that it would be best if I were to stay at home and take care of him and, hopefully soon, our new family. Even today, I couldn't quite remember why I agreed to it. I'd always loved working. I loved being independent. But I'd been very much in love, and it seemed to make sense. If I were to get pregnant, I'd want to take some time off to be with the baby anyway.

Only, I didn't get pregnant. And the second I quit my job, my husband's attitude changed—as if my worth had somehow diminished and he could treat me any way he wanted.

But that was all in the past now. Even so, if I were being honest, it still hurt to think about everything I'd been through with him.

Grace Cointreau was Grace Deveraux again—not that that was doing me many favors these days. My brothers literally made a mess of everything. Some people were wary of associating with the Deveraux name, and after what those idiots had done, I really couldn't blame them. I'd encountered many hurdles when I was setting up the business. Thank God I had a very generous nest egg I'd saved up, because I hadn't wanted to ask my parents for any money. I was far too proud for that.

And speaking of fresh starts... I hurried to my desk and opened my laptop. Maybe it was a millennial thing, but I didn't like to check emails on my phone. I clicked on my inbox. *Darn.* There was no reply.

I'd recently seen an ad from a horse ranch specializing in assisted therapy. They were looking for someone to invest in their business, and I was very interested.

After my divorce, I went to therapy for a while—they used painting and dogs for healing purposes, and it had been wonderful. Gaston and Felicia's ranch served the same purpose—psychological therapy.

I'd sent them an email last week, and they replied that they'd get back to me but hadn't done so yet. I wanted to know details and if someone else was interested too.

Despite the hour, I decided to call them right away. Knowing me, by tomorrow morning, I would forget all about it and throw myself into the marketing of my new skincare line. To my delight, someone immediately answered.

"Hello."

"Hi, I'm Grace Deveraux."

"Oh, Ms. Deveraux. Yes. This is Gaston here. Sorry, we've been meaning to get back to you, but we've had our hands full."

"I figured it would be easier if I called."

"Yes, yes. Good idea. Thank you for calling and for your interest."

"Listen, I won't keep you long. I'd like to make an appointment so I could come visit the ranch."

"Sure, sure. I'll talk to my wife about it and see what the schedule is in the upcoming week. Do you prefer evenings or mornings?"

"I'm flexible. And I have a question. Is anyone else interested?"

"Yes, Zachary LeBlanc." The name was familiar, of course, and not just because LeBlanc was a common name in New Orleans. The LeBlancs and the Broussards were very well known in our community. One of the brothers, Xander, had been the one to put the paper trail together to prove my brothers had swindled money.

"I see" was all I said.

Why would a LeBlanc be interested in this? The Orleans Conglomerate had dozens of businesses already, and this would be so out of their realm.

"We're going to coordinate it so that both of you see it at the same time, if that's all right?"

"Sure, that makes sense."

For them, at least.

"By the way," he continued, "some guy called named Marcel."

"Right..."

"He said he's working with Zachary LeBlanc and started asking us about you."

I blinked, certain I'd heard him wrong. "I'm sorry, asking about *me*? Asking what?"

"If we've met you, what kind of person you are, if we can see ourselves doing business with you. If we've heard about your brothers'... er, ah... endeavors."

Well, not a total surprise. It wasn't as if the town hadn't been talking about it, but still, that was extremely unprofessional. Obviously, he wanted to give them a bad impression of me.

"I found the whole thing very odd," Gaston continued.

"Yes, it is," I agreed. I kept my fingers crossed that he would hold this against Zachary. I already disliked the man on principle. Who would do that to someone else simply because they were interested in the same investment opportunity? "Mr. Gaston—"

"You may just call me Gaston."

"Right. I'm an open book, and you can ask me anything."

There was a pause, and then he said, "There's been a lot of bad news concerning your brothers in the last year."

I closed my eyes, taking a deep breath. Oh, if I had a penny every time I heard that. "Yes, I know. And I want you to know that I hold them responsible for what they did too. It was wrong."

"It was indeed. People say that they tricked a lot of people out of money."

In layman's terms, yes. In legal terms, it had almost been a Ponzi scheme. It was only because my brothers could afford the very best of lawyers that they narrowly escaped any legal repercussions, but they had to leave the city. No one around here would do business with them again.

Even while we were growing up, I'd never seen eye to eye with them. They were always looking for the quick way to do things. Then as we got older, it was how to make bank without really doing anything. That was perhaps one of the reasons why I hadn't wanted to go to the same schools they did. I'd wanted to pave my own way even then. The right way.

"Well, my wife and I have been talking..."

"Gaston," I said quietly. "*I* would be the one investing in your business. The risk is on my side, but if you feel insecure about it—"

"No, no, no. You know what? Let's forget I ever said anything. I don't even know why I did. That Marcel guy must have gotten in my head."

I gritted my teeth. I couldn't believe I hadn't even met Zachary LeBlanc, yet I already had a bone to pick with him.

"We're a small business and know that anyone who invests does so because their heart tells them to, not because they're expecting any big profits," he went on.

That was true. I hadn't even asked to look over their financials yet. I would eventually, but I didn't expect to find anything great.

"Do you have any experience with animal-assisted therapy?" he asked me.

"Only dogs. I find the whole thing very endearing. I went to therapy after my divorce," I found myself saying, then closed my eyes. *Why did I say that?* I tried to never share anything personal with people I wanted to work with. I didn't want to be perceived as weak or something worse. "What I meant to say was, I know how helpful animal-assisted therapy is. I think your work with veterans and kids is truly admirable, and that's really why I wanted to help out." They especially focused on post-traumatic stress disorders in veterans and anxiety in children.

"Thank you. That's very nice to hear. Listen, my wife is feeding the horses, and I don't think she'll be back very soon, so I can't give you a definite date right now."

"Don't worry. You already said that you'll get back to me. But if we could arrange a visit next week, I'd be very grateful," I said, applying gentle pressure. That was the way I did things, and it usually worked out for the best.

"And one last question, actually. Do you need to secure financing in order to invest?"

That was a legitimate question. Securing financing could be tricky in cases like this.

"No. It's from my own personal funds."

I thanked the heavens every day that the skincare business had taken off the way it did.

"All right, then. See you next week."

"Thank you, Gaston."

After hanging up, I was tempted to google Zachary LeBlanc. I knew it wasn't uncommon in business circles to ask around about people—how else did you find out about someone you might be investing with? But I didn't want to sour the rest of my evening. I'd just have to deal with him when we met at the ranch.

Sometimes it felt as if New Orleans was a small town, especially when it came to old families like mine or the LeBlanc-Broussards, and people loved to talk. But what he did was definitely crossing the line.

Whatever. The day was over, and I wouldn't dwell on it.

I took a deep breath and got up from behind my desk, leaving the office before I could find something else to work on. The second I stepped out into the street, I looked to the right and to the left, taking in the evening air. It was fresh but warm as well. New Orleans' summer humidity could be ghastly, and I thanked God I had air-conditioning in the office. This tight skirt and flimsy blouse weren't the best choices for this hot weather.

I had the whole evening to myself tonight, and I was going to use it to treat myself to my favorite jambalaya at a small fusion restaurant just around the corner. Life was good, and I wasn't going to let anyone convince me otherwise—not even Zachary LeBlanc.

CHAPTER THREE
ZACHARY

I liked going out to the bayou. However, I usually went there on weekends, typically fishing with my grandfathers. After retiring from running the Orleans Conglomerate many years ago, they took up the sport. I enjoyed spending time with them, listening to their tales of the days of old. They had lots of wisdom to impart, and I would ask them for business advice when I was in a conundrum. Even if I didn't follow it, I wanted to hear their thoughts.

But driving to the bayou on a workday in the afternoon was a shit idea. Instead of three hours, I needed four. Whatever. I would make good use of my time and call my niece, Bella.

My brother Chad was picking her up from school, and they should be home by now, so I called him on my car's speakerphone.

"Hello," he answered.

"Hey, can you pass me to Bella?"

He chuckled. "Right. You two and your phone dates. Sure."

It had been a few days since we spoke at our dinner. I'd been trapped in meetings, but I didn't want to postpone this any longer, nor disappoint her in any way.

"Uncle Zachary." This was her serious voice, which immediately alerted me that she truly wanted to discuss something. Sometimes Bella used her uncles to get her way in things that Chad didn't allow, such as watching the next Harry Potter movie—which was far too dark for a kid her age—or eating too many sweets. But her tone was different. Ever since Chad and

Scarlett had Simone, the rest of us were paying even more attention to Bella, figuring she might be jealous. But she'd grown into her role as big sister perfectly.

"Hey, cricket. What do you want to talk about?"

"Is it true what they say in the family about you?"

"Can you be more specific? They say a lot of things."

She giggled. "That's true. They say that you're very good at managing crisis situations."

Where is she going with this? "Yeah, that is true."

"Good, because I have a crisis."

"What's going on?" I heard Chad ask.

"Daddy, I asked you to step farther away. This is between Uncle Zachary and me."

I barely held back laughter.

"Okay, okay," Chad grumbled in the background.

Bella was silent for a bit before speaking again. "Several girls at school are saying that my friends aren't cool. They don't want me to be friends with them anymore. And they say that if I don't do that, they won't include me in what they do."

I hated how kids could be. "What do *you* want, Bella?"

"I don't want to drop my friends. I think they're cool."

I adored this girl. "There's your answer, then."

"But how do I deal with the other girls so they don't drop me?"

"Why don't you want them to drop you?"

"I guess they're the cool ones."

Poor kid. The pressures of school.

"Do you have fun when you're with them?" I asked.

"Not always. I think they're very mean."

"Do you like the activities you do together?"

"Some." I could hear her questioning her answer.

"Could you do them without them? Maybe even with your other friends?"

"Yes, I could do them with my other friends."

"Listen, Bella, you don't have to be friends with anyone if you don't want to. Don't let your peers force you into anything you don't want to do."

"Really?" Her voice brightened. "I thought that once the cool girls wanted me to hang out with them, I *had* to do that."

"No, you don't."

"I didn't know that was an option." She sounded perplexed.

"You always have options, cricket. I promise you."

"Yes! I don't have to dump my friends, and I don't have to hang out with the mean girls either. Thank you, Uncle Zachary. You truly are the best."

I chuckled. "Anytime. Sorry it took me so long to call you."

"It didn't take you that long. Just three days."

I liked how exact kids were. No wonder she got along so well with Xander. Then again, she got along with everyone in the family—and we spoiled her rotten, of course.

I expected her to give the phone back to Chad, but she didn't. She just hung up, making me laugh. She had a good head on her shoulders even though she was barely ten.

I was tempted to call Chad back to tell him not to worry about anything. Lately, he tended to worry whenever Bella wanted to talk about something exclusively with us. Then I remembered that I still hadn't spoken with Marcel. And considering that I was about to meet this Grace Deveraux in person, it was high time I got some information. I asked Siri to dial him, and he answered after a few rings.

"Hey, Zachary. I was about to call you."

"Good. So, you have some info?"

"Of course. You know I never fail. I'll lay out everything chronologically. Grace Deveraux went to an all-girls prep school."

"Yeah, I've heard about that. Skip to the most recent info. I don't need her entire life story."

"She worked in the Deveraux company for about eight years after graduating, right until she got married. After that, she immediately quit her job. Unless you count attending social events as a job. That was all she did for the past few years. Four of them, to be exact. Then she and Roger Cointreau divorced. She started a skincare company last year, after the divorce. If you ask me, it's more of a vanity project."

"You don't know that," I said, cutting him short. I didn't like the tone he was using.

"Fair enough. I didn't have time to dig into financials or anything."

"Is she working with her brothers in any capacity?"

"Not that I could find. Honestly, I think she's just a socialite who wants to look good."

That got under my skin. Marcel was good at what he did, but lately he was pissing me off. I was paying him for information, not opinions.

"Is her company self-funded?"

"Yes. No investors. Then again, with the Deveraux name, it would've been impossible to get any."

I agreed with him on that. It was a simple fact. They were the black sheep of the city.

"Thanks for all the info."

"Anytime. You want me to dig more into the financials?"

"I'll let you know if that's necessary." I didn't want to waste too much time with this because I wasn't going into business with her.

I arrived at the ranch a short while later. There was already another car in front of the fence. I immediately got out, grabbing the box of pralines that I'd gotten some time ago for Gaston and Felicia. During my first call, they told me how much they liked the LeBlanc & Broussard pralines, and I took the hint.

This place had good bones. The property was huge, with trimmed grass that butted up to the bayou that flowed at the edge of the property. There were horses outside, leisurely moving around, and several cabins spread about where they hosted patients during camps.

Even from this distance, I could tell that the cottages had seen better days. Several shingles were missing from the roofs, and the wood on the front porches needed improvement.

I jogged toward the main building and immediately saw a stunning brunette next to an elderly couple who I assumed were Gaston and Felicia. I could only see her profile, but it was impressive. She was wearing a tight skirt and a fancy blouse. Her dark hair reached to the middle of her back. As I approached, I noticed that she had thick dark eyebrows and red lips. I glanced down and cocked a brow. Who in their right mind would show up to a ranch in stilettos?

A few seconds later, I made the connection. This had to be a Grace Deveraux.

"Hey, everyone. Sorry I'm late," I said. "I'm Zachary."

Gaston waved his hand. "Don't you worry. Ms. Deveraux just arrived also."

"I'm Felicia," his wife said, and I shook hands with them both.

"These are the pralines I promised," I told them, holding out the box.

"Oh, aren't you a delightful young man," Felicia said, grabbing it from me.

Then I turned to face Grace Deveraux. Her features were striking. I was certain that I'd never seen her before in my life because if I had, I would've remembered her. She didn't smile as she held her hand out to me.

"Nice to meet you," I said in a cool voice.

"Likewise."

I shook her hand briefly, and then she pulled it back—yanked it almost. I cocked a brow. This was an interesting start. Obviously she wasn't happy that I was here.

"Let's go inside so we can tell you a bit about what we do," Felicia suggested.

"Why don't we go see the stables first and look around the property while the sun's still up?" I suggested.

"Son," Gaston said, "the humidity is even worse out here in the bayou than in New Orleans. We'd be cooking. We can chat first, and then when the sun sets, we can go. I've got good mosquito repellent."

"I'd still prefer to go now," I admitted.

"Well, then, Mr. LeBlanc," Grace cut in, "why don't you take a walk by yourself and look around while Gaston, Felicia, and I have a chat inside?"

I stared at her. Why was she antagonizing me?

"The suggestion was for all of us," I emphasized.

"I, for one, prefer to take Gaston's advice. After all, he's the one running this place and knows best. Unless you expect us all to simply do your bidding?"

Whoa.

"Is there a problem here?" I asked her.

"You tell me."

Gaston and Felicia looked at each other. I was beginning to think Marcel hadn't jumped to conclusions for no reason.

"Shall we go inside, then?" Felicia asked. "I made some sweet tea."

"Sure," I said.

Grace gave me a sardonic smile.

What the hell is going on?

Once we entered the foyer, I could see that the house looked better on the inside than the outside.

Gaston gestured to the room. "This is where we live."

"You only offer camps, right?" I asked.

"You've looked on our website!" Felicia said. She sounded thrilled.

"Yes, of course. I asked around a bit before I even called you."

Next to me, Grace huffed. I looked at her again. Her eyes were icy. How could a woman so beautiful be so stuck up?

Felicia looked at Gaston, who shrugged. Grace was shooting herself in the foot. She was being completely unprofessional. Not my concern, though. In fact, it worked in my favor.

"Having camps makes the most sense. I mean, we're three hours from New Orleans, where most of our clients come from. No one would come for just an afternoon session," Gaston explained.

"We do weeklong camps with kids who love, love, *love* our horses. And then we also do camps for adults and veterans. We handle those a bit differently, space them out and so on. In here, we have the group therapy sessions." She pointed to four empty rooms. "It's also where we have meals for everyone."

"How many therapists do you have?" I asked.

"We recruit for each camp as needed, though most are repeats. Depending on the size of the camp, between five and ten."

This ranch was a valuable asset to many people, and the fact that they managed it all on their own was impressive.

Felicia added, "Clients work mostly with the animals, like a working ranch. They'll brush them, clean the stalls, and of course ride the horses around the perimeter. Physical work with animals is very healing."

"That is quite an endeavor," Grace said. "How long have you two been doing this?"

"It's on the website," I said. Had she not checked it out at all?

She bristled. I had no idea why I'd put her on the spot like that. It was unlike me, but she'd already ticked me off. Besides, she'd been doing the same to me. I figured she was fair game.

"We've been running it for thirty years," Felicia said, unfazed. "I studied psychotherapy myself, and I wanted to do something different. Not many people were offering this at first. After my parents passed away, I had a small inheritance I could invest. And that was the last time we had any money to pour into this place. That's why it needs a thorough renovation."

"Do you have trainers for the horses?" I inquired.

"No, we do that by ourselves," Felicia replied. "We weren't properly trained for it, but after so many years, it's become second nature. We've never had any issues with our animals misbehaving."

"And you've never had any liability issues?" Grace asked. It was a smart question, I'd give her that.

I stood a few steps behind so I could take a good look at her. Her shoulders were rigid, her chin slightly jutted forward in a commanding way.

"No, not even one," Felicia replied.

Grace nodded. "It's something I'd take a closer look at in the eventuality of a collaboration," she went on, and both Gaston and Felicia frowned. Grace was definitely not winning them over, but that was fine by me.

They gave us a full tour of the house, going into great detail about how they organized therapy sessions. It took about two hours even though there were just a few rooms.

"We could show you the cabins," Gaston said, "but honestly, most of them are pretty run-down. It's the reason why we haven't really booked anything this summer. We realized we needed a total overhaul before we could have people stay over again."

I didn't like the sound of that. Why did they wait until the last minute?

"I'd still like to see them," Grace said, "just to get an idea of what the investment would be."

"Then let's go," Gaston said, he and Felicia walking back to the front door.

Grace didn't even look at me as she stepped past me. I wanted to ask what the fuck her deal was but held back. I was simply here to assess if this was worth my investment. If she had a problem with me, it was up to her to tell me.

CHAPTER FOUR
GRACE

"As you can see," Felicia said apologetically after showing us two of the cabins, "we truly need to renovate them."

I smiled, turning around to face them. Honestly, they'd scared me when they said they weren't offering camps this summer because the cabins were too run-down.

"Felicia, these aren't too bad. Nothing a good team can't fix."

I was speaking directly to the two of them. I couldn't even stand looking at Zachary LeBlanc. I couldn't understand why this man was affecting me so much. True, he'd played dirty by having someone contact Felicia and Gaston. But I'd endured much worse over the years. I stayed a few feet away from him because his nearness unnerved me.

On top of being annoyed with him, he exuded a strange energy—*and probably some pheromones too,* said a small voice in the back of my mind. It was impossible not to notice how attractive he was. But that didn't matter. He was still a jackass, no matter how iridescent his blue eyes were or how muscular his arms were. I'd checked him out in more detail than I'd intended to. In my defense, though, the man was wearing a T-shirt.

"Are all the cabins the same size?" I asked. This one had two bedrooms.

"No, we have smaller ones, too, with just one bedroom. Some of our veterans need more privacy than others. The kids mostly just want to bunk up."

"It's a good mix." I smiled, looking around again. I'd had to be careful in my heels, as the floorboards had spaces between them, and I didn't want to stumble. The walk over was cumbersome too. I had to stay on my tiptoes almost the entire way or I'd sink into the ground.

The cabin was all wood and *really* hot. They needed a proper AC system. I couldn't believe they'd been built without one, as the bayou had always been hot and humid in the summer. It had two doors opposite each other so occupants could get a good draft, but it wasn't enough to cool a cabin down. Plus, in the heat of summer, the bayou could get really buggy too.

"This place has great energy," I said, and their faces completely opened up.

Oh, thank goodness. They'd looked so stern back in the house. Then again, I'd put my foot in my mouth a few times. I wasn't really behaving like myself. On the drive here, I'd managed to work myself up into a frenzy thinking about Zachary LeBlanc bad-mouthing me.

"Could we go see the horses?" I inquired.

"Sure."

"I love animals," I added with a sheepish smile. They were kind, gave pure, unconditional love, and just wanted to be loved back. No hidden agendas.

Once we stepped out, I looked down at my feet. I should've brought sneakers to change into, but it completely slipped my mind. As proficient as I was at wearing heels, I still kept my eyes firmly on the ground so I didn't trip over something.

The stables were quite some distance away from the cabins. I was hyperaware of every step Zachary took. Even though he was walking behind me, I swear I could tell whenever he was getting nearer. I was certain he wasn't close enough for me to feel his body warmth, and yet I did.

We went into the stables. Only half the horses were inside. The other stalls were empty.

"May I pet one?" I asked.

"Sure," Felicia said. "Do you have any experience with horses?"

"I used to ride as a teenager."

I went to the nearest horse—he was mostly white, but his mane was gray. I stretched out my palm, right over his shoulder. Peace filled me instantly. I could completely understand why these noble animals were used in therapy.

"Do you have a vet on call?" Zachary asked.

"Yes," Felicia replied. "He doesn't live far away." She went on about the animals and the checkups they got. I could tell they were very well taken care of.

I glanced out of the stall. Zachary was looking straight at Felicia and Gaston, taking in their conversation. He didn't particularly show an interest in the horses. *Strange.* Why did he want to invest in this place, anyway? It wasn't a big moneymaker and wouldn't make him the profits he was used to. Was he doing it to look good, for charity reasons? That was entirely possible. Most of the people I grew up with came from old money. They spent most of their time doing activities that made them look good, kind, or generous.

A buzzing sound filled the air, and Gaston took out his phone. "Oh, we need to take this. May we leave the two of you alone for a few minutes?"

"Sure," Zachary said. "We'll be right here."

"We'll go outside the stable to have some privacy," Felicia added.

As they left, I focused on the horse in front of me. The silence was peaceful at first but soon changed to uncomfortable. I decided to make conversation.

"You don't like horses?" I could've picked a positive topic, but honestly, I didn't want to make an effort. There was no reason to pretend that I wanted to be on good terms with Zachary.

"I do. Watching them from a distance is enough, though."

I scoffed. This man unnerved me to no end. But why?

The horse jutted his head backward. I was getting angsty and he was feeling it, so I stepped away. I didn't want to upset the animal for no reason.

"What's your problem?" Zachary abruptly asked.

I turned to him, fighting a scoff. He damn well knew what was bothering me. "I think you know."

His eyes went wide. "No, I don't. That's why I'm asking. You've been impolite ever since I introduced myself." His eyes were steely now yet still so damn gorgeous. Immediately, I looked away from them. "The way you're acting is bordering on unprofessional, but honestly, that's your problem. Just know it won't win you any points with Felicia and Gaston."

Unfortunately, he was right.

I could feel my blood pressure rising. *Breathe in, breathe out. Come on, Grace. You've dealt with worse. Why are you letting this guy rile you up like this?*

"You took care of that anyway, didn't you? Tried very hard to bad-mouth me."

"What are you talking about?" He actually looked like he was confused. *Nice act.*

I folded my arms over my chest. "They told me that a guy named Marcel called to ask them about me. Very pointed questions and interesting ones."

Zachary's eyes bulged, then narrowed. "I asked Marcel to look into you. I thought he was being judgmental, but now I see that he was completely correct."

"About me?"

"Yes. You are rude, spoiled, and probably doing this as a vanity project."

My emotions got stuck in my throat. How dare he?

"You know nothing about me!"

Why did my voice sound strangled? Damn it, I wanted to be strong.

You've been through worse, Grace. Your ex was much, much meaner than this.

I cleared my throat, trying to get a grip on myself.

Zachary shook his head. "Doesn't matter. Whatever reason you're pursuing this project isn't my business, as I intend to win anyway."

"Really? Why are you even bothering? Clearly this project isn't a fit for the portfolio of the Orleans Conglomerate." I flexed and unflexed my hands. God, I hadn't been so worked up in a very long time.

"I'm glad we've settled our opinions of each other," Zachary said in a cool voice. "Let's just proceed with the tour."

I couldn't do it. I knew myself well enough to realize I wouldn't regain my composure to finish this and would likely wind up making a fool of myself. Which was why I turned on my heels without another word to Zachary and walked out of the stables.

Felicia and Gaston were talking to each other, clearly having finished the call. They both stopped when they noticed me approaching.

"Hi. I'm truly sorry, but I need to go," I told them. "I got a call, and I'm urgently needed back in the city."

Felicia's face fell. This sounded like the made-up excuse it was, but I was too upset to come up with something better.

"But I'd like to make another appointment so I can look at everything thoroughly," I went on. "I'm still very interested, and I'd planned to discuss ideas with you today about what type of investment would make sense and how I could help best. But I need to be on my way."

I wanted them to see how important this would be for me, but right now, I couldn't even gather my wits. I shouldn't have scheduled so many meetings before coming here because I was exhausted. Zachary and exhaustion were not a good combination.

"Of course," Gaston said. "I'll walk back with you to your car."

"There's no need. I'll find my way." I felt like a coward, leaving like this, but it was better than the alternative.

I bid both of them goodbye before walking away. The humidity was truly insane out here. I struggled to breathe until I reached my car. Once inside, I immediately turned on the air-conditioning. I could finally take a deep breath.

I simply sat in silence for a few seconds, wondering if I should go back after all. But no, it would make things even weirder.

Oh, Grace, this isn't like you, running away like this.

Zachary's insults were still ringing in my ears. The nerve of him. I couldn't believe he'd dared to say all those things. He knew nothing about me. Absolutely nothing. Not who I was. Not what I'd gone through. He had no right to talk to me like that.

But none of that mattered.

I was going to come back here as soon as possible and show Gaston and Felicia that I was the right person to partner up with—not that infuriating jackass.

CHAPTER FIVE
ZACHARY

The next morning, I called Marcel first thing. I'd stayed for two more hours out at the ranch after Grace left yesterday. I even had dinner with Gaston and Felicia. I had a good feeling about the whole thing. It would require more of an investment than I'd initially figured, but that was all right. I'd told Gaston and Felicia that I would outbid Grace no matter what she offered. They were shocked but pleased.

I couldn't believe Grace had darted out like that. In fact, the whole interaction with her had been completely bizarre. But something that stuck with me was that she accused me of having Marcel bad-mouth her to Gaston and Felicia. I couldn't see him doing something so unprofessional, which was why I dismissed it when she first said it. But then again, why would she lie?

He answered immediately, as usual. "Morning, Zachary!"

"Listen, I'll make this quick. Yesterday evening, I went out to the ranch. Did you by any chance call the owners to tell them anything about Grace?"

"Yes, of course. Even asked them if they knew what her good-for-nothing brothers had been up to last year."

I instantly saw red. "Why the fuck would you do that? I just told you I needed information about her."

"Because that was part of my gathering information. I wanted to know if she'd already been in contact with them."

"That was not in the scope of what I asked you to do."

"You asked me for information. I have my methods. It's never been a problem before."

"Yeah, well, your methods reflect on me." I couldn't keep the anger out of my voice. In fact, I wasn't even trying.

"I don't remember you ever complaining about me getting you what you needed before. Why's this different?" he questioned.

"Well, now I am. This is unacceptable."

"Why are you even wasting time with that place? It's a decrepit, run-down ranch. It will never be a moneymaker. There's no profit in it."

"I pay you to give me information, not your opinions. And I pay you to do that subtly. Do you understand that?"

"Whatever, dude," he huffed. "If you don't like my methods, that's your problem."

"No, it's yours. This is the last time I'm collaborating with you."

"Are you shitting me right now?"

"I don't condone such behavior. It's beneath me."

He scoffed. "You LeBlancs always think you're better than everyone else, don't you? Well, you're not."

What? I was dumbfounded. What had gotten into Marcel? Or was this his real opinion of me and my family, and I was just now finding out?

"As I said, I don't give a shit about your opinions. But a word of warning: none of your clients will like this type of behavior. It's a very lazy, unprofessional way to get information."

I was fuming by the time I hung up. Fucking hell, I was never going to use Marcel's services again. I would ask Xander how he surveyed businesses. In fact, I decided to head to my brother's office in the business district right then. Maybe I should've taken him up on his offer to look into Grace's endeavors in the first place.

I hadn't paid him a visit in a while, so it would be nice to catch up. I liked that all of us were within walking distance in the Quarter. I met with the rest of the family far more often than Xander. He'd always done things his own way, and I respected that.

Of course, going to see him on a whim turned out not to be my best idea, as my brother wasn't in his office.

"I'm truly sorry. Did you have an appointment with him?" his assistant asked.

"No, not at all. I just figured I'd drop by and see if he was here and had some time to chat."

She looked at me like I was speaking a foreign language. Yeah, that was definitely not my brother. If I wanted to see him, I knew I had to get on his calendar. That was just how he worked.

"Should I tell him you dropped by?"

"Don't worry, I'll talk to him later."

I could head back straight to the Quarter, or I could grab a coffee nearby. Since I couldn't get this business with Grace out of my mind, I figured it might be best to take a minute to myself before going back to work. Maybe I'd be able to focus on something else once I had some caffeine in my system.

I stared across the road and suddenly thought I was seeing things. Was it my imagination, or was Grace Deveraux sitting outside the coffee shop across the way, talking on the phone? I zeroed in on the figure and realized it truly was her.

I walked straight over to her even though I didn't know what I was going to say. But I wanted to get to the bottom of why she'd been antagonizing me at the ranch. No matter what Marcel did, her behavior had been completely unprofessional, and while I might be laid-back, I definitely wanted to call her out on it.

She'd pocketed her phone by the time I reached her and was sipping from a cup of coffee. I stopped right in front of her, and she looked up. Her demeanor instantly changed. Her smile fell, and she looked upset.

"Zachary," she exclaimed. "Did you follow me here?"

I jerked my head back. "What the actual hell? Why would I do that?"

"I don't know. What are you even doing here?"

She seemed angry. And that instantly pissed me off. Did she really think the world revolved around her?

"I was in the neighborhood. My brother has offices here."

"Oh, I supposed you've come to ask for more information about me from the infamous Xander LeBlanc?"

I opened my mouth to give her a scathing reply, but the truth was that was exactly what I'd been doing. "What's your problem?"

"I already explained that to you."

"No, there's more to it. That in no way excuses your completely unprofessional behavior back at the ranch."

"You have some guts calling me unprofessional," she said, rolling her shoulders back and rising to her feet.

"When you have a problem with someone, you ask them to talk in private, like a professional. You don't start making snide remarks in front of others, huffing and puffing."

"Right," she said, tilting her head. "Anything else? I'm taking mental notes."

"I could write you a whole damn report on this. Fucking hell, you Deveraux people."

She rolled her shoulders back again, jutting her chin forward—the same commanding stature she'd worn at the ranch. "Don't you dare." Then she scoffed. "You know what? This conversation is over."

"Suits me," I replied sardonically. "I did what I came to do."

"Which was what? Insult me?"

"No. Telling you that there is a way to do things, and it's definitely not yours."

"Thank you for the information. How generous of you to share it with me. Now, if you'll excuse me, I have a very important call to make," she said.

Her tone was dismissive, which only riled me up more, but I had no more patience for this. I'd wasted enough time on Grace Deveraux. This was going to stop right now.

Why did I even care so much? If anything, this was going to work out in my favor. I was going to invest in that ranch, and she and her entire family were going to continue to be shunned—apparently for very good reason.

Chapter Six

Grace

On Sunday morning, I went to visit Mom and Dad. They'd moved out of the city into a gorgeous mansion a few years ago. Lately, though, they'd been spending more time in the city, using their old residence as their weekend and vacation home. The two were only one hour apart.

"Darling, you haven't touched your food," Mom said.

I barely stifled my laughter. There was enough on my plate for two.

"I ate a lot, Mom. Your gumbo is still my favorite."

"It's the beans, I'm telling you," she said with a smile. "I taught Theresa how to make it exactly like me. We're so lucky that she's still with us after so many years."

"She's amazing," I agreed. Theresa had been working as a cook for my family for as long as I could remember. She was honestly like a grandmother to me. I was happy she was still with my parents.

They'd decorated this house the same way they had the one in the Garden District, in an art deco style that fit both of them well. They didn't like classic furniture, but they weren't ready for a totally modern setup either.

"Darling, how have you been?" Dad asked.

I met up with them once in a while—more often now that I was divorced—but this was the first time we'd gotten together in a few weeks.

"Busy."

"So I've heard," he said. "I called your office the other day, and they said you were still working even though it was dinnertime."

I nodded. "Sometimes I do spend my evenings at the office."

"Darling, there's no need to overwork yourself," Mom said. "You could always go back to working with your dad. You know how much he needs you."

I sighed. I really didn't want to start this conversation with my parents again. I didn't like hurting their feelings.

"I love you two," I assured them, "but I want to do my own thing. Besides, Dad is doing great in the company without me."

Dad was looking at the table, both arms on the armrests of the chair. "All my life I worked hard, Grace. I didn't mind. I liked it. I liked honoring my forefathers and knowing that I'm keeping their legacy safe. But right now, there's no one left to take over that legacy. Except you."

Oh, and cue the guilt trip again. My childhood had been full of this kind of pressure and the expectation that the three of us would continue the family tradition of working at Deveraux Industries. It focused on clothing manufacturing, which I'd enjoyed, but that had been a different part of my life.

"Have you heard from Kyle and Beau?" I asked them.

"No," Dad said sternly. "And I hope I never do again. The mess they made nearly sank the company and tarnished the family. I can't believe they'd dare play with the family name like that. Five generations of Deverauxes built this company from the ground up, and they almost destroyed it with their antics."

"Are you in contact with them?" Mom asked me.

"No. I haven't spoken to them in more than a year." Not that we were close before. Ever since I got married, things between us had drifted apart even more. If that hadn't happened, maybe I would've been aware of what they were up to. But both my brothers had been very dismissive of me, even when we'd worked together. When I told them I was leaving, they'd made it clear that there was no place for me if I ever decided to come back.

Dad sighed, reaching for a scone. "It's a good thing Xander LeBlanc exposed them when he did. I should thank him next time I see him."

I wasn't feeling very pro-LeBlanc right now. "You'd thank him for meddling in something that wasn't his business?" I couldn't help but ask, thinking about Zachary.

"He stopped your brothers from embarrassing us even further, and that's good enough in my books."

"I don't know where I went wrong with those two," Mom said quietly. "I keep thinking and thinking and—"

"Mom, don't be hard on yourself. You're both excellent parents." I picked up my napkin and wiped at the corner of my mouth. "Listen, I need to go back to the city. I promised my friend we'd go out for drinks in the Quarter."

"Good for you," Mom said. "I've been worried about you lately, always cooped up at work."

"Well, the weekend is for relaxing." I was only half lying. I'd work a bit in the morning.

I kissed both my parents, smiling as I headed to the kitchen before leaving. "Hey, Theresa. I wanted to say bye. See you again next week?"

She turned to me, looking me up and down. "Grace, are you sure you don't want me to pack some of that gumbo?"

"It's not necessary, but thanks."

"Hm," she said.

Theresa looked the same as she had my entire childhood, with her curly blond hair pulled into a ponytail and a robust physique. I had many fond memories of her combing my hair and giving me advice on boys when I was a teenager. Mostly how to stay away from them.

"You know, I can make your favorites if you stop by the house more often," she called out, referring to my parents' residence in the Garden District. She was perpetually upset that I wasn't eating enough. Truth be told, these days, I did often forget to eat. I'd lost a few pounds without even meaning to, but I planned to put them back on tonight with some alcohol and a sweet treat or two.

"I'll keep that in mind," I said, sending her an air kiss as I left.

I drove straight to the French Quarter, wondering how life could change so drastically in such a short time. A little over a year ago, I was unhappily married, hoping for a positive pregnancy test. In retrospect, I was glad it never happened. Divorcing Roger would've been far more difficult if we had a child together.

I hadn't been in the Quarter for a while, and I was already looking forward to it. Technically, I was way too early—I was meeting my friend Lais at eight o'clock, and it was barely five—but that was quite all right. I wanted to roam the streets a bit, maybe head into a shop or two. Being born and bred in New Orleans, I knew almost every shop, of course, but occasionally something new popped up.

I parked at the edge of the Quarter, near the river, because I wanted to take a walk along the water. It *could* end at Café Du Monde. I hadn't been there in eons. I walked at a quick pace, looking over my shoulder every time I heard a bicycle coming along. I was wearing my high heels again, as well as a dress. Mom appreciated when I looked nice visiting them, and I liked to make her happy.

The bells of the St. Louis Cathedral rang in the distance. As I passed Jackson Square, I instinctively looked that way. There were droves of tourists around the church. I'd just decided it would be easier to go left and not go to Café Du Monde and deal with the foot traffic when a familiar figure caught my attention.

Zachary LeBlanc was talking on the phone at the edge of the river, feet wide apart in a macho stance. He was laughing. He looked so different from the previous times I'd seen him. If possible, he was even more handsome.

Oh, stop it, Grace. There are plenty of handsome men in this city. Why do you have to keep ogling him?

Well, because he kept popping up in my life and making it more difficult. But that was neither here nor there. I wasn't going to let the sight of him ruin my evening. I was going to have fun.

And yet, instead of turning left as I'd planned, I headed straight to Zachary. Last time, I'd been blindsided by him and caught off guard. Now, I could finally be the one surprising him and also give him a piece of my mind.

I stopped directly in front of him. He noticed me right away and said, "I'll call you back, Bella, okay? Yeah, I promise." He lowered his phone and turned around. "Hello to you too."

"It's not nice being blindsided, is it?"

He groaned, pocketing his phone. "Grace, let's give this a rest. I think we said enough."

"No, *you* said enough. I just stood there, shell-shocked, taking all the insults you were hurling at me."

"It's not like I didn't give you the opportunity to speak," Zachary said.

Goodness, why was this man so damn infuriating?

"You were the one who cut the conversation short," he added.

I swallowed hard. What could I tell him? That insulting others didn't come easily for me? And that I certainly couldn't do it on the spot?

"You have no right to insult me or call me out on my work ethic." *Ugh. Why am I pursuing this?*

"I didn't insult you," Zachary said, not even a bit placatingly. "I merely laid out the facts."

"You're assuming that your opinion is an actual fact. It's infuriating. Because you're—"

I stumbled backward. I wasn't even sure how. One moment I was stepping back, and the next, I was simply flying backward. I moved my hands in an erratic pattern, trying to regain my balance, but the opposite happened.

Cold gripped my body as I realized I was falling into the Mississippi River.

CHAPTER SEVEN

ZACHARY

I heard the splash, but I didn't put two and two together right away. But then it dawned on me: Grace had fallen into the damn river!

Holy fuck!

She dunked under the water and then resurfaced, gasping. I didn't even think twice before jumping in. Jesus, the water wasn't warm at all. Swimming with shoes on was insanely hard. When I came up for air, I realized the current had already carried her a bit. She was swimming against it as hard as she could, but the Mississippi was stronger.

I could swim faster than her and managed to reach her what felt like years later, grabbing one of her hands. That wasn't helpful, though, because the current was now carrying us both.

"We need to get to the shore," I told her. "There's no point trying to swim against the current. Let's just let it carry us, and we'll find a place to get out farther down."

"Yes, yes." She was frantic.

"Grace, I'm here. Just breathe in deeply. We'll get to the shore."

I searched for a spot where we could easily grasp the edge; otherwise, we'd just hit it and then be carried on downriver. I noticed a fallen tree farther down. That would definitely stop us.

"See that tree?" I shouted over the sound of the rushing water.

"Yes," she yelled back a few seconds later, just in time because we were approaching it at a rapid speed.

"Hold on to my left arm when we're close, and I'll grab it for both of us."

I was hoping for the best: that the tree was safely secured, or at least heavy enough that we wouldn't topple it into the water over us.

"On my count, grab my arm," I instructed Grace.

"Okay." She sounded panicked now. Most people probably would be. But having been an EMT, I'd seen a lot—though I'd never actually practiced for this type of emergency.

"Three, two, now." I grabbed the trunk with my right arm. The current felt a million times stronger when we weren't moving with it. "Can you grab it?"

"Yes," Grace said, putting one arm on the trunk too.

"All right, let's slowly untangle our arms and grip it with both."

"We could topple it." She panicked.

I looked at the other end of the trunk. "It's secured. It'll hold us." Grace looked like she didn't believe me. "I promise nothing bad will happen. Now grab it!"

She nodded furiously, her lips blue. The water was fucking cold!

Slowly, we moved ourselves up the trunk toward the shore. I climbed out first.

"Give me one of your hands," I said.

"I can't hold myself with only one arm."

"Then I'll grab your wrists and pull you up."

She looked up at me. "I'm heavier than I look."

"I'll manage. On the count of three." I bent down and put my left hand on her right arm, then grabbed the other one. "Just let go of the trunk when I say, okay? One, two, three!"

I pulled her up with ease. She practically slammed into me once I set her down. She was barefoot, having lost her shoes in the river. Exhausted from the physical effort, we both fell onto the grass. Her body was soft and hard at the same time. I only half managed to break our fall, so she was lying on top of me.

For a few seconds, neither of us said anything. I took in her appearance. She was white as a sheet. Her pulse had probably gone through the roof, but she hadn't swallowed water as far as I could tell. Now that I'd determined she wasn't in immediate danger, other details registered, such as how soft her breasts were against me. She was definitely not wearing a bra. She was gorgeous even like this—completely disheveled and in a state of shock.

"Grace, you're safe."

She nodded but didn't look convinced.

"Want me to help you up?"

That seemed to snap her out of it. She looked down at my chest and back to my face in horror, then immediately rolled off me.

"Oh, I'm so sorry. I, um...This was..." She didn't finish her sentence. Instead, she put a hand on her chest. It was rising up and down even more rapidly.

"You're still in shock," I told her calmly. "But you're safe now. We're on the ground, and nothing happened. We're not in danger."

She closed her eyes, taking a deep breath and furrowing her thick eyebrows. Her lips were downright kissable.

Jesus, man, get a grip. I couldn't believe where my train of thought just went.

She opened her eyes and sighed. "Thank you, Zachary. Truly. How are you so good at this?"

"When I was a teenager, I trained as an EMT, and I volunteered as one until I finished college. Some things you don't forget."

"Wow, I lost my shoes." She pointed at her feet. She wasn't going to get far like that. "Do you know what happened? One minute we were talking, and then suddenly I was falling."

"There's no railing, and you lost your balance."

"Oh my God! You jumped in for me?"

She was trembling. I needed to get her back to her place, changed, and warm before she went into hypothermia.

"I'll call an Uber and take you home."

She shook her head. "No, I'll just go by myself."

"Grace, I want to make sure you're okay. States of shock can manifest even after the event has passed, and I'd rather not leave you alone."

"All right," she said, nodding again.

"Our electronics are probably dead." I reached into my pocket to find out this was true. I'd get a new one tomorrow.

Grace gasped. "Oh no, you're right."

"Listen, I have a proposition. You wait here; I'll find a cab."

"But do you have any cash?" She was looking around, still not coherent of the entirety of the situation.

I felt my back pocket, which was bulging. "My wallet is still here. Soaked, but it'll do. I won't be long."

"Okay."

She was still glancing about when I said, "I'll be right back," then hurried off.

I didn't like leaving her alone, but I didn't have a choice. I looked left and right. This was a relatively deserted stretch. I liked that even less. I had no idea how long I'd have to walk to find a cab, but it was my best plan for now.

I was lucky, as a cab passed me only a few feet down the street.

The guy looked me up and down and said, "Hell no. You'll ruin my back seat."

I took out my wallet. "Listen, all the money is soaked, but it'll dry up. I'll give you enough to clean the car and buy yourself dinner."

His eyes widened. "Let me see the money first."

I took it out, flaunting the wet bills in front of him.

"That's good. I'll take it."

"We need to go by the river first. There's a woman waiting for us."

"What the hell did you two do? Fall into the Mississippi?"

"Exactly."

The man turned white instantly. "Jesus, you're lucky you made it out."

"I know. Come on, let's go get her."

Grace was still in the spot where I'd left her, holding her knees with her arms. She was still in shock. It was a good thing I was going home with her.

"Grace, cab's here." She immediately jumped to her feet at my words. "Can you walk?"

"Yeah. Don't worry about it."

Before I could offer to carry her, she darted toward the taxi.

I slid next to her on the back seat. "What's your address?"

She named a prominent area in the warehouse district. I was surprised. I would've taken her for the type to have a mansion in the Garden District.

We didn't speak during the drive to her place, which thankfully didn't take that long. When we exited the cab, I looked around, taking in the view. Grace lived in a luxurious condo in a redbrick building.

"You have your key?" I asked when we stepped into the foyer.

"My bag!" she responded with distress. "No, I lost my bag. Oh no!"

"Grace, don't worry. All that's replaceable, yes?"

She nodded in agreement as we approached the concierge. He did a double take when he saw us. "Ms. Deveraux, are you okay?"

"Hi, Donald. We fell into the Mississippi. I honestly don't have anything on me, ID or keys. My purse is at the bottom of the river." She sounded so forlorn. "Do you think you could let me into my apartment?"

"Of course, Ms. Deveraux. I usually ask guests for ID, but since he's with you..." He was obviously teasing her, seeing how upset she was and trying to lighten the moment.

"How generous of you," Grace said, and Donald laughed. He clearly felt at ease enough with her to joke around.

She didn't seem at all like the haughty socialite I'd taken her for. Anyone else could've been a real bitch if something like this happened to them. Instead, she was appreciative and trying to maintain her composure even though she obviously wanted to sit down and cry.

Donald got a set of keys from under his desk and then went with us to the elevator. Grace lived on the top floor. We thanked Donald for assisting us as he opened the door to her condo. I tipped him generously.

Once inside, I noticed how big her place was, with modern decor. It was tasteful and comfortable, not overly done or pretentious.

"Zachary, I have a washing machine and a dryer in the smaller bathroom, so you can take care of your clothes in there. It's probably going to take a couple of hours, so you can shower in the meantime."

"I'm going to take you up on that. The Mississippi isn't the bayou, but it doesn't smell much better. And a warm shower sounds inviting."

Grace lifted and sniffed her dress. "You're right. I think I can just toss this dress in the garbage. It's supposed to be dry clean only." She stroked her arms, looking at me and swallowing hard. I could see her eyes softening, the shock of the evening finally dissipating.

"Thank you for jumping in," she said quietly. "You didn't have to do that."

"Grace, I wasn't about to let you drown or be carried away by the river. The water is tricky, and I didn't know how good of a swimmer you were. I would never have let you manage that on your own."

"I'm a decent swimmer, just not when I'm panicking. That could've ended so badly." She pulled her hair to one side before putting her hands over her face.

On instinct, I walked closer. The back of her neck was exposed, and I put my thumb there, resting my other four fingers under her hair on her neck. Her pulse was erratic.

Even though we both smelled like scum, I couldn't help but lean in. This woman was alluring to me in a way I couldn't explain.

"Don't be hard on yourself, Grace. Ninety-nine percent of people can't think straight when their life is in danger."

She lowered her hands, glancing at me. "Thanks. Why don't you go take a shower, and I'll get you a robe. I guess you'll have to wear that until the clothes are dry." She tiptoed away from me, rubbing the back of her neck in the exact spot where I'd touched her.

"Do you want to have dinner while we wait?" I asked. I still had a credit card in my wallet and could order something from DoorDash. Or from our restaurant for that matter.

"Oh no!" She turned around with her eyes wide. "I was supposed to meet my best friend for drinks at eight. What time is it?" We both glanced at the clock on her oven. It was six thirty. Her shoulders slumped. "I don't feel like going."

"I'd advise against going anyway. After what you've just been through, your nervous system needs a chance to calm down."

Grace smiled, and I realized it was the very first time she'd smiled *at me.* She'd smiled at Donald earlier, and even at Gaston and Felicia at the ranch, but not at me. "You really talk like a doctor. It's very calming."

"I'm glad it's helping."

"I need to contact Lais, but without my phone... I'll send her an email. I can also check how we can order something from the laptop. I haven't done that in ages. I always use apps."

"Mind if I shower in the meantime? I can't stand how I smell."

"Sure. What do you want to eat?"

"I'll have anything. Just order whatever you normally eat."

"Okay."

She led me to the master bedroom, which was an explosion of pink and violet. I hadn't really expected that of a businesswoman in her thirties, but I was starting to realize that maybe I did have the wrong idea about Grace.

"Word of warning: everything in my bathroom smells like roses."

That made me laugh. "Honestly, I don't care. It's much better than smelling like swamp."

"True. You've got towels there. I'll show you where the washer and dryer are after you're done."

"Perfect. I won't need long."

I'd done such a great job keeping my eyes off her chest until now. But as she lowered her arms, I got a full view of her nipples pushing against the fabric. I barely bit down a groan. It was a visceral reaction.

Fucking hell.

I drew in a deep breath. She immediately noticed where I was looking and crossed her arms over her chest.

"I'll put a robe on my bed," she said quickly before disappearing.

I was ogling a woman who was getting over being in shock. Real nice.

I stepped into her shower, turning on the water and sniffing her shower gel. It smelled exactly like her. It felt as if she was here with me, and my cock stood to attention right away. Fantastic timing. I gave it a few squeezes, but it did absolutely nothing for me. I refused to jack off in her shower, though.

I lathered myself with the damn shower gel twice. I was going to smell like roses for the next year, but I was fine with that as long as I got rid of the smell of that river water. A few minutes later, I stepped out, grabbing a towel and drying myself properly.

When I opened the door to the bedroom, I saw a robe on the bed. I could tell by looking at it that it was far too small, but I tried it on nonetheless. I couldn't even put my arms in it.

"Grace?" I called.

"Yes?"

"I can't wear your robe. It's too small."

"Oh, I didn't think of that. I just figured it would be too short. Grab more towels from the bathroom and cover yourself as best you can."

I wrapped one around my lower body and draped another one over my shoulders before walking to the living room, carrying my soggy clothes in one hand. "Where can I wash these?"

Grace was staring at me, her mouth hanging slightly open. My ego was very happy about that. She liked what she saw.

"In the bathroom in that bedroom." She pointed to a door next to the couch.

This bathroom was much smaller than the master, with a combo washing machine and dryer. I tossed everything inside.

After she set the "Express" program, we returned to the living room. "I'm going to take a shower too," she said. "If the food comes in the meantime, please open the door."

"Sure."

She swallowed hard. "Maybe don't let them see you."

"Why?" I said, deciding to tease her. "Are you afraid that word will get out that you've got a naked man in your apartment?"

She instantly blushed, opening her mouth and then closing it again. Her lips looked even more kissable than usual. She was still drenched in muddy water and smelled like it too. And yet I was blindly attracted to her—the woman who fell into the Mississippi because she was too busy insulting me to pay attention to where she was stepping.

I was clearly losing my mind.

"Just, you know, don't make anyone uncomfortable," she stammered.

"Wouldn't dream of it," I said.

The pizza arrived while she was in the shower. It was already cut. I found plates and cutlery easily and arranged everything on the small round table by the kitchen.

Grace came out wearing a long dress that nearly swept the floor. Her hair was wet and pulled up tightly on top of her head.

"Food is here," I said.

"Great. I've never ordered from this restaurant before, so let's hope it's good."

"It's hard to get bad pizza."

"I didn't know what your favorite was, so I got a mix of cheese and pepperoni."

"Grace, I'm very easygoing. I eat anything," I said once we both sat down. The dining table was the only thing that wasn't huge in this apartment, which made me think she usually dined alone.

"Really? That was not the impression I got of you," she replied.

I laughed. "Want to start sparring again? I'll have a slice of pizza, and then I'm good to go once my stuff is dry."

"No, God, don't go." Her shoulders slumped. "I'm so sorry about tonight."

"Grace, let's make a deal."

She raised her eyes to me. "I'm listening."

"Let's give it a rest for tonight. We don't need to talk about the river, the ranch, or anything else. I just want to make sure you're okay. And as soon as my clothes are dry, I'll leave, and then we can pretend this never happened."

She looked at me intently for a few seconds before nodding. "Sounds like a fair deal."

"Glad you think so. Did your friend see your email?"

"Yes. She hangs on to her phone as much as I do, so she immediately replied. She's a bit sad that I couldn't make it but understands. So, what were you doing in the Quarter?"

Grace

"I took my niece to the voodoo museum. Turned out to be a shitty idea."

Zachary took his niece? That was nice. "Why was it bad?"

"Because that stuff is fucking scary," he said, and I started to laugh. He seemed like a totally different man than the one I'd met at the ranch and in the coffee shop near my office. Who knew he could actually laugh and have fun at his own expense? Or perhaps he was making an effort right now because I was still out of sorts. "When you saw me, she'd called to tell me that she was scared shitless. Anyway, let's change the subject. What did you do today?" he asked.

"I had lunch with my parents."

"They moved back to New Orleans?" he asked as he took a bite of his pizza.

"No, they still live outside the city. They only come to New Orleans on weekends."

"You visit them often?"

"Honestly, no."

He raised a brow. "You don't get along with them?"

I sighed. "I do. I just don't really have time. My business is taking up a lot more time than I thought, but I love every minute of it. Though I could be a better daughter and see them more often now that I'm the only kid they've got left around here."

"No one is in contact with your brothers?"

I looked at him intently. "Are you fishing for information?"

He shook his head. "No, Grace. I was simply trying to make conversation."

I swallowed hard. "Sorry. My brothers are a sore topic even now."

"Noted. I won't bring them up again."

"I'd appreciate that. For what it's worth, I'm truly sorry for the problems they've caused. I have to say, I'm not even sure who exactly they stole money from."

"Not us," Zachary said. "But we've always been a bit at odds with Kyle, especially since we were in school."

"Most people seem to have taken an instant dislike to him." I tried to remember back to my own childhood. "I never really spent a lot of time with my brothers. Probably because I was a girl, I guess, and younger than them."

We both ate rather quickly, which was a clear indication that we'd both been hungry. Once we finished the pizza, I said, "Oh, I forget to ask if you want something to drink. I have some orange juice in the fridge."

"Sure. I need something to wash down the pizza."

I felt very nervous all of a sudden, being with this hot-as-hell man here in my apartment, especially when he wasn't being infuriating. Because then it was very hard to ignore the way my body reacted to him. It was even more difficult to deny to myself that I was attracted to him. It was a purely physical impulse because he was a very good-looking man. *And* he'd just been my knight in shining armor. My hormones were wreaking havoc.

A beeping sound filled the apartment. "That was the dryer. Your clothes are ready."

"Perfect. I'll be right back."

Several minutes later, he joined me in the kitchen fully dressed, bringing the plates with him.

"Thank you," I said, placing them in the dishwasher.

He stacked the two pizza boxes, saying, "I'll take these with me and throw them away when I go downstairs."

"No need." I immediately grabbed them to give myself something to do besides ogle this man. I shoved them by my trash can as I heard him pour some orange juice.

As he gulped it down, I turned around. Oh yeah, even watching the liquid go down his throat, his Adam's apple bouncing up and down, was enough to make my skin sizzle.

What the ever-loving hell is happening to me?

"Grace?" Zachary said. "Are you okay?" He walked over to me, rounding the kitchen island until he was right in front of me.

"Yeah, sure. Why?"

"Because you've gone very quiet, and you seem to be avoiding me."

I licked my lips, glancing up at him. "No, I'm..."

"Do you have a headache?"

I blinked. "What? No. Why are you asking that?"

"Is your vision blurry?"

"No."

"I'm checking for signs of shock or concussion."

"Oh, right." That was okay as long as he didn't see the signs that I had the hots for him...

I felt so off-balance. I couldn't understand how just a few hours ago, I'd lunged at him to give him a piece of my mind, and now I couldn't focus. Maybe I had hit my head after all.

"I'm fine, Zachary. Really."

He captured my wrist and put two fingers right over my pulse point. Then he looked up at me, swallowing hard. I sucked in a breath, licking my lower lip before biting it. He zeroed in on my mouth and grinned, and at that precise moment, I realized that he knew exactly how attracted I was to him.

Before I knew what was going on, his lips were on mine. The kiss was as hot as it was surprising. *Oh my goodness.* His mouth was exquisite. It tasted like orange juice. The way he moved his tongue against mine was driving me crazy. My entire body was burning, and my panties were instantly wet. I pressed my thighs together, completely shocked by my body's reaction and by the fact that he was kissing me in the first place.

He stepped back with a groan. "Fuck."

I didn't say anything, but that one word seemed to sum this up pretty nicely.

"Grace... Fuck, that was out of line. That was... I don't even know what it was."

"Neither do I," I whispered.

He looked up at me and shook his head. "I have no excuse. You're in shock, and I'm taking advantage of you."

Huh? That's what he's thinking? That didn't sound right. On the other hand, what did I know? Perhaps I was still in a recovery state, and that would explain all my strange reactions to him.

"Right."

"Since you don't seem to be in any danger, I'll leave. That's better."

I nodded, taken aback by what just happened. "Thanks a lot for everything, Zachary."

"If you do start to feel any symptoms like having difficulty breathing, go to the ER, okay?"

I nodded like a weirdo because I didn't know what else to say. The man had just given me the hottest kiss of my life, and now he was giving me instructions to go to the ER. The whole thing felt bizarre.

"Right. Thanks for the pizza and the shower," he said.

"You're welcome."

He walked with his back toward the door, turned to open it, and then said, "Good night, Grace."

"Good night, Zachary."

CHAPTER EIGHT

ZACHARY

Dinners in the LeBlanc-Broussard mansion were always crazy. Granted, every time we got together here at the house, it was loud and insane, but for some reason, evenings were even more so. The entire gang was gathered at the huge table in the living room.

Even though I hadn't grown up in this house, when I thought of home, this was the first place that came to mind—not even my own house. My parents and both sets of grandparents lived here. We all thought they were going to kill one another when our parents first came up with the idea, but it worked surprisingly well. It helped that the place was huge, so everyone had their own wing. They met mostly for meals. Mom was still at the gallery every day. The grandmothers were at their fragrance shop, and my grandfathers went fishing every chance they got. Dad was living his best life since he retired from running the company.

"Zachary, darling," Isabeau said. "I've been meaning to call but forgot. Did you move forward with your idea with the ranch?"

"I went to see it."

"What was your impression?"

"It's run-down and needs a big investment, but they're doing a good thing. I have several ideas for the place."

Xander stared at me. He was sitting closest to me at the table. "I still don't get it. Why don't you just write them a check and be done with it?"

Bailey, his fiancée, laughed. "Oh, Xander. It's not always about the money."

"I know that, but these people have been running that place forever. Clearly they know what they're doing. Why would you even need to get involved?"

"I want to," I told him.

"Is Grace Deveraux still interested?" Celine inquired.

"Yes. I met her, too, when I was there." And twice more, but I left out that detail.

"After you mentioned her, I did a bit more asking around," Isabeau said.

I gritted my teeth. "I would rather you stop doing that," I replied, just managing to keep my voice level.

"Why? What harm could it do?"

I didn't want to get into the whole issue with Marcel, so all I said was "It's not necessary."

Even though Grace and I were at odds, I could understand her point of view. I'd be furious, too, if someone called a potential business partner to insinuate that I wasn't a trustworthy party.

Isabeau turned to Georgie, Julian's fiancée. "Darling, I hope it's okay that we're talking about the Deverauxes."

Georgie had dated Kyle at one point, and he'd been a complete jackass to her. He constantly put her down and ended up cheating on her.

"Yes, yes. Don't worry. I've actually never met Grace. Kyle only mentioned her a few times to say that she'd gotten married, and…" She frowned. "I didn't like the way he spoke about her. Almost as though he didn't like his own sister."

"I don't know why those boys turned out like they did. Their parents are good people," Dad said.

"Anyway, people are saying that Grace is actually quite charitable and a good person. She just had a rough few years with the divorce and then the whole scandal with her brothers," Isabeau went on. "What was your impression?"

That she's smoking hot and a spitfire. "I didn't interact enough with her to form an opinion," I said.

"Want me to look into her financials?" Xander asked.

"No," I said a bit too forcefully.

He frowned.

Anthony chuckled.

Beckett was grinning. "Careful, guys. We're pissing off our brother, and I'm not even sure why."

"I know you all want to help, but no one needs to look into anything, okay?" I insisted. "This is just going to be a passion project. If I get to do it, fine. If Grace ends up partnering with them, I won't sweat over it."

That wasn't strictly true. I really wanted to invest in this, though I couldn't explain why.

Although, after our kiss, everything changed. I couldn't understand what the hell had been going through my mind, and I wasn't going to try any longer. But I was starting to accept the fact that there was no denying my attraction to Grace Deveraux. It had started off as something purely physical—especially since I'd pegged her so wrong in the beginning. But she'd simply had her guard up because we'd started off on the wrong foot.

"I personally think that this would be a great side project for you," Mom said. I tilted forward so I could see her. "You've always had different interests than the rest of us, and I think this is a very nice investment."

Sometimes I thought Mom secretly wished I'd have become an EMT or a doctor so she wouldn't be the only one who wasn't involved in the Orleans Conglomerate. But she never told me that to my face.

"We'll see how it goes," I said, then looked at my grandfathers. "So, how's fishing going?"

"Fantastic. We found this great spot. I don't know why the fish congregate there," Grandpa Felix said.

Grandpa David nodded. "It's our new favorite spot. Let's hope others don't find it."

I was feeling a bit guilty that I didn't go out with them as much lately, but Dad was on it.

"I'm going to join you this weekend," Anthony told them.

"Me too," Beckett replied.

Those two were always a duo. But I supposed that was to be expected. They'd been very tight growing up too.

"Sure. The more, the merrier," Felix said. "We can even make a little competition, see who gets the most fish."

"We're always up for that," Anthony said lazily.

Beckett groaned. "No, I always get my ass beaten. It's an unfair competition. You two"—he pointed to our grandfathers—"spend half your time out on the bayou."

David laughed. "You boys can always join us."

The competitive streak was strong in the family. But that made for great conversation, and it shifted the focus off me and Grace.

Once I left the house, though, my mind was back on her. Fucking hell, the more I tried to forget about the way she tasted, the more details I recalled. I was barely fighting the temptation to contact her. I didn't have her phone number, but I had my ways of obtaining it. And yet I knew it was a bad idea.

When I got into the car, I decided to call Gaston. My new phone was more sophisticated than the one I'd lost in the Mississippi, and I was still getting used to it, but I liked it. Thankfully, all my contacts and other information had been backed up to the cloud, so I was able to transfer everything over as soon as I'd purchased it.

I hadn't heard from Gaston in a while, and I wanted to know what was going on. He and Felicia had both made a great impression on me, but I had a feeling that they weren't handling all this like a business. He answered after a few rings.

"Good evening, Zachary," he said.

"Hi, Gaston."

"It's great that you're calling me. I've been meaning to get in touch with you, but Felicia and I were busy this week. We bought a new horse, Starlight."

"Congrats," I said. "How come? You aren't opening this year."

"No, but this was too good an opportunity to pass up."

I needed to take a really good look at their cash flow. I couldn't imagine it did them any favors to buy a horse in a year with no income. I didn't plan to run this as a profitable operation or anything, but still, I didn't want to run it in the red. It was just a passion project, but I wanted it to be able to finance itself so it wouldn't always need cash infusions.

"How about you drive out to the ranch to check him out sometime next week?"

I didn't say anything for a moment, then asked, "Is that necessary?"

"Yes. It's good for you to meet the horses, and we can discuss some more about the investment with Grace as well."

Well, that piqued my interest. "She's coming too?"

"I haven't spoken to her yet, but she seemed to really like the horses, so I'm assuming she'll be thrilled."

"Then count me in," I said without hesitation—which was when I realized exactly how deep in trouble I was.

CHAPTER NINE
GRACE

I was so excited that I couldn't even sit still in my car as I drove slightly faster than was legal toward the ranch. I loved horses! Business-wise, it wasn't smart for Gaston and Felicia to acquire a new horse when they didn't plan to open for the season, but it probably took time to train them properly. Whatever, I was excited!

This time, I dressed appropriately, going home after work to put on sneakers and jeans so I didn't have to mind my step everywhere I walked.

After my mishap in the Mississippi River, I had a little cold the next day, but otherwise I was fine. I didn't tell my parents about the incident—why worry them? A small scratch that was healing on my arm was the only reminder of last weekend, as well as my new phone.

I thought about Zachary and how he heroically dove in to save me and how big of a deal that really was. I should've done something for him, but it took a while to get new identification and credit cards, since all my stuff was in a bag somewhere at the bottom of all that water. If I ever saw him again, I'd offer to buy him dinner. It was the least I could do.

I arrived a bit earlier than Gaston suggested, but I was far too excited. I hoped it wouldn't bother them. After parking, I noticed Gaston out in the paddock with a gorgeous pitch-black horse. I wondered if it was the new one.

He gestured for me to join him, and I practically broke into a run. It was a good thing it wasn't very sunny today; it meant we could stay out here for longer because it wouldn't be hot.

I looked up at the sky. *Hmmm...* It wasn't just *not* sunny. It was dark enough that I feared a storm would follow. Had they announced bad weather on the radio and I missed it? Oh, who cared? I could get my fix with the animals before it started to rain.

"This is the new horse?" I asked.

"Yes, this is Starlight," he announced proudly.

"He's beautiful. Can I pat him?"

"Let's try. He's a bit shy but didn't have a problem with me and Felicia."

I stepped closer, waiting for a sign from Starlight that he was uncomfortable, but I didn't get any. I gently put my hand on his mane. "Hi, Starlight. Nice to meet you."

"He's going to make a great addition. We don't have many black horses."

"Is there a reason for that?"

"Some kids are afraid of them. But when I saw Starlight, I knew we needed him. If I've learned one thing over the years, it's that you buy horses when you find them. You don't start to search for one when you need it."

The rest of the horses kept circling Starlight but didn't get too close. Gaston seemed to know what I was thinking, because he explained, "They'll accept him before long. It's only his second day."

"He's got his own feeding space in the barn?"

"For now, yes. When he's ready, he'll eat with the rest. By the way, Zachary should arrive soon."

My entire body stood to attention as I whipped my head toward Gaston, taking a deep breath. "He's joining us?"

"Yes. Didn't I mention that?"

"No." I mentally reviewed my appearance. I didn't look my best, but he'd seen me soaking wet. This was progress.

I was suddenly on edge. My stomach constricted, and my breath came out a bit labored. I didn't know how things were between us. Confusing, that was for sure.

"I don't like these clouds," Gaston said. "It's gonna start pouring. I'm betting we're in for a storm."

"They didn't say anything about it on the radio that I'd heard." But I was never listening to the weather channel.

"I don't trust the weather forecast any more than I trust economists making forecasts. Neither of them ever get it right."

I started to laugh. "Gaston, you're onto something."

I focused on Starlight while I was still processing that Zachary was going to join us. The horse seemed to sense that I was getting antsy, because he leaned into my touch. I pressed my forehead against his. "You're going to do great."

"There he is," Gaston called.

And just like that, not even Starlight's touch could calm my body's response. My heartbeat accelerated, and all my muscles somehow locked up. I took in deep breaths, my palms already getting a bit sweaty.

"Sorry I'm late," Zachary said.

Why was even his voice attractive? The man was such a complete package. I was appreciative of what he'd done for me after the river incident. I wasn't discounting the fact that that could've gone way wrong and I'd be dead. Yet I wasn't ready to totally let my guard down either. I had been fooled once before and hurt badly in the end. I wasn't saying the two men were similar, but I still needed to be cautious.

Finally, I turned around to face him. He was watching me with a twinkle in his eye and a half smile. He didn't seem surprised that I was here. Had Gaston told him?

"Hi, Grace." He stopped a few feet in front of me, checking me out. He didn't linger, though I felt as if he'd just undressed me with his gaze. What was that about?

"Hey. This is Starlight. Isn't he great?"

He looked at the horse as if this was the first time he was seeing him even though I'd been standing right next to him the whole time.

"I like him," Zachary said. He did a whole circle around him, looking but not touching.

"You can get closer," Gaston said. "He's docile."

"That means he won't need as much time in training, right?" Zachary asked.

Gaston shrugged. "I'm not judging that until I've seen how the first training session goes."

Thunder rumbled across the sky. I winced. Starlight took a few steps back but then immediately relaxed.

Gaston looked up. "What did I tell you? That weatherman. I don't know why they still keep them around."

"I'm sure the clouds will pass," Zachary said nonchalantly.

Gaston snorted. "I've been out here on the bayou for a long time. Clouds like that don't just pass. They pour and pour until everything's soaked."

"Should we get the horses inside, then?" I asked, wondering what Starlight would think of a cold rain and more thunder.

"Yes," Gaston replied.

Zachary came up next to me, patting Starlight's mane as well. I felt myself breaking out in a sweat even though I was certain the temperature had actually cooled off a bit since I arrived. When our arms accidentally touched, I felt even hotter. Yeah, a cold shower wouldn't be bad... even if it came in the form of rain.

"I'll call Felicia, and she and I will take the horses in." He eyed the two of us. "Actually, how comfortable are you two herding horses?"

"I can lead Starlight in," I said.

"That'll work," Gaston said. "Zachary, you could take two."

I liked seeing Gaston in action. He was confident but led with a soft authority, which I always preferred.

"I can take two as well," I offered.

"Let's not stress Starlight too much. He isn't used to the group yet."

"I'll take good care of him." He was right about that.

Gaston was leading four horses himself. I looked back and noticed the others were simply following us. That was interesting.

Starlight leaned into me more with each round of thunder, seeking comfort. I patted him, whispering quietly, "It's okay, Starlight. Just a thunderstorm." I was certain he'd lived through quite a few in his lifetime, but this being a new place, it was probably unsettling for him.

Once we got the horses inside, the thunder intensified, then we heard the unmistakable sound of rain hitting the roof. *Tap, tap, tap, tap.*

"As I said, that weatherman should be fired," Gaston grumbled.

Zachary started to laugh, looking at me conspiratorially before we brought each horse to their place. I liked how Gaston spoke as if there was just one universal weatherman.

"All right. We'll just leave them all in here," Gaston said.

"Should we feed them?" I asked.

He put his hands on his hips. "I'm going to bring some hay later on. Was supposed to do it earlier and forgot, and I don't have enough to feed all of them."

I wanted to spend some more time in here. I wasn't ready for whatever came next, which surely included more time with Zachary... and without horses between us as a buffer.

"Right, you two. I'll give you blankets for cover, and we can make a run to the house. Felicia started cooking some hearty stew this morning. We'd love to have you both for dinner."

"Oh, that won't be necessary," I said. "Although, we could talk more shop," I corrected myself, realizing that this was as good as an opportunity as any.

"I'm good with stew," Zachary said. He was looking at me with amusement in his eyes. Why? Even more perplexing was my body's reaction. It was practically simmering.

Oh Lord.

Gaston gave us each a huge blanket. I wasn't certain it was really necessary—until he opened the door. My God, it was pouring.

"We'll get wet anyway," I said.

"We'll manage. We've had worse," Zachary added. He glanced at me again, and this time I did start laughing. The memory of us in that river wasn't something I was going to forget anytime soon.

The main house was quite a distance away, and the ground was already damp. We were sloshing around with every step. Even though the day had been hot, the rain was icy. I decided on the spot that I didn't like cold rain, and it did not equal a cold shower.

The second we stepped inside the house, I used a blanket to dry myself and caught Zachary's eye. He swallowed hard, his eyes fixated on a point below my neck.

I looked down at myself. I was wearing a bra without padding, and my nipples had decided to perk up and say hi. I tried to cover myself with the blanket as much as possible, but I was simmering yet again despite being utterly cold on the outside. I didn't dare meet Zachary's eyes.

"You should lose that blanket. It's only going to make you feel colder."

He was right, of course. I dropped the blanket in the same spot Gaston and Zachary had left theirs, then crossed my arms over my chest.

When I heard Zachary take a sharp intake of breath, I risked a glance at him. He was fixating on something again, but what could it be? Certainly not my boobs—I was covering those. Whatever it was, his pupils had dilated. The urge to be closer to him hit me like a ton of bricks.

"Oh, there you are. You made it. You don't even look that bad. I was afraid that rain soaked you. Grace, darling, do you want a blow-dryer?"

"That would be great," I replied. I could also use it on my shirt.

"I have one right there in the bathroom." She pointed to a small wooden door, and I immediately darted toward it, taking a deep breath as I stepped inside, closing the door behind me.

The blow-dryer was on a shelf above the sink. Grabbing it, I looked at myself in the full-length mirror on the door. I actually wasn't that wet. My shirt was only soaked because my wet hair was on it and lying over my breasts. The bottoms of my jeans were soaked, too, but other than that, I was good.

I plugged in the dryer, putting it on the hottest setting. I missed having my product with me because my hair was going to look insanely frizzy, but it didn't matter. Tonight was about finding out what Gaston and Felicia wanted and what they expected from a partner—*not* about looking my best or impressing Zachary. I would be eternally grateful to him for what he did and making sure I got home okay and was safe. But right now, I had to keep my head in the game.

When I stepped out of the bathroom, I noticed that the house smelled absolutely amazing. I remembered where the kitchen was from the tour last time I was here. The three of them were gathered in there.

"There you are," Felicia said. "The stew is waiting in the slow cooker."

"It's still early, woman," Gaston said, and I realized it was only six o'clock. "No one has to eat now except the horses. I need to take the pallet out and feed them."

"I'll do that," Zachary said at the same time I exclaimed, "I want to feed them."

Gaston clapped his hands. "Perfect. Then I can help Felicia finish dinner faster. What do I have to do, darling?"

"I'll throw a salad together. Bring some pickles and other veggies. Maybe you can whip up an appetizer," she suggested.

Gaston jerked his head back. I barely managed to stifle laughter. Clearly he'd expected something along the lines of "Oh, there's nothing for you to do."

"Grace and I will take care of the horses while you do that," Zachary said.

Huh, that twinkle was back. What exactly did this man have in mind?

Our kiss flashed in my head. My entire body vibrated at the thought of repeating it. But that was highly unlikely, wasn't it? Then again, so was our first one. Sometimes I still wondered if it had really happened.

"All right, I'll bring you two raincoats," Gaston said.

"Will they fit us?" I asked.

"Yes. They're one size fits all. We have quite a few for our guests, since the weather can be unpredictable. It's much better than a towel or an umbrella. Just your face gets wet."

Gaston led us to one of the seminar rooms and opened a closet. It was full of coats. Zachary and I each grabbed one and put them on. Mine was a bit too big, but it would do. I pulled the hood up and was ready to go.

Gaston took us out through the back door. "You can take this one," he told me, pointing to a small haystack. "Zachary, if you grab one of the big ones, that'll be enough for tonight's feed.

"All right," Zachary said.

He bent down and easily lifted the stack. *Yummm.* I couldn't see his body properly, but I could imagine his muscles were stretched taut right now.

"You can break into a run, Grace. I'll catch up." Zachary said.

"Oh. You don't mind?"

"Not at all. I'm going to be slower with this."

"I'll wait for you at the stables, then."

I ran through the rain, my face freezing after only a few steps. *Holy crap.* I was breathing hard by the time I arrived at the stable.

"Hey, horses," I greeted. "Hi, Starlight." I pulled at the string under my chin and lowered the hood so he'd recognize me. "We're here with dinner."

Zachary came in only a minute or so later.

"You were fast," I said.

"Glad I made it. Couldn't even see what was right in front of me."

That's right, he couldn't shield his face, since he was carrying the heavy pallet. As soon as he sat it on the wooden table next to the door, I became acutely aware of the fact that we were completely alone. He lowered his hood too.

"They have a feeding dock for all of them. I noticed it earlier."

"I did too."

"I'm going to feed Starlight separately," I said, reaching for the hay, intending to take a few handfuls, but Zachary caught my wrists with both hands.

I sucked in a breath.

"Grace."

God, he sounded exactly like he did when we kissed.

"Hmm?" I asked noncommittally.

"Let's talk first."

My ears started to ring a bit. I realized it was because my pulse had quickened.

"About what?"

"The ranch, the kiss—your pick, but we need to talk."

CHAPTER TEN

GRACE

"Let's feed the horses first."

I didn't need to look at him to know he was smiling. Why was my discomfort making him laugh?

"Fine."

I filled a bucket for Starlight while Zachary took care of the main feeding area. I lingered in Starlight's stall. It wasn't fair to the others, but he was my favorite. I was rooting for the new kid. I started combing his mane, which was very soothing for me, too, and he seemed to like it. I didn't realize that I'd lingered too long until Zachary appeared in the doorway of his stall.

"You really took a liking to him, huh?"

I nodded. "Yeah. He's very sweet, though a bit shy. But that's just because you're new, isn't it, Starlight?"

"Have you ever owned horses?"

"No, but my parents took me riding when I was a kid. They refused to buy horses, though. Dad was actually against me riding too. He thought it wasn't very safe."

"Bad accidents can happen," Zachary said in a stern voice, then softened it. "Grace, I didn't want to put you on the spot earlier."

I whipped my head toward him. He was standing with his feet wide apart, arms crossed over his chest. How could he look sexy even in that god-awful raincoat?

"Really? Because you did seem to enjoy yourself a bit."

The corners of his mouth twitched. "Sorry."

"That I caught wind of it or that you did it?"

"Both," he said, and now he was full-on smiling. "But I didn't want to make you uncomfortable. We don't have to talk about any of that. I just wanted to clear the air because everything was..."

"Insane?" I suggested.

"Yep." He snapped fingers as if he'd been searching for that word all along. "Perfect way to put it."

I laughed. "Hmm. Let's just leave it at that, okay?"

I returned my attention to Starlight's mane, but there wasn't much for me to do. I'd combed it perfectly. He currently had much better hair than I did.

"Sure. Whatever makes you comfortable. You look great in that raincoat, by the way."

"Really? Because I have never felt less sexy—ever."

A loud groan resounded throughout the stall. It took me a second to realize it came from Zachary.

"You're fucking sexy no matter what you wear. Even when I took you out of that river, all I could think about was not ogling you like a damn Neanderthal."

I sucked in a breath, repeating the same stroke on Starlight's hair because I didn't know what to do with my hands. His confession took me by complete surprise.

"Well, you fooled me," I whispered. "You seemed very focused on getting me to calm down."

"I can multitask," he said without hesitation.

Right! Clearly there was no stopping whatever this was, so I decided to play by the same rules. I didn't even know what they were, but I could improvise.

Looking him straight in the eye, I said, "You don't look too shabby in your raincoat either."

His eyes lit up. "I'm glad you noticed."

"Hard not to."

"Really? I'd say this makes it difficult enough." He motioned to the coat.

"Yes, but I do have a good memory and an excellent imagination. Like you."

He bent at the waist, tilting forward toward me. "I like this side of you, Grace."

I swallowed hard. "I like it too. Wasn't even sure I still had it."

His smile fell. Straightening up, he frowned. "What do you mean?"

"I haven't done this—teasing—in years. Forgive me if my skills are rusty."

"I assure you they are not. I could tell you I have proof, but it's best not to talk about this anymore."

It was on the tip of my tongue to ask what he meant when it dawned on me.

Wait. Does he have a hard-on?

Jesus, Grace. Why did your mind jump right there? He could mean a million other things. Maybe his pulse is racing or something along those lines.

"You've been divorced for a year, right? Longer?" he asked.

My shoulders slumped as I lowered the brush. There was really no point in brushing anymore. Starlight's mane couldn't possibly look any better.

"Ah, can we talk about anything else?"

He nodded. "Of course. Sorry, none of my business."

"I don't have anything to hide, and it doesn't make me uncomfortable, just sad," I said as we walked out of the stall. "But yes, even though I've been divorced for longer than a year, I haven't been out on a date. Honestly, I threw everything I had into my company. At the time, it was my only way to survive. It was very important to me that my business succeeded so I could regain my self-esteem," I explained as we headed toward the door. We didn't leave the barn, though. It was still pouring rain.

"You should be proud of what you've accomplished. From what I know, your business is a great success. I was stunned when I first looked up how young the company was. You're a very good businesswoman."

I tilted my head. "And you weren't expecting that from the socialite who just does things for her ego, were you?"

Zachery closed his eyes, shaking his head before opening them again. "I truly apologize for that. Marcel's words coupled with our first interactions gave me the completely wrong impression. I usually don't jump to conclusions like that."

I was willing to give him the benefit of the doubt because he'd jumped in the Mississippi River for me.

"I gathered a lot of experience in the family's company before I got married," I said.

"And then you quit."

"Yes. It was one of my husband's wishes that I become a full-time wife."

"Why did you do it?"

The obvious confusion on his face made me second-guess myself all over again. I guess I was just trying to keep the peace in our marriage at the time, but that wasn't something I wanted to tell Zachary.

"Honestly? I don't know. I thought at the time that's what good wives are supposed to do. I didn't realize his intentions, though."

"Interesting. And you didn't like it? Being a stay-at-home wife?"

"No, not at all. I always loved working even though I wasn't seeing eye to eye with my brothers on many things. To be fair, maybe that's one of the reasons why I quit. I wanted some distance from them. They were more like my husband than like me, I came to find out later."

He nodded once. "Makes sense. From what I know of Kyle, I wouldn't want to be around him either."

"You don't need to sugarcoat anything. I know who he is, and I make no apologies for him. He's always had a chip on his shoulder somehow regarding Dad. Wanted to prove that he could do better."

"Even if it was illegally," Zachary said through gritted teeth.

"Sounds that way. He and Beau were very eager to get me out of the company and make it clear that there was no place for me." I glanced at the floor. It bothered me that I'd never had the sibling relationship that other kids had in their families. But everyone's upbringing was different, so I tried not to dwell on it too much.

"What the actual fuck!" Zachary exclaimed. "That's pretty shitty of your family, in my opinion. One thing I know is that not one of my brothers would try to undermine any of us in business. That's just not our way. We have one another's backs." His voice was hard, like he couldn't possibly accept what I told him.

"Then your family has a bit more heart than my brothers. Anyway, my husband—I only realized much later on—wanted me to stop working so he could have the upper hand. You know, if he controlled the finances, he'd control me. Bit by bit, he started to chip away at my confidence." I couldn't bring myself to look up from the floor. "He started very subtly, telling me what was okay to buy or not. Then he got angry when I'd use my savings." I shook my head, finally looking up to see the coldness in Zachary's eyes.

Why am I telling him this? It's not like we're friends.

"That son of a bitch." His visceral response actually made me feel good. How strange was that? It was like he really cared.

"I'm happy it's all over, honestly. And I'm happy we never managed to get pregnant." I closed my eyes. "Sorry, I don't know why I said that. It's very personal."

"Grace." His voice was soft. When I opened my eyes, I realized he'd stepped closer. "I'm sorry for everything you've been through, and I'm very sorry for being such an asshole to you. It wasn't my intention to put you down."

"Well, I wasn't exactly welcoming either. I can imagine that having someone continuously make snide remarks would put you on edge. I'm sorry too."

It was hard to form a coherent thought with him so close. He smelled like rain, and mud, and hay, and horse, and I somehow loved it.

"The snide remarks weren't helping." He winked. "Still, I don't want to excuse myself. When you're an asshole, you're an asshole. And I was an asshole, so the excuses don't matter."

"Thank you. I appreciate that even though I do have my share of blame."

"Right." He tilted his head to one side, breaking eye contact. Taking a deep breath, he added, "Want to run back? The rain doesn't appear to be slowing down."

As if on cue, another lightning bolt flashed across the sky, followed by a roll of thunder.

"Yeah. This is only getting worse. How are we going to drive back in this weather? Visibility is zero."

"We're going to probably need twice as long to make it back to the city." He was looking outside the barn, obviously trying to decide what to do.

"Maybe we shouldn't stay for dinner," I suggested.

"Let's go back to the house. I think that dinner will help pass some time so maybe the rain will subside a bit. I'll race you," he said.

I burst out laughing.

"Right. You're a foot taller than me. That would be a very unfair race. Unless you give me head start." And then I darted out of the barn without looking back, securing my hood around my head.

The rain was even colder than before, and my teeth were chattering by the time I reached the main house. I burst in unceremoniously and then stayed put for a few seconds, trying to catch my breath. Zachary came in right after me.

"Good God. It's terrible out there."

"I agree," I said.

I immediately opened my raincoat and shrugged it off. Even though it wasn't wet on the inside, I felt very cold. Fortunately it was long enough to cover my jeans.

Felicia hurried toward us. "Thank goodness you're back. I was wondering if something happened. You were out longer than we figured."

"We're good," Zachary said in a confident tone that invited no further questions. "Something smells tasty."

"Dinner is ready. And you can just leave those in the corner."

We did as she said. Zachary was right next to me as we followed Felicia through the house. Once we entered the kitchen, I could see the wooden table was full of goodies.

"Felicia, this is a feast," I said.

The appetizer was a crab salad, which I was dying to taste. The main course was indeed a stew. I spied black beans, sweet potato, and shrimp.

"Come on, you two. Sit down. All went well at the stables?" Gaston asked.

"Yep. Horses are well-fed. Starlight's hair was thoroughly styled," Zachary said, winking at me.

I blushed. "I couldn't help it. He seemed to like being fussed with."

"You have a knack for horses, Grace," Felicia exclaimed. "You're welcome here anytime. The horses will love you. And you can join whatever activities you want, whenever. There's no need to notify us."

Her comments humbled me. I was happy she trusted me so much.

The atmosphere at the table changed a bit as conversation shifted to talking shop. Good. I took a look at Zachary, but he seemed very relaxed. He reached for bread as Felicia put crab salad on each plate.

"I'd definitely love that. I wouldn't want to just be financially invested in this, but also personally. Not to make any decisions, of course," I added quickly, looking at Gaston and Felicia. "You're the experts here, but I'd like to be involved."

"If I'm honest," Felicia said, "we do need someone with good business sense. We've been winging it for thirty years, which is possibly how we ended up in this conundrum in the first place. So any knowledge would be helpful."

"I'd be more than willing to share."

Zachary was suspiciously quiet. When I looked at him, he said, "Me, too, of course. There's no doubt about that. I don't know as much about horses as Grace, but I'm very good at business."

"What would each of you suggest we improve?" Felicia asked as I took the first forkful of crab salad.

"You're a very good cook," I offered once I'd swallowed. She beamed from ear to ear. "As for changes, well, first things first, I'd say that all the cabins need air-conditioning."

"Yes, they've become quite unbearable in the summer," Felicia said.

"And I suggest making some of the cabins bigger for groups that want to stay together."

"I was going to suggest that as well," Zachary said. "Kids, especially the teenagers, prefer to do things as a group. They want their privacy, too, but not too much."

"You know, we do get more and more teenagers," Gaston said. "And that definitely has merit."

Zachary and I both had plenty of suggestions as dinner went on. It didn't feel like we were competing—more like we were collaborating.

After we gulped down the food, I leaned back in the chair and put a hand on my belly. "I'm about to explode."

"We've got dessert too. Apple pie," Felicia told us.

"Oooh, I can always make space for apple pie."

She brought the dessert to the table, with vanilla ice cream on the side. "I'm sorry this is a bit unceremonious, but Gaston and I usually slice our own portions and spoon whatever we want of the ice cream on top."

"My brothers and I do the same whenever one of our grandmothers makes pie," Zachary said. "With so many of us, there's nothing left after everyone gets their servings."

Felicia and Gaston looked at each other. I felt like they were going to announce something, and I was instantly on edge.

"We have an idea," Felicia said. "Why don't you both participate in this project? You clearly have good ideas, and you could work well together." She hesitated on those last few words. I didn't blame her, since we'd been at each other's throats during our first visit here.

"I'd be good with that," Zachary said, which completely shocked me.

I swallowed hard, feeling put on the spot. Could I do this with him? I considered it for a split second before realizing it wasn't possible. After the way things had gone with Roger, I didn't want to risk anything. Never again would I depend on anyone else or have to ask for approval. I wasn't sure any of it would actually apply in this case, but my body instantly shifted into fight-or-flight.

"The idea does have merit," I said, "but I'd prefer to go into it by myself, if at all."

My announcement was met with silence. I realized they were expecting me to explain my reasoning, but what could I say? I got too burned by my ex-husband?

"It was just a thought," Felicia said in a low tone as we all helped ourselves to the apple pie.

More thunder rolled in—louder than before. The windows clattered, and I nearly dropped my fork.

"This is turning out to be one big damn storm," Gaston exclaimed. He looked out the windows. "It's going to tear out trees at this point."

"The wind was strong when we came back from the stables," I said.

"It's not just strong," Zachary said, glancing at his phone. "Weather channel says it's fifty miles an hour. It's definitely going to tear out trees."

"It's going to be madness driving back," I whispered.

"No way are we letting the two of you go back to New Orleans tonight. It's unsafe out there," Felicia said. "You'll get blown off the road! And what if a tornado pops up? You'll have nowhere to go."

I looked at her and saw the worry and concern all over her face. Zachary still had his head tilted to his phone, but he'd raised his eyebrows, indicating that Gaston's assessment was indeed accurate.

"What do you suggest?" he asked.

"One of the cabins is still fully functional. You can spend the night there," Gaston said. "It's not big, but it'll be comfortable for you two. Has almost all the amenities except air-conditioning. But you won't need it tonight because temperatures are dropping. You can drive back in the morning. We'd offer to put you up here at the house, but there's just one bedroom, and that's ours."

I swallowed hard. The thought of rooming with Zachary in a cabin was enough to make me hyperventilate. Our smoking-hot kiss flashed in my mind, as if it had just happened.

On the other hand, I truly didn't want to drive back.

I nodded. "I'll take you up on your offer. Thank you."

"I'll stay too," Zachary said. "Thanks to both of you for looking out for us. All the news outlets say the traffic is already madness. Some roads have been closed down because of flooding. Apparently, the rain is already too much for the sewer system."

"Excellent. Since neither of you are driving, how about I bring a bottle of our best brandy? Gaston made it. And we can finish all of this pie while we're at it too," Felicia suggested.

"I'm up for some brandy," I said. "Kind of need it. That cold seeped into my bones even though I didn't get wet."

"Not a brandy type of guy, but if Gaston made it, I'll try it," Zachary added.

"It's a party, then," Felicia concluded.

Chapter Eleven

Zachary

Gaston and Felicia were very good at entertaining. They shared stories about what dinner and lunchtime looked like during camp season, how crazy and loud it all was. They loved the joy they brought to the kids' faces and the restoration that the peacefulness of the ranch gave to the veterans still fighting their demons from war.

Grace seemed to relax, too—especially after the second glass of brandy. Then again, we'd had enough food and pie that we could down a whole bottle and I doubted anyone would get even tipsy. I kept wondering why she'd so quickly shut down the idea of both of us supporting this project. It seemed almost like instinct, as if the alternative simply wasn't thinkable. I didn't even think it was because she'd be collaborating with me; it was more that she couldn't give up control to anyone. I wanted to get to the root of it, but I didn't want to bring it up now in front of Gaston and Felicia. I'd have plenty of time to address it later.

"Right, I think it's time for you two to go to the cabin," Felicia said. "The rain has eased up a bit, but who knows for how long? I think you can make it there just with an umbrella."

Grace yawned. "That would be amazing. I'm actually pretty tired."

"No wonder," Gaston exclaimed, pointing to the grandfather clock opposite him. It was almost midnight.

"There are fresh towels there," Felicia said. "My sister was supposed to visit, so I put them there for her. Unfortunately, I don't have any pajamas or anything like that to give you."

"We'll manage," I told her confidently.

"The couch is comfortable enough but not very big," Felicia commented.

"I'm sure it'll be fine," I said. "Which cabin is it?"

She gave us a key with the number 14 and pointed to the right. "It's the first one you see there. It's the one that's in the best condition. You can't possibly miss it. If you need anything, please call."

Three lightning bolts flashed in the sky. Thunder cracked soon after.

"You'd better be quick. I have a feeling it's going to start pouring again," Felicia said.

"You're right," Grace replied as we left the house.

She walked in front of me at a quick pace. There was mud everywhere. Even the air smelled cold. I quickly unlocked the door when we reached the cabin, and we both closed the umbrellas before stepping in. Grace immediately turned on the light, and I barely bit back a groan.

"Oh my. This place is much, much smaller than I imagined," she said.

The couch was tiny. I was certain that even after pulling it out, I wasn't going to fit. The entire place was downright claustrophobic. The bedroom was just off the main room. There was no door to separate them.

Grace bit her cheek, turning slightly toward me. As we chucked our shoes at the door, she offered, "You take the bedroom."

"What?"

"Zachary, you can't sleep here. Look at this couch."

"Then I'll sleep on the floor, Grace, but you're not sleeping on the couch."

"You're going to be awake the whole night, tossing and turning."

"I'll manage."

She curled her lip up and smiled. "Yeah, but then I'll hear you from the bedroom, which has no door. Then I won't be able to sleep either."

"And you can manage that?" I teased.

"Considering you're willing to break your back, I could risk a night of bad sleep because I'll hear you complain about it. Let's ask if any other cabin is inhabitable. I don't need much."

"Grace, you saw the other cabins. They're teardowns."

Her shoulders slumped. "You're right. So, you're okay with this?"

I was not fucking okay. But if there was one thing I'd learned, it was to make the best of circumstances. Complaining about something wasn't going to make it better, and I couldn't find a solution this late at night. Driving back to New Orleans was completely out of the question.

"Yes. Do you want to shower first?" I asked.

"I was just going to suggest that."

She walked away so quickly that it made me think my presence was unnerving her.

"Grace, I can sleep in the car if it makes you feel better," I suggested.

That would be even shittier than the couch, but I didn't want her to have to put up with this if it made her uncomfortable. That was the last thing I wanted to do after what she'd revealed about her ex.

She turned around. "What? Don't be ridiculous. It's going to be fine. I'll pretend you're not here."

I started to laugh despite myself. "And why is that?"

"Because it's the first time I'm sharing sleeping quarters with a man who's not my husband."

"Grace..."

She put her hands on her hips, shaking her head. "I don't know why I said that..."

I couldn't stand not being close to her, so I took a few steps forward. I wanted to look her in the eye, so I bent my knees until I was eye level with her.

She smiled. "You don't have to do that. I can look up."

I straightened up, and she wasn't averting her gaze anymore.

"Tell me what you need, and I'll make it happen," I said.

She narrowed her eyes. "You can't."

"Just try me."

"I'd like two beds here."

"No, you're right. I can't make that happen."

She winked at me, which meant she was more at ease. "See? I'm going to take a shower."

"Fine, I'll set up the sofa bed."

After Grace closed the door to the bathroom, I set the couch cushions in the corner of the room and wrangled the rickety frame out of its enclosure. When I finally got it open, I took one look at it and knew there was no way I could fit. I tested my theory, lying down on it. My feet hung off the bed. I angled myself, thinking that might give me more room—nope. To make matters worse, it was hard as a rock. Maybe the floor *would* be better.

Whatever, I'd just have to power through.

Grace was taking her sweet time in the shower, which was fine with me. I found some linens in a dresser next to the TV and plenty of blankets. I put everything I needed on the sofa bed, including three pillows, although I couldn't see how that would make things any better. At least it was just going to be one night.

Grace came out a few seconds later, fully dressed, then gasped.

"Zachary. Oh, come on." Her eyes focused on the couch. Clearly she was seeing the same problem I was. "That's... I don't even think you can fit diagonally on it."

"I can't. I tried. Don't worry, I've had worse."

She cocked a brow. "Really?"

"No, I just wanted to make it sound better."

"Well, Mr. Smooth Talker, jump in the shower. It takes forever for the water to get warm, and I think it still is, so don't waste too much time."

"I'm on it," I said, heading toward the bathroom.

While I showered, I kept thinking about how this could work out. I wanted to be involved in the ranch, but I knew Grace did too. I had to get to the bottom of why she couldn't see us working together. We'd apologized, and I thought we'd cleared the air. She knew I meant her no harm, especially after our swim in the river. Maybe she still thought I was an asshole.

I came out with the intention of addressing this, then nearly swallowed my tongue because Grace was lying down on the couch with the covers up to her chin.

"I've decided this is my spot," she said. "I already made the bed, but this is comfier, and I'm small. I fit on it perfectly, see?"

I noticed her head was on one of the pillows and her toes were peeking up from under the covers. She'd painted her nails red, and I liked it.

"Grace," I said carefully.

"Nope. Really, I won't hear anything different. Bed is yours. I'll sleep here. I won't toss and turn. And even if I do, I checked, and it doesn't creak. I guess that's a perk. The only one I can think of," she rambled.

I walked over to the edge of the sofa bed where she was lying. "You're not sleeping here."

"Yes, I am. It's decided."

I bent over her, looking her straight in the eye. "You are not sleeping here."

"What are you going to do to stop me?"

I reached out for her with one arm, lifting her off the bed. With the other, I grabbed the blanket she was clinging to for dear life, but that wasn't going to help her case. I carried her and the blanket toward the bedroom.

"Zachary." She sounded frantic. "Zachary, you're..."

It took me a few seconds to realize why she was frantic. Grace wasn't wearing her jeans anymore. And she either had the world's tiniest underwear or she wasn't wearing them either. My hands were firmly gripping her naked ass cheeks.

I groaned as my cock stood to attention. I'd gotten hard so fast, it was damn painful. I felt as if I was going to burst out of my jeans.

"What the fuck, Grace," I said, lowering her onto the bed. "I'm sorry, I didn't realize."

"I tried to warn you."

Her face was reddening as she scrambled to pull the covers around her, but she only managed to push them away completely. She was wearing black panties and her T-shirt from before. No bra. Those nipples... Christ.

I'd been fixating on them ever since we'd gotten caught in the rain coming back from the stables the first time. I'd been able to push the image out of my mind during dinner, but now it was going to be impossible.

"Ugh, why can't I get this blanket to cover me?"

I tugged at the blanket, intending to help, but accidentally brushed her thigh. Her skin instantly turned to goose bumps. She drew in a sharp breath, and I stilled completely. She pressed her thighs together, and I knew exactly what that meant. Even the small contact had excited her.

"Grace..."

"Zachary, I..."

I couldn't hold back any longer. I put a knee on the bed, between her feet. She instantly opened her thighs invitingly. I lost all sense of decency and kissed her so fiercely that she lost her balance. Somehow, I needed her even more than last time.

Chapter Twelve

Zachary

I lowered myself over her. The fly of my jeans was right over her pussy. She moaned at the contact, and I couldn't believe that she was so turned on already. I moved my pelvis back and forth while I circled her tongue with mine. She still tasted like brandy and pie. I wanted to explore her body, cover her with kisses. I couldn't stop at her mouth. The thought was unthinkable.

I put one hand on her right thigh, drawing my fingers along one side, then the underside. I liked how receptive her skin was. She still had goose bumps. Then she rolled her hips, seeking friction against the fly of my jeans. She was desperate for an orgasm. The thought nearly made me explode.

"It's the first time I'm sharing sleeping quarters with a man who's not my husband."

Was it possible that she hadn't been touched in so long? That would explain why she was so on edge already. I was honored that she was trusting me, wanting this. I paused the kiss, tracing a line to her ear.

"Grace," I said. "Babe, we need to stop."

"No," she moaned.

I had no idea where I'd found the self-restraint to even suggest that.

"I want you so damn badly," I confessed.

"I want you too."

Fuck. My self-restraint completely melted away at that.

"Are you wet?"

"Yes, yes," she whispered as if she could barely believe it herself.

Wanting to check for myself, I pushed two fingers inside her panties and groaned. She was so wet that my fingers practically slipped away. *Fucking hell.* I took my hand out of her panties and then pulled them down. I'd intended to pull them past her ass but managed to rip them completely. Grace sucked in a breath.

"I want your pussy naked and exposed for me so I can make you come the way you need."

She whimpered, nodding desperately.

"Lie back down. I want to kiss you."

I paused, straightening up so I was on my knees between her thighs, which were spread open for me. She was waxed clean, and her pussy was pink and inviting. Her breathing was labored.

"Take off your shirt."

She arched her back, immediately doing as I said, and pulled it over her head. Her hands got tangled in it, which gave me an idea.

Her breasts were exquisite. I leaned over once more, taking one nipple into my mouth. She moaned.

"I've been fantasizing about these all day," I said between licks.

She rolled her hips back and forth once more, as if she couldn't possibly stand to be still, as if she already had too much energy stored in her body and needed to release it. I moved to the other nipple.

"Zachary." Her voice was a plea and a protest at the same time.

I moved away so I was kneeling between her legs again. I ran my fingers up and down her inner thighs, right up to her pussy, then teased her clit with my forefinger. Her entire body shook as she closed her eyes tightly, pressing her lips together. Even her stomach seemed to clench. This woman was going to come the second I touched her clit again, I was sure of it. But I wanted to be inside her when that happened.

Then realization hit me.

"Grace." Her eyes flew open at my tone. "I don't have any condoms."

She swallowed hard. "Are you clean?"

"Yes."

"So am I, and I've been on the pill forever. It's good for my skin. We don't need anything."

"We don't?"

"Just touch me. Please. Don't stop touching me."

I couldn't resist, not after she was begging so beautifully. I pushed my jeans down just enough to free my cock and then laid on top of her again.

"I'll make you come, I promise. But I want to be deep inside your pussy when that happens. So pink and fucking soft and wet."

I groaned when I positioned my crown at her entrance. Then I drew the length of it over her clit, wanting to coat myself in her wetness so that I slid inside her easily.

"Zachary... oh my God."

Even this friction on her clit was too much, so I positioned my head at her entrance again and pushed inside. Grace came the next second, tightening around my cock so much that my vision blurred. Her face turned completely red, her mouth open wide as a guttural sound filled the room. She tried to move her wrists farther apart and nearly tore her T-shirt. I felt more than saw her legs move frantically on the bed. I couldn't get past how intense this already felt. Her inner muscles worked my cock so much that I was in danger of coming already.

I blinked several times so I could regain my vision. I didn't want to miss any detail of Grace coming this beautifully the second my cock was in her pussy. When I pulled back, then slammed in again, she cried so loud that I realized she hadn't even finished coming. I fucked her through her orgasm, watching her climax intensify more on every thrust.

She seemed in control of her body again a few moments later as she came down from the cusp. Perfect time to change positions. I put one of her ankles on my shoulder, tilting her pelvis slightly backward. She moaned at the change of angle. I liked how easy I could access her clit like this. I immediately brushed my thumb on it.

"Zachary!" she panted. She sounded as if she could barely string two syllables together, like she was still delirious with pleasure. It was all I wanted.

She attempted to free her hands, but I leaned forward enough so I could grab the shirt tightly. "No."

Her eyes flew open. "I'll do whatever you say, just please don't stop."

If she was going to continue begging like this, I'd blow any second now. I moved in and out of her, watching her face but also taking in the way her body changed on every thrust.

I could tell the moment she went from simply enjoying the sensations to bracing herself for another orgasm. First, she tilted her head back just a smidge, jutting her chin forward. She bit her lower lip and closed her eyes, then turned her head sideways, burying it in one of her arms. Her breasts were completely flushed. Her nipples turned, if possible, even harder. I knew that without even touching them. I twisted one between my fingers, and she whimpered.

Bringing a hand down from her nipple to her clit, I brushed it with two fingers, drawing out moan after moan. My cock felt on fire already. She fueled me on insanely fast. I wasn't going to hold back because I knew she wouldn't need long to come.

"Zachary, oh my God." She undulated her back almost in a spasm. She needed a break or she'd get too overstimulated, so I took my hand off her clit and slowed my thrusts.

Her eyes flew open, and she looked me directly in the eyes. I fucking loved this moment, pushing in and out slowly while she had her eyes on me. She was trying to anticipate my next move. At the same time, I knew without a doubt that she trusted me implicitly to drive her over the edge and give her all the pleasure she needed. The way she gave herself to me without any fucking restraint nearly brought me to my knees.

Grace always seemed to hold her cards close to her chest, but not at this moment. Right now, she was surrendering to me in this godforsaken cabin next to the bayou.

Her inner muscles started to tighten around my cock again. I decided that this was how I was going to make both of us come—by fucking her exquisitely slowly.

"Zachary, what are you doing to me? This is..." Her voice shook before turning into a cry. She seemed to lose control of her body again and yanked one hand out from under her shirt. I didn't chastise her or make her put it back; she needed freedom to move so she could ride this out completely. She lowered her leg from my shoulder, then pushed herself up onto her elbows. I realized she wanted to make this faster, but I grabbed her hips with both hands.

"No, babe."

"Zachary, please." Her voice shook so badly that I could barely make out what she was saying.

"I promise you'll come so damn hard. I fucking promise that. But you need to trust me."

Her entire body was trembling, but she nodded and lay back down. I kept her hips up slightly, a few inches from the bed. I continued to fuck her at the same rhythm, pulling out slowly, pushing in even slower. I felt her muscles grip my cock on every inch that went in. It was out-of-this-world good.

Then she started to shake even more. Her breath hitched. I was so close that I could practically feel my climax. The anticipation was killing me, but I didn't want to rush. Not at all. I wanted us to savor every second.

I looked straight at her, not breaking eye contact. When I pulled my cock out completely and brushed the length of it over her clit, she moaned, dropping her head back before crying out loud. "Fuck yes."

Her sounds could be heard even from miles away. I was sure of it. It was a gorgeous sight—an experience that I'd remember for a long time.

Then I slid back in as her climax tore through her body. I joined her this time. My release was so powerful that I couldn't even move properly. Relief filled every cell. This was pleasure unlike anything I'd ever experienced. It brought me to my damn limit, and I cried out right along with Grace for everyone out on the bayou to hear us.

CHAPTER THIRTEEN
ZACHARY

The next morning, it was very hot inside the cabin. Grace was sleeping peacefully next to me. My phone showed it was ten o'clock. We hadn't gone to bed until after sunrise, but I couldn't sleep any longer, so I got up.

I put on my boxers and moved to the living room, checking my messages. I had an unread text from Felicia.

Felicia: Good morning. We're out with the animals. We've put a basket with breakfast in front of the door because we didn't want to wake you up. I hope you had a good night. I know the couch couldn't have been too comfortable.

Zachary: Thanks for breakfast.

I tossed my phone onto the couch as I went to open the door. The basket was chock-full of food. On top there was bread and small jars of jam. I brought it in, putting it on the small table next to the wall, and then I heard footsteps. Grace was walking in slowly, a sheet wrapped around her. She looked gorgeous. Her hair was in complete disarray, her eyes heavy with sleep.

"Good morning," I greeted.

"Hey."

"Felicia left breakfast at the door."

"That's so thoughtful. What time is it?"

"Ten o'clock."

She gasped, her eyes suddenly wide and alert. "Crap. I need to tell the office that I'm not going in today."

"Good thinking. I forgot it's not Saturday. I'll do the same. Although, I could probably get there in the afternoon."

She turned around in a half circle to face the bedroom, then turned back to face me and blinked.

"I forgot where my clothes are."

"You weren't wearing any pants when I carted you off the couch, so I'm guessing somewhere in here."

Grace licked her lips and smiled, quickly looking down at her feet. She walked with small steps to the side of the couch, grabbing something from the floor. She dug her hand into her bag, taking out her phone.

"I've got six missed calls. I can't believe this didn't wake us up."

"After last night, we certainly needed our rest," I teased.

She tapped on her phone before setting it on the couch, then glanced at me. "We did, didn't we? So, what goodies did Felicia prep for us?"

"Lots of things. Have your pick."

I watched her intently as she came closer, but she didn't make eye contact. She peeked in the basket, taking out bread and a small jar. "Peach jam. I love this. Haven't had it in a while. Are there plates anywhere? Oh, wait, Felicia put some in the bottom of the basket."

We took them out carefully before sitting down.

"Good thinking on her part. Everyone probably eats at the cafeteria, right?" Grace said as she lathered on a lot of butter followed by peach jam.

As she took the first bite, she sighed. "Ah, this is exactly the boost of energy I was hoping for."

I gave her a half smile. "Why? Do you have a certain activity in mind?"

She instantly blushed. "I wasn't... That's not what I..."

I moved closer to her and pushed a strand of hair from her face. "I was teasing you, Grace. You're tense this morning."

She licked her lips and then lowered the half-eaten slice of bread to her plate. Her shoulders slumped. "I'm all over the place this morning. I should've showered first. It helps me wake up."

"You're adorable with your wild hair and holding that sheet around you as if you're determined not to let me see anything."

She tipped her head up to me. "That is kind of the point."

I raised a brow. "You do remember I already saw everything, right?"

"Oh, you're being mean to me this morning," she whispered.

"Not at all my intention."

"Right... Well, since I'm not going to work today, I could spend some more time with the horses and chat with Felicia and Gaston." She was mostly talking to herself.

"Do your neurons always fire up so quickly in the morning? Because I've got to say, I'm a much simpler creature. The only thought going through my mind is 'How can I convince you to stay indoors with me?'"

She started to laugh. "That's the sugar, trust me. Wakes me up fast. I'd love to know what the horses do in the morning."

"I see. So, you choose the horses over me."

"Zachary, honestly. I can't blush this early in the morning."

I leaned in, whispering in her ear, "I can do one better. I can make you come right now."

She nearly choked on her food. A split second later, I realized she truly was choking. She put the plate down, bending slightly over the table.

"Fuck, I'll get you some water."

I grabbed one of the bottles Felicia had put in the basket and opened the cap, handing it to Grace. She took a deep breath and then downed some water.

Once her fit had passed, she glared at me. "You are dangerous for me, Zachary. Quite literally."

Leaning in, I tugged at her earlobe, but she stepped back. I could feel that she was pulling away. Last night, we'd both given in to our impulses and our needs, but this morning, something had changed. I straightened up and waited patiently, looking at her.

"You want to talk?" I asked.

She sighed. "We should, right? But I feel like I need to get my bearings first so I can put my thoughts in order. I'll hop in the shower."

"Sure. I'll go in after you."

I took a step back, watching Grace move around the couch once more, gathering her clothes.

After she went into the bathroom, I decided not to waste any more time. I did part of my morning workout routine right there on the floor of the cabin. It consisted of push-ups and jumping jacks. I wasn't even paying attention to my surroundings until I heard Grace whistle.

"Well, well. That's a sight I love walking out of the bathroom to."

She stood in the doorway, watching me without shame. I stopped in the middle of doing a crunch and immediately pushed myself up to my feet.

She licked her lips before tugging at the lower one with her teeth. "How can you be so damn sexy, hmm? Especially wearing just boxers?"

"I, for one, think I'm overdressed. I can drop these, too, but I want to shower first. I worked up a sweat."

She stepped away from the bathroom door. I winked at her before going in and jumping into the shower.

While the water ran over me, I thought about the conversation ahead. Grace had fun last night—I was sure of it. So why was she retreating now? I wasn't used to playing games. Granted, I usually just went on casual dates and had one-night stands that I wasn't interested in repeating.

But now I wanted a repeat—very much so.

After stepping out of the shower, I heard Felicia's distinctive voice and realized we were no longer alone in the cabin. I wanted to throw her out and just keep Grace prisoner here for a few more hours.

I opened the door, and Felicia looked straight at me.

"Perfect. If you're both ready, we can head out. It's a gorgeous day! Poor Starlight got a right scare yesterday and needs some loving." At the last part, she looked pointedly at Grace, and I smiled.

Grace looked over at me. "By the way, your phone kept ringing while you were in the shower."

I immediately grabbed it from the couch and checked the messages.

"Damn it. I forgot I had a big meeting scheduled today. If I leave now, I should make it in time." How the hell did I forget?

Felicia's face fell. "Right. Grace, are you still staying?"

"Yes, of course. Starlight needs me, and I'd really love to spend more time here before I head back."

"Fantastic. Then I'll wait for you outside. I want to check if there was any damage to the cabin during the storm."

That sounded like a bullshit excuse, but she must have realized that we needed a moment together. I wondered if she could tell what had happened here last night.

After she left, Grace narrowed her eyes and tilted her head playfully. "Are you sure you can't stay?"

"Unfortunately not. I can't postpone it because I've got execs coming in from all over the area. Our shipping business has run into some logistic issues, and my brothers and I want to work things out with the people directly involved."

I moved closer to her. I couldn't understand how this woman seemed more beautiful to me every time I saw her.

"But my previous offer still stands. We'll just have to move the party"—I wiggled my eyebrows—"to New Orleans."

"Zachary," she whispered, shaking her head.

"You've had time to think," I concluded.

"I just... Last night was amazing, but I don't know. This is a time in my life where I need to be by myself."

"Right."

If that was her decision, then I was going to respect it even though I didn't like it one bit.

"Can I ask you something?" I said.

"Sure."

"Why won't you even consider us both investing in this place?" I really had to know if my suspicions were warranted.

She sighed. "I realize I was probably too blunt at dinner. It wasn't my intention. I just..." She ran her hand through her hair. I wanted to bury my fingers in it, then tug her head backward and kiss her, but it wasn't what she needed right now.

"For so long," she continued, "my identity and everything I did were somehow tied to someone else—first to my family's company, then to my husband. For the first time in my life, I'm doing things completely on my own, and I like it. So, any project I'm embarking on—"

"You'd rather do on your own. I get it."

"You do?"

"Yes."

"And you're not mad?" she asked quietly.

"Grace, why would I be mad?"

She shrugged. "Why not?"

"It's your choice. I respect it."

We heard footsteps, and we both fell silent as Felicia came in.

"I'll be right out," Grace told her, hurrying toward Felicia. She turned to look at me. "Have a safe trip back, Zachary."

"Thanks, and you too."

I didn't like that I was heading back to the city with things between us like this, but I knew it wasn't the right moment to push.

That didn't mean I was giving up, though.

Chapter Fourteen

Grace

It was late in the evening by the time I arrived back in the city. I'd decided to spend the whole day with the horses, and it was fantastic. Not only did I help with grooming and feeding them, but Felicia let me ride one of their longtime fillies. It was so refreshing, healing even, and I hated to leave.

As I entered the city, Lais texted me.

Lais: We're still on for an evening of watching Netflix at your place... or did you have another mishap?

She was going to have a field day when I told her about everything with Zachary. I was bursting with excitement to tell someone. I almost couldn't believe it had happened at all.

Grace: Yes, I'm going to be home soon. Is 7 a good time for you?

Lais: Perfect.

We'd originally planned another evening in the Quarter, but I needed some time to decompress, and I couldn't face the Quarter on a Friday evening. I wanted something more laid-back. Lais and I used to have a lot of girly evenings together before my awful marriage, and that seemed like a perfect way to spend our time tonight.

I arrived home with half an hour to spare, so I ordered our usual cheeseburgers with curly fries. I had popcorn ready to go too.

Lais arrived on time, as usual. When I opened the door, she looked me up and down and exclaimed, "There's a strange energy about you."

I laughed. "You and your energies."

She shrugged. "We live in New Orleans, darling. If we don't believe in voodoo and energy, then who should?"

I didn't think much of the city's obsession with the supernatural, but I knew I was in the minority.

She raised a brow. "So, did I get it right that you only came back from the bayou today?"

"Yes."

"Why?"

"We should eat first," I said, pointing to the burgers and the fries I'd laid out on the small coffee table in front of the TV.

Lais's eyes widened. "This is a serious conversation if it requires food first."

As we both sat down on the couch, I dug into my cheeseburger. I hadn't eaten anything since our late breakfast. Felicia had offered to cook dinner before I left, but I didn't want to linger that long.

"Girl, come on. First tell me and then you eat." She'd only taken one bite.

"I wasn't joking when I said I need some food."

Lais cocked a brow but then dutifully bit into her cheeseburger again.

"Did you seal the deal?" she asked after she'd swallowed.

"Not exactly."

"Then what happened out there?"

"First things first, you know there was a storm, right?"

She sucked in a sharp breath. "Oh my God, you got caught up in that. Girl, we need to sharpen your storytelling skills. You need to do a much better job. Were you hurt in any way?"

"No. But it wasn't safe to drive back, so I didn't."

Lais narrowed her eyes as she took a sip of her drink. "What else are you not telling me?"

"Felicia and Gaston didn't tell me that Zachary was joining us too."

Lais gasped. "Wait, so he got trapped there too?"

I nodded.

"You kissed again, didn't you? I knew it was going to happen."

"We didn't just kiss," I whispered.

Lais looked stunned as she pushed the rest of her food to the side, full attention on me.

"Grace Deveraux, did you finally, *finally* break that awful dry spell you've been having?"

"I did."

"Hallelujah, hallelujah," Lais chanted, and I burst out laughing. "That's the best news ever. Do you have any champagne? Something we could celebrate with? I could have a Sazerac or five. In a pinch, even a tequila shot would do."

"I have none of that," I confessed.

"Oh, never mind. I'm so happy. It was high time you got some."

I chuckled. "You've made your opinion clear on that. I just wasn't ready."

"And now you are?"

"Honestly, I'm not sure."

Lais frowned. "I don't understand."

"It was a very spur-of-the-moment thing. The hosts only had one cabin that was livable, so we had to share it."

"This sounds like a movie." We both giggled at her comment.

"That's the perfect way to describe it."

"How was it?"

I turned to her and sighed. "Fantastic. I didn't even know sex could be like that."

Lais's face fell. "You're telling me that bastard was bad in bed in addition to being bad at everything else?"

I pressed my lips together. "I don't want to talk about Roger."

"Right. Sorry."

"It doesn't even matter either. I feel vindicated now, like I've crossed something that was holding me back."

"Well, we don't need to talk about *he-who-should-not-be-mentioned*, but that man did a number on you, and I am just thrilled to see I've got my bestie back in all her glory."

"Yeah. I definitely found my self-perseverance, my self-esteem. I feel like I can hold my own again, and I am so happy!" I was sipping my drink when Lais asked her next question.

"So, Zachary LeBlanc first won you over with his kissing skills and then with his sexual skills. When are you seeing him next?" She was so funny, and I just loved her. She'd stood by me through it all, and there was no better friend in the world than her.

"I'm not. I mean, I don't think there will be a repeat."

Lais didn't reply right away. Instead, she began munching carefully on her cheeseburger again.

"What are you thinking about?" I asked, feeling a bit unnerved. Lais didn't usually just go radio silent, so she had to be mulling over something.

"I just wouldn't have thought that you'd want a onetime thing. Especially since this was pivotal—life-changing, even."

I chewed on a fry, thinking about it. "Well, trust me, I'd planned this to be a zero-time thing. I just got my life back on track and need to focus on me."

"I know that. But you can do both. This is the first time in a very long time that I've seen you so excited. Like there's actually a little light in your eyes. I haven't seen that in *forever*."

I didn't reply because I knew what she was saying was true.

"That light went out three days after your wedding," Lais added.

I shuddered. That coincided with the day Roger asked me if I wanted to quit my job.

"I don't want to talk about the past."

"Sorry. I was just making a comparison. The point is, the light is back now. I wouldn't be discarding the possibility of more sexy interludes with Zachary LeBlanc."

I grabbed another fry, munching on it. "I think he's the type who does one-night stands." I felt oddly sad at that. "And honestly, I'm not a friends-with-benefits kind of person. But we haven't discussed anything."

"So then why would you assume that there wasn't more?" Lais asked in a sharp tone. "You've been assuming a lot of crap about this guy, and none of it turned out to be true."

"I don't know. He doesn't seem the type who wants to settle down..."

Lais waved her hand. "No one wants to settle down until they actually do. If I had a penny every time an ex told me he wasn't ready for more and then went ahead and married the next person he dated, I'd be very rich indeed."

I winced. This happened to her three times. I couldn't understand how she had so much bad luck.

"On the bright side, you're not divorced. It's better to wait for the right person to come along rather than rush into marriage."

"I thought we weren't talking about the past anymore," Lais said, looking at me pointedly.

"You're right. We're not."

She popped the last fry into her mouth. "And you're not going to see him again at all?"

I leaned back on the couch, setting my bowl of fries on my lap. Unlike Lais, I liked to savor them and eat very slowly.

"I don't see how that could happen. I mean, our paths don't really cross."

"Except for that one time you fell into the river, that other time he kissed you, and this last time when somehow both of you ended up sleeping in the same cabin."

"That wasn't a coincidence, though. In hindsight, it was obvious they were going to ask us both to come to the ranch. I just don't understand why I didn't realize it." I set the fries back on the table and grabbed my drink. "So, since I fessed up about everything, how about starting the next phase of the evening?"

"What are we watching?" Lais asked. "What are you in the mood for?"

"No vampires."

She pouted. "You're such a grouch."

"But that's always what you want to watch, Lais."

"I know, I know. But I'm not alone. Many people are obsessed with vampires. And it's not just because I live in New Orleans."

"Let's watch something fun. A documentary?"

Lais groaned. "Only you could use 'fun' and 'documentary' in the same sentence. I totally veto the documentary, but I could watch an actually fun rom-com."

"The choice is yours," I said as I clicked on the TV and pulled up the Netflix app, then handed the remote to my friend.

While Lais was browsing through the top recommendations in the rom-com section, my phone vibrated. My team had been up in arms today. I'd never taken a day off, and they'd bombarded me with emails. I'd even stopped the car a few times on the road to reply to the lengthy ones.

But this time it wasn't a message from my team. It was from Zachary.

Zachary: How did it go? Are you back?

My heart somersaulted for no reason.

Grace: Yes, a little while ago. It was a long day, but I loved it.

Zachary: Spoiled Starlight some more?

I laughed.

Grace: You know it. That baby boy hasn't had such shiny hair ever in his life, I bet.

Zachary: What are you doing tonight?

I took a picture of the TV.

Grace: Spending time with my best friend and trying to decide what to watch. You?

He sent me a picture of the Mississippi. My heart started racing.

Zachary: I left the office and ended up walking along the river because it's less crowded, and now I can't stop thinking of our little adventure here.

Our little adventure. That was such a nice way to put it.

"Why are you giggling?" Lais asked. "Why is your team even spamming you at this hour?"

"It's not my team," I replied.

"It's Zachary!" she surmised.

"Why would you guess that?"

She laughed. "Your voice sounded a little bit coy. I'm your best friend. I know you."

My phone vibrated again.

Zachary: Everything with you is unexpected, and I fucking like that.

I turned my phone to Lais, who grinned from ear to ear. "That doesn't sound like someone who considers last night a one-night stand. I bet he's going to try and flirt the pants off you."

I licked my lips. "You think?"

I reread his message, then decided to reply with the truth.

Grace: I'm not even sure how these things happen. I promise I don't plan them like that.

Zachary: I know. Are you going to hit the Quarter tonight?

Grace: No, I'm too tired.

Zachary: Even after the lazy morning? Then again, last night's activities stretched until late.

I couldn't help laughing.

"He's starting to flirt, isn't he?" Lais asked.

I nodded.

"And?" she inquired. "Are you going to flirt back?"

I grinned at her, pressing the phone to my chest. "I'm considering it."

"Oh, hallelujah, hallelujah," Lais started again.

"Don't chant victory too soon."

She pressed her lips together immediately, assuming a serious demeanor. "No, you're right. Don't want to get ahead of myself."

"Let's start watching something," I said.

Lais and I chose a rom-com. I snapped a picture of the screen as the title appeared and sent it to Zachary. His reply made me laugh.

Zachary: Shudder. Rom-coms are at the top of my shit list. Have fun.

I expected him to continue texting, but he didn't, and so Lais and I watched Sandra Bullock and Hugh Grant for the fiftieth time in silence, sighing at our favorite scenes. We'd first watched this when we were teenagers, and we laughed at it still. There was something eternally romantic about those old rom-coms.

I yawned several times as the ending approached. Lais looked at me out of the corner of her eye.

"You're already sleepy. I thought we were going to have a party tonight and watch several movies."

"I thought so, too, but I had a long day." And as Zachary pointed out, a short night, but I didn't feel comfortable sharing too many details with Lais. Once upon a time, we did that—when we were in the throes of dating. But after I got married, I shared less and less. I was too ashamed.

"Then I'm going to go, but you still owe me that night out in the Quarter, okay?"

"How about next week?" I suggested.

"Either Friday or Saturday works for me. I'll make you keep the promise."

"I haven't promised yet," I pointed out, batting my eyelashes.

She put her hands on her hips.

"I won't bail on you again, I promise."

"No more swimming sessions in the Mississippi." She wiggled her eyebrows.

I chuckled as she headed to the door. "Good night, Lais."

"Good night," she said before leaving.

I yawned again and rose from the couch, moving my body a bit because I'd gotten stiff. After I cleaned up our mess, which involved throwing what was left in the garbage and the dishes in the dishwasher, I hopped into the shower. It was my absolute favorite way to relax. My daily pampering routine. I'd once read that the average person showered in less than four minutes, and I couldn't even comprehend what that meant. Mine were at least fifteen minutes long.

I applied lotion thoroughly after I came out. Even though it had been humid out in the bayou, my skin was still dry. As I massaged my inner thighs,

I had flashbacks from last night. I almost couldn't believe how alive I'd felt. How incredible Zachary had been with me.

After putting on my silk nightgown and fluffy slippers, I searched for my phone in the bedroom, needing to set the alarm, then remembered I'd left it in the living room. When I grabbed it from the coffee table, I noticed an unread message.

Zachary: Rom-com over?

Suddenly, I wasn't just relaxed but happy. The sentiment caught me by complete surprise. How could I be happy just because he was texting me?

Grace: Yep. And Lais left too. She's suspicious about why I'm so tired.

Zachary: You didn't tell her about last night's activities?

I giggled as I typed back, sitting on the couch.

Grace: I did, although I didn't give her many details.

Zachary: Don't remember them? Because I'm more than happy to remind you of every single one of them. I've committed everything to memory.

Oh, my bestie was right. This was definitely not the behavior of someone who only considered it a one-night stand.

I bit the inside of my cheek. Had I been too quick to label it?

Grace: Don't worry. I remember every detail too.

Zachary: Perfect. That means I made an impression.

I started to laugh out loud. Zachary was quite different from what I'd imagined.

Grace: How did your meeting go?

Zachary: Good. But next week will be rough.

Grace: Fingers crossed it goes by quickly.

Zachary: Oh, it will, because I'll play our night together in my mind every time someone annoys me. That'll put me right back into a good mood and annoy them in return.

I grinned.

Grace: That's a fantastic tactic. I'll use it too.

Zachary: You can text or call whenever you do, and then we can reminisce together.

Heat pooled between my thighs at the thought. Holy shit, that sounded almost like dirty texting.

My heart was hammering out of my chest as I imagined getting out of the meeting and just calling Zachary for a quick, what, dirty exchange? I was truly losing my mind. He was probably joking, and here I was seriously considering it.

Zachary: Don't be surprised if you get a random call from me during the day.

Okay, so he wasn't joking. I could shut this down, of course, but I was enjoying myself far too much. I hadn't done that in a while. Yet with Zachary, it was almost like an instinct. I couldn't stop myself, so I didn't. That's why I replied with sass.

Grace: The same holds true for you. Brace yourself.

Zachary: Will do.

Chapter Fifteen
Zachary

The following week was a bit of a shit show. This time of year always was. Everyone was rushing to fulfill orders before business ramped back up in September. That meant our ships needed to arrive on time—every delay cost us money. I hoped the meeting we'd had last week helped with the logistics and that we'd circumvented the quota issues that were pending. As one of the country's main shipyards, it was important that everything ran smoothly. We safely transported containers of goods and were highly respected both domestically and internationally. It had been a legacy operation of the conglomerate for decades.

On Monday morning, the first meeting was insane. We had a delay with one of our biggest transports, which would cost us a lot.

I needed to blow off steam somehow. So, right before my second meeting, while I drank my fourth coffee of the day, I texted Grace.

Zachary: Week started off awful, but I'm still in a good mood, remembering the way you looked on that bed, completely naked for me.

To my astonishment, she replied right away.

Grace: Zachary, I'm in a meeting.

Zachary: So they're wondering why you're blushing?

Grace: They'd better not.

I didn't say anything else, though. I hadn't thought this through. Clearly we needed a better arrangement. We couldn't randomly text; there was a high chance the other one was busy.

Zachary: Buzz me when you've got a break.

Of course, she texted me while I was in a meeting three hours later. This one wasn't going smoothly either, but it wasn't a total shit show like the other one. Why couldn't anything ever be easy?

Grace: It's not even noon and I'm already on edge. If only someone could take the edge off.

Fucking hell.

I'd never had a hard-on in a meeting. But there was a first time for everything.

I drew in a deep breath and then turned the phone over with the screen down. I shouldn't have looked at it.

It took me a few moments to push the image of Grace with her legs wide open out of my mind. Then I decided to text her back; otherwise, I'd be thinking about it for the rest of the meeting.

"Just one second. I need to reply to something urgent," I said in a serious tone, picking the phone back up.

Zachary: When do you have your lunch break?

As soon as I hit Send, I flipped the phone back over and set it to the side. Astonishingly, I focused perfectly on the meeting after that. But the second we were finished and I was alone in the meeting room, my thoughts raced back to Grace. Grabbing my phone, I saw she'd texted me twice.

Grace: One.

Grace: Damn it. I won't have a break today.

I groaned. The impulse to flirt with her was overpowering.

Zachary: The evening, then.

She didn't reply.

I spent the rest of the day in a huge negotiation with a potential business partner. It was six o'clock by the time I finished. Almost everyone on the floor had left. Six o'clock was the unofficial end of the workday here. I didn't encourage extra hours, as I'd seen enough people burn out early in their careers because they'd worked far too long for years. I didn't want that for any of my employees. Burnout could sneak up on you unnoticed.

I texted Grace.

Zachary: Fucking long day.

Grace: Mine is still ongoing.

Zachary: That's not good.

Grace: What are you going to do about it?

My pulse shot up for the second time today, and it wasn't because someone was annoying me. Rather, I was seriously considering tracking Grace down.

Jesus, I was starting to lose my mind. It was one thing to flirt; it was another to barrel into her office.

Zachary: I can take the edge off right now.

Grace: Through the phone?

Zachary: Hell yes. We don't even need to call. Texts are enough.

I was getting turned on from the prospect of it alone.

Grace: Zachary! I'm about to start a conference call again.

I wondered if it was the truth or if I was pushing too much. Maybe it was a mix of both, so I decided to backtrack.

Zachary: Then good luck. I'm off for the evening.

We texted back and forth for the rest of the week, and it was the damn highlight of every day. I didn't push as much as I did on Monday because I realized that I needed to ease Grace into this—whatever *this* was. I couldn't define it yet, but one thing I knew for sure: I wasn't ready to forget what happened at the ranch.

After a record six-hour meeting on Friday, I was headed to the mansion to have dinner with the whole family. Later, I was going into the Quarter with Anthony and Beckett to blow off steam.

As I went down to my car, I texted Grace.

Zachary: My day is done. What are you doing tonight? I'm going to be in the Quarter.

Grace: Me too. I promised Lais I'd go out with her, and I can't bail again.

I smiled triumphantly. One way or another, I was going to see Grace tonight. Getting into my car, I drove straight to the Garden District because there wasn't much time left until the family started dinner. My mind was on Grace the whole drive, which made it pass by quicker than usual.

Mayhem reigned inside as usual when I arrived. Besides both sets of grandparents, Chad, Scarlett, Simone, and Bella were already there. Then I noticed Anthony and Beckett, too, along with Xander and Bailey. Only Julian and Georgie were missing, along with my parents.

"Uncle Zachary!" Bella exclaimed when she saw me. "You know what just happened?"

"No, tell me."

"Dad agreed to let me watch *Goblet of Fire*."

I whistled loudly, nodding at Chad, who, by the looks of it, had simply decided the fight was taking too much out of him. He seemed resigned.

"Scarlett said she'll watch it with me," she went on. "Do you want to watch with us too?"

Ever since I told Bella that I'd watched all the movies, I'd risen to the ranks of a very beloved uncle. I was still battling with Xander and Julian for the top spot, but they both only watched it because Bella made them. I'd actually seen them when the movies first came out and had always been a fan. Watching them with Bella was like reliving my own teenage years.

"Sure thing, kid."

"Yeeeeeees!"

Everyone was gathered in the sitting area around the fireplace. They hadn't lit it during the summer months, of course. The weather was sweltering enough, and the family simply refused to use AC, which was driving me crazy. There were huge fans hanging from the ceiling, but it wasn't nearly enough.

"Uncle Zachary, Gran Isabeau said that you'll have a horse ranch."

I sat down on the couch, and Bella perched on my lap. I liked that she still did that. She claimed she was too old for far too many things, but not for sitting on my lap.

"I don't own it yet, but I'm in talks to invest in it."

"Can you take me there too?"

I looked at Chad, who simply nodded. He took Simone from Scarlett's arms, keeping her on his chest. She giggled, leaning into him.

I gave my brother shit for a lot of things, but I wouldn't promise Bella something he wasn't comfortable with.

"We can arrange something. I don't know when that'll be, though." I was always very careful with what I told Bella. Kids were very exacting, which took me a while to learn.

"How's that progressing? Have you gone back to the ranch again?" Beckett asked.

"I did, yes. I was there last week. I looked at a new horse they acquired, and we got some more intel on their renovation plans."

"We?" Anthony asked, a brow cocked. "Was Grace Deveraux there again? Is she still in the running?"

"Yes, both of us are still in the running."

"Have you made an official offer?"

"No. It hasn't been a priority at all this week. I don't think it has been for Grace either."

Beckett looked up from his glass of scotch. "What makes you say that?"

I cleared my throat. "Just a hunch."

"Did you get a better idea of how she is as a person?" Isabeau asked.

"She's nothing like her brothers. Though I'm not entirely sure about her motivations to buy the ranch, considering she owns a cosmetics company."

"And you run the shipping branch of the Orleans Conglomerate," Celine pointed out, "which is not exactly related."

"True, but my EMT background... You know what? Never mind. It wouldn't be fair for me to guess Grace's motives. But I wouldn't count her out of the running. Felicia and Gaston certainly like her."

Isabeau's eyes actually *glinted*, as if lights had popped up in them. "What do you think? You like her too?"

"Sure."

My grandfathers were sitting on the couch adjacent to the one where my grandmothers were sitting, and the two of them exchanged a glance. I could swear Grandpa David was fighting laughter. That meant they'd already talked about this.

"But that's not relevant," I added quickly. "We started off on the wrong foot, I'll say that."

"What do you mean?" Isabeau asked.

"I had Marcel look for information on her. It was the wrong thing to do. I don't agree with his methods."

"I warned you about him a while ago," Xander said.

"That's true. You did," I admitted, turning to him. "The only problem with you, brother, is that you've warned me about so many things that I lose track."

Xander shook his head. "He's not a decent guy."

"Yeah, I've learned that the hard way."

"That poor girl. What did you do to her?" Isabeau asked, and I turned my head toward her. She was frowning.

"You don't even know what happened, yet you're siding with her?"

Isabeau shook her head. "You know I always side with the family. But I've heard from trusted sources that her ex-husband was a shithead."

I jerked my head back, and Bella clapped. Chad groaned.

Isabeau had a very loose filter, but she kept the swearing to a minimum around Bella. She'd tried it while we grew up as well, but she gave up as we became teenagers.

She winced. "Sorry. Bella, that's a bad word. Don't repeat it."

Bella didn't even bother to nod. She was just grinning, and I knew she'd already added it to her vocabulary.

"Why do you say that?" I asked Isabeau. I had a feeling that Grace hadn't told me everything. And why should she?

"He didn't treat her right, and when they divorced, he put a detective on her. Then, when he couldn't find much, he started to make things up. I really don't know the whole story, but it didn't bode well in the end from what I've heard."

Fuck, fuck, fuck. This was a million times worse than what I'd imagined, and it explained why Grace had been so upset about Marcel.

I cleared my throat. "Well, it's not the same thing, obviously, but Marcel called the owners of the ranch and implied that Grace wasn't to be trusted."

Isabeau crossed her arms over her chest. "I thought we taught you better than that."

Mom and Dad came in just then. "Sorry we're late," Mom apologized. "That gallery event took longer than expected."

"Don't worry, Mom," I said nonchalantly. "You're not missing much. Just Isabeau giving me a hard time."

"Oh, well, she's always been very good at doing that, which made me look like the best mom on the planet." And that had been true.

"Well," Celine said, "whatever you do, just make sure you don't give that poor girl more grief. She's had enough to last her a lifetime."

"It was a mishap. I've made sure it'll never happen again," I assured them.

"That's what I was hoping to hear. Anyway, I heard she has great business sense. And that her family's company increased their profits a lot in those years when she was involved," Isabeau said, then glanced at her phone. "Julian just texted and said he and Georgie can't make it. Means we're all here. Celine and I are going to bring the food. Anyone want to help?"

"I'll come with you," I offered. Anthony and Beckett joined us too.

As we went to the kitchen, Isabeau asked, "Are you going to see Grace again?"

The honest answer was "Fuck, yes." But Isabeau didn't have to know everything.

"Not sure. We didn't discuss any more meetings with Felicia and Gaston. The next step is going to be to make an offer. Although, I need more information regarding the actual cost of the renovations they're planning. We've seen and talked a lot but haven't discussed any numbers."

Isabeau looked over her shoulder as we went into the kitchen. "Well, if you do see Grace, could you tell her about our fragrance shop?"

"Why on earth would he do that?" Anthony asked.

"Rumor has it that the poor girl hasn't dated since her divorce. We could give her a nudge by making one of our special lilac perfumes for her. I found her story very endearing. And if we can help her find the right one, then why not?"

I was absolutely *not* going to tell Grace about their shop at all. I didn't want her to have a perfume, especially not one with lilac. Not that I truly believed my grandmothers when they said it had special powers to bring people together, but why risk it?

"I'll see if I can find a way to put that in the conversation," I said.

Was the look in Isabeau's eyes triumphant, or did it just seem like that to me?

Anthony whistled, and Beckett clapped my shoulder. "Dude, you should consider yourself lucky that she's not offering to make a lilac perfume for *you*. You know, to attract 'the right one,'" he mimicked Isabeau, who instantly bristled.

"Oh, you three, just keep mocking us," she replied.

"We're not mocking, Isabeau," Anthony said, but Beckett tilted his head.

"I was. Sorry, I just can't take that story seriously." He chuckled.

"Lilac doesn't work on men," Isabeau explained.

"Yes, we only use it in women's fragrances," Celine added as she put jambalaya in bowls.

"Well, now we're relieved," Beckett said in a sarcastic tone. My youngest brothers couldn't read Isabeau and Celine as well as the rest of us. I wanted to warn them that all three of us were in trouble.

"We have something else for men," Isabeau said.

Fuck, I knew it.

"And what is that?" Anthony asked, and he at least had the good sense to sound a bit terrified. Maybe he could read Isabeau's intentions better than I thought, but it was too little, too late. "You know what? Never mind. We don't wear colognes anyway."

"No, you don't," Isabeau said sweetly. "But you do get all those soaps from us all the time."

I could practically feel my brothers panicking next to me. I was panicking a bit too. Yeah, that was the power of Isabeau LeBlanc and Celine Broussard. The three of us were grown-ass men, CEOs of our respective branches. Yet our grandmothers had the power to make us cower.

"What?" Beckett asked sharply. "You would tell us if you put something in them, wouldn't you?"

"Why would we?" Celine replied. "After all, those things don't work," she continued, mocking my brother. It was too funny.

"Fucking hell," Anthony groaned.

"Now, boys, let's take the jambalaya and the rice with beans to the living room," Isabeau ordered, effectively ending the conversation.

I exchanged a glance with my brothers, but neither said anything. Our grandmothers could be joking, of course, but I was going to thoroughly check my soaps once I got home.

Chapter Sixteen

Zachary

By the time I left with Anthony and Beckett, it was about nine o'clock.

"Should we grab a drink at Julian's bar?" Anthony asked.

That was the name we used for the Lucky Bar because it was where we all went most often. In the past, Julian was there on Friday and Saturday evenings, too, to keep an eye on business. But lately, he hadn't been making as many appearances.

"Sure," Beckett replied.

"What have you two been up to?" I asked.

"Same as usual," Beckett said with a shit-eating grin. "I won't be staying long, though. I've got a date later, if you get my drift."

"So do I," Anthony added.

I wasn't bothered by that in the slightest because I had plans of my own. And I didn't necessarily want my brothers to know about them. They wouldn't understand.

When we arrived, the Quarter was already packed.

"Anyone else think we live in the best city in the world?" Beckett asked as we headed down Bourbon. Many people avoided this street, especially on Friday and Saturday nights, but I liked the energy. This early in the evening, there weren't that many drunkards. They came out later.

"We're lucky," I replied.

As we walked down Bourbon, I texted Grace.

Zachary: Hey, are you already in the Quarter?

Grace: Yes, we're at a place on Chartres.

She sent me her location pin.

My entire body filled with tension. I'd planned to head over once my brothers and I parted ways. But now that I knew exactly where she was, the pull was simply too strong.

"Let's head down Chartres," I said.

"Why?" Anthony asked. "That's not the shortest way to the Lucky Bar."

Beckett replied nonchalantly, "We could switch things up a bit. Check out the competition for Julian now that he's spending Friday evenings cooped up at home."

"Don't be so judgmental," I said.

I could definitely see the benefits of being cooped up with Grace right now. And that thought alone was insane. I'd always relished being a bachelor, doing what I wanted when I wanted without having to check with anyone. But things were beginning to change.

As we turned on Dumaine and approached the location she'd sent, I kept looking around for Grace. They were at the outdoor bar, of course. Most everyone was outside on the street because it was so damn hot at this time of night, and even with AC, it was hot inside. It wasn't easy to spot her.

But then I heard her voice, and she sounded annoyed.

"No, really, we're good. We don't need any drinks."

"Oh, come on, really? Two single women coming out looking like that? I know women like you. It's what you came for, so someone can buy you drinks."

The moron sounded inebriated. Who the hell talked like that to women? He thought he was going to pick someone up with those lines? More likely he'd pick up a punch to the face. And I wasn't opposed to being the one who delivered it.

Grace was standing between two buildings on a narrow pathway. She looked fucking stunning in a gold dress that was short enough to send my imagination running wild. She was wearing high heels, too, and the shoulder strap from her purse crossed her chest. Her hair was pulled to one side with curls cascading down her shoulder.

The woman next to her had to be her friend Lais. I headed straight to them. They both had their shoulders hunched and had moved back until they'd almost reached a wall.

Why the hell was no one else stepping in? If I'd heard Grace, then so had a group of men who were just two feet away. Then again, this was Friday night in the French Quarter. People usually tried to stay out of trouble, not get themselves into it.

"Fuck off," I said the second I was close enough for him to hear me.

He snapped his head in my direction. His eyes were bloodshot already. He was a big guy, but not bigger than me.

"You fuck off. They're mine. I saw them first."

"What the fuck? You think women are some sort of property? Get the fuck out of here."

He sneered. "Isn't that what we're all doing out here in this heat? Looking to get laid?"

"No, we're fucking not," I said.

"Zachary," Grace whispered. The relief in her voice chilled me.

"Fuck off," I told the guy again, "and don't make me say it a third time."

He crossed his arms over his chest. "Or what? I don't need both of them. You can take whichever you want. I want Goldie here. You can take the other one." He pointed at Grace, and I saw red. "And you won't stop me."

He took a step toward her.

Grace shrieked as I raised my fist and punched the guy right between his eyes. He wobbled backward until he reached the wall opposite from the one Grace and her friend were propped against.

"Are you insane?" he asked.

"Fuck off."

"Get checked, man."

I laughed without humor, but he scurried away.

Once he was out of sight, I turned to look at the two women. "You two okay?"

"Yes, now, thanks to you," Grace's friend said. "I'm Lais, by the way. Nice to meet you."

"Likewise. I'm—"

"Zachary LeBlanc," she finished for me.

"Have we met before?"

"No, but I've heard about you." She glanced at Grace, who had a hand on her chest, tugging at her pendant. Clearly she was still unsettled.

"Grace, are you okay?"

She nodded, but it wasn't very reassuring.

"What the fuck just happened?" Beckett's voice came from behind me as he and Anthony joined us.

"Where were you two a few seconds ago?" I asked.

"Looking for you. One second you were with us, the next you just disappeared. Thought we lost you in the crowd. Then we saw you clocking that guy," Anthony said.

"He deserved it," Lais cut in. "He was making us very uncomfortable, and Zachary here was our knight in shining armor."

"Lais, Grace," I said, "these are my brothers, Anthony and Beckett."

"Grace Deveraux?" Anthony asked.

"Yes," Grace replied, nodding.

"Why don't the three of us grab drinks?" Lais suggested, pointing at my brothers. They immediately nodded.

That worked for me. I wanted to take Grace somewhere private and make sure she was really okay. She seemed almost uncomfortable here. Was she not used coming out to the Quarter on weekends?

"I want a Pimm's," she told Lais.

"And I'll take a Sazerac," I added.

"Dude, Julian is going to skin us alive if he hears we drank Sazerac somewhere that's not his bar," Anthony said.

"I'll take the risk." I rarely drank any other cocktail.

"We'll be right back," Lais said.

Anthony looked at me and Grace with a frown. Beckett raised an eyebrow. They'd put two and two together but at least had the decency to keep their mouths shut—for now, anyway.

Once they were gone, I turned to Grace, putting both hands on her shoulders. "You're shaking."

"I'm not even sure why. That guy was pushy, but..." She shook her head. "The way he spoke to us was insane. Like we were his property, and he was going to pick one of us no matter if we wanted it or not. It chilled me."

"Nothing happened," I reassured her. I moved one hand to her cheek, touching it with the backs of my fingers. "Want us to leave?"

"No. I really did promise Lais that I'd hang out with her. We just arrived a while ago. We haven't even managed to get our first drink. Alcohol will help—liquid courage and all." She looked up at me. "Thanks. You know, I never actually put myself in positions to be rescued, but you've had to do that twice now."

"My pleasure. Although, I'd rather not do it a third time. I don't like the thought of you being in danger." My words surprised the hell out of me.

Grace stilled, blinking rapidly.

"So, you're out with your brothers," she said, clearly attempting to change the conversation.

"Yes. We had dinner at our parents' and grandparents' house."

"Where were you heading?"

"My brother Julian's bar on Dumaine."

"Then don't let us keep you."

"I want to make sure you're okay. I won't leave before that."

She laughed but without humor. "Then you might be in for a long wait."

"I don't mind."

"I'm really not sure why that guy creeped me out like that. But whenever I hear someone talking to me like I'm property... well, it brings back memories."

I instantly remembered what Isabeau told me. Of course that would be triggering for her. That fucking moron. I'd clock him again if he were still here.

"He won't be bothering you again," I promised.

"Not as long as we have this sexy bodyguard with us." Her eyes flashed.

"Bodyguard," I repeated. "I can live with that. What do you say to me being your bodyguard for the rest of the evening?"

"Very smooth."

"Grace, I've been trying to be smooth all week. I'm hanging by a thread."

"What are you talking about?" she said, but her expression was lighting up. This was working. "You've been *shamelessly* flirting all week."

"Grace, you haven't seen shameless."

"Oh. Oh!" She covered her mouth with one hand. I pushed a strand of her dark hair behind her ear.

"All right, here we go," came Beckett's voice.

Instinctively, I dropped my hand and straightened up, but Anthony saw us. His eyes fell on Grace's cheek where I'd been touching her. Lais was smiling big, also looking between us. Beckett seemed blissfully unaware of anything as he handed me the Sazerac.

"You have one too," I said, pointing to his drink.

"Couldn't let you be the only one getting the end of Julian's wrath. Besides, it's not bad to check out the competition. See if he still has the best Sazerac in town."

"Your brother owns the Lucky Bar?" Lais asked him, and Beckett nodded.

I was damn proud of our oldest brother. He'd been the one to perfect the Sazerac recipe. It was voted the best in town year after year.

"Cheers," Lais said, and we all clinked classes. "What a nice surprise to run into you, Zachary. Of course, circumstances were unfortunate."

"What about us?" Anthony asked her.

"We're just collateral something," Beckett informed him.

Lais laughed. "Of course I'm glad to meet you too. But I've heard so much about Zachary from Grace that I was dying to meet him."

Silence reigned between us for a few seconds. Both of my brothers stared at me.

"Really? You've heard a lot about him, huh? So, what exactly did you hear? We're curious," Beckett asked her.

Lais seemed to realize she'd spoken out of turn because she cleared her throat, looking at Grace, deferring to her.

"Lais is up-to-date with the fact that we're both interested in the horse ranch," Grace explained.

Even though Beckett had the good sense to stay quiet, I knew what he was thinking: that was definitely not *hearing a lot*. It was just the bare minimum. But thankfully he didn't press.

"Right," Anthony said, chugging down his bourbon. We had something of an obsession with the liquor in the family. Probably because we'd grown up watching our granddads, David and Felix, down one in the evening as they chatted about business. Bourbon always seemed very sophisticated.

"So, Lais, what do you do?" Beckett asked.

"Oh, I'm an accountant. I know it sounds boring, but I promise *I'm* not boring. So, what do you guys do?" she asked, pointing first to Beckett and then Anthony. "I know Zachary here is running the shipping side of the family business. And you two?"

"I'm in charge of all the bakeries," Beckett said.

Anthony cleared his throat. "And I run everything else that doesn't fit into a category, which I thoroughly enjoy. There's a bit of everything. Mostly, I'm focusing on music venues, though."

"Like jazz bars?"

"No, it's bigger than that. Some are speakeasy places—very similar to bars but focusing on music. Others are actual music venues where people go to concerts and things like that, mostly in arenas."

"That's impressive. So, I have a proposition," Lais said before she downed her drink. My brothers had done the same too. Damn, they were quick. "Why don't you two and I go to the Lucky Bar to grab one of those Sazeracs? This one's shit."

I laughed, taking a sip of my own.

"I wouldn't say it's shit," I said, "but it's nowhere near as good as Julian's."

"I'm sure Grace and Zachary have more details to discuss about the ranch," Lais continued.

I knew Grace was blushing even without looking at her. When I did look, her cheeks were indeed tinted red.

Anthony cocked a brow. "What would they have to discuss?"

Beckett elbowed him. "Yeah, great idea. Let's go. Neither of us can actually stay too late."

"Don't worry. I can always entertain myself or come find these two." Lais winked at me. Clearly she didn't think we'd linger here at all. "Now, let's go. I haven't had your brother's Sazerac in a while."

Chapter Seventeen
Zachary

"Well, Lais is even less smooth than you," Grace said, sipping from her Pimm's as the three of them walked away.

"If my brothers didn't catch on before, they will now for sure."

"Catch on to what?" she asked, and I could tell she wasn't faking her confusion.

I pointed between the two of us. "This."

"I'm sorry. I had no idea Lais was going to run her mouth. She usually doesn't. She's a very discreet person, but I think she was just very relaxed tonight and—"

"Don't worry about a thing. You look like you feel better."

She nodded. "The Pimm's is helping. Won't you drink your Sazerac?"

"I just wanted a taste. Lais was right. I'm not even sure how they call this a Sazerac. I can get you another Pimm's if you want."

"Yes, please. Actually, I'll come in with you. I don't feel comfortable staying out here on my own."

I put a hand on her back and then moved it up to her shoulders, pulling her closer. It was fucking possessive, but I wanted everyone here to get the damn message. She was off-limits to everyone. She was mine and mine alone, and that was it.

We stepped inside and went straight to the counter.

"Will you drink something with me too?" she asked.

"I'm driving. Otherwise, I'd take a bourbon on the rocks."

It took a while before our turn came, but then we got the drinks right away.

"Want to go outside again?" I asked Grace.

It was claustrophobic in here. I had to pull her even closer because there wasn't much space. I didn't mind, but this wasn't relaxing.

"Sure. It's hard to breathe in here."

She took a few sips as we headed outside. I could feel her relaxing more with each one.

"Grace, I'm not trying to prod, I promise, but is there a reason this incident scared you so much?"

She lowered her eyes to her glass. "It's not normal, is it?"

I shook my head. "I don't like the word 'normal.' It's just that I'm trying to understand what happened."

"I honestly don't know. The way he cornered us... My ex got a bit like that toward the end. I'm not even sure how that happened because he didn't used to be like that." She bit her lower lip. "For a long time, I thought it was something in me that made him react like that."

"Oh, for fuck's sake, Grace. Don't think that for a second."

She shook her head. "I don't, not anymore, but when the person you married is starting to change behaviors and become meaner and more hateful to you, you start wondering what you're doing wrong." She looked up from her glass, putting on a smile, but something wasn't right with it. "But I'm forgetting all about it. Let's not mention it again. Friday evenings are for fun."

"Grace, you don't have to pretend for me. If you don't feel like staying here, we can always go. I just wanted to better understand what happened. I like to see you smile, but this"—I pointed to her mouth—"this isn't your real smile."

It instantly fell. "You can tell?" she asked.

"Yes. There's a big difference. You light up completely when you smile genuinely, and this was just—"

"For show," she finished. "I know. It's my high society smile," she said, but now she was smiling for real. "I perfected it when I was fourteen and went to my first cotillion. I enjoyed myself, but it was a little bit awkward. I felt like I never truly fit in with everyone else."

"Kudos for even going. Mom suggested it once, and we all turned her down. I believe she then went on a rant about how unfortunate it was that she didn't have any daughters."

Grace laughed. "Mom always told me that I didn't have to go if I didn't want to. But I didn't want to let her down, you know?"

I was starting to understand that she sometimes did things because she didn't like to displease others.

"You're a great person, Grace."

She tilted her head, then straightened it, taking a sip of her drink. "Do I detect surprise in your tone?"

"No, not at all."

"There's prejudice because of my brothers. I swear to God, every time I'm out in the Quarter and I say the name Deveraux, people do a double take. Not everyone assumes I'm related to them because the name isn't so uncommon in the South, but enough put two and two together."

"Anyone giving you grief?" I asked bluntly.

"If I say yes, what will you do?"

"You don't want to know."

The corner of her mouth lifted. "You have a dangerous side, don't you?"

"I like to call it protective."

"Yes, let's go with that. Protective sounds much better." As she downed her second Pimm's, she rolled her shoulders back. "I'm starting to feel my body go soft already. I'm not really used to coming out to bars to drink."

"I thought it was a favorite pastime for all New Orleans locals."

"No, I didn't even do it when I was in college."

"Where did you study? Loyola?"

"Of course. You?"

"Same."

She looked around several times.

"What do you need?" I asked.

"A comfy place to sit."

I laughed. "Sorry to disappoint, but I don't think there's a bar in the whole Quarter that can boast comfortable seating. Not even Julian's bars. I swear those chairs are torture devices."

"Ha! See, I knew there was a reason I don't like going out even though I do enjoy drinks."

"I have a proposition," I said.

"I'm listening."

"Let's take the party somewhere else."

"Such as?"

I didn't even hesitate. "My house."

Grace looked down at her feet and then back up. Fuck, I wanted to push this. I wanted to flirt, and I definitely wanted to kiss her, right here and now. But I needed to be certain that she wanted it. The last thing I would do was corner her somehow. She was special and needed to be treated as such.

"Sure. Is it close?"

"No. Actually, it's in Lakeview."

"Lakeview. I haven't been in that neighborhood for a while."

"We can leave anytime you're ready."

She showed me the empty glass. "I'm ready."

"All right, then let's go."

"I'll text Lais to let her know I'm leaving." She took out her phone and typed out a quick text, then put it back in her back. "Okay, I'm all set."

I'd parked at the edge of the Quarter, near the Mississippi. Walking out of the area was more difficult than walking in had been. The crowds had doubled. I kept a hand firmly on Grace's back as we maneuvered past all the people.

"Oh my God," she exclaimed when we finally came out of the Quarter. "That was a bit insane."

"I agree. My car is right here."

I took a good look at her for the first time tonight as I opened the passenger door. She climbed in, and her dress rode up a few inches. Her legs were endless. The memory of her completely naked in that bed was branded in my mind.

Pace yourself, Zachary. She only agreed to come for drinks. And if that was all she wanted, that was fine. Honestly, I just wanted to spend time with her.

After I climbed in, she asked, "How come you live in Lakeview?"

I shrugged. "No reason. Just found a house I liked there."

"I took you for the Garden District type," she replied.

"That's too close to my family's mansion. I love them to bits, but I wouldn't want to live two streets away."

Grace laughed. "I totally understand. I'm close to my parents, too, but I wouldn't want to live next door either."

"Some of my brothers have stuck around the Quarter. Julian actually owns a house *in* the Quarter, and Chad isn't very far away in Marigny. Xander is in the business district, but I wanted to find the perfect house and didn't really care where it was."

"That's smart."

The rest of the city was just as alive as the Quarter but thankfully not as crowded. I parked right in front of my house.

Grace smiled. "Oh, I can see why you like this."

From the outside, it resembled the mansions in the Garden District. It was a revival colonial style with columns, a huge wraparound porch, and a balcony on the second floor. The yard wasn't fenced, but the gardening team kept my perimeter trimmed to perfection.

"Wow. This is a surprise," she exclaimed as we walked through the front door.

It was completely modern on the inside. The living room had floor-to-ceiling shelves with a mix of books and wine bottles as well as rum and scotch. I had a huge dining table that was, quite literally, shaped from a tree. She drew her fingers over the surface.

"It's so elegant even though it's raw."

"What can I tempt you with?" I asked as she sat down at the head of the table.

"This is really comfy," she said. "It has armrests too."

She glanced at me, pressing her lips together. "I want to taste your favorite bourbon."

"On it." The bottles on the shelves were for display only. I had a separate bar area in the dining area. I put ice in two glasses and poured bourbon into each before returning to Grace.

"Cheers," I said, clinking my glass to hers.

"What are we toasting to?"

"An unconventional start."

"And for you luring me to your home."

I grinned at her as I sat at the corner of the table. "I did well, didn't I?"

"Yes, very smooth. Well done."

I swallowed hard before taking another sip. She did the same.

"Grace," I said, "I wasn't joking about wanting you to be comfortable. You seemed on edge out there."

She nodded, playing again with the pendant at her neck. I found the gesture extremely sexy, especially because it reached right into her cleavage. I had an insanely good view. I only saw the tops of her breasts, but it was more than enough.

"I know. I mostly went because Lais likes going out. But honestly, this is more my type of relaxing. Staying home with a drink, maybe a good movie or a book. I'm a very homey person. Although, I do get a bit of cabin fever in my apartment. Should've looked for something bigger."

"Why didn't you?"

She took another sip. "I just wanted to move out quickly. I took the third option that the realtor showed me. I loved the building and the location, but I'll move into something bigger as soon as I can."

She uncrossed her legs and then toed off her shoes. "This is much better!" She played with her bare feet on the raw wood floors, then started to shimmy in the seat.

"Want to move onto the couch? That's even more comfortable."

"Sure, why not? Let me just put my shoes away."

"Forget them. They're fine where they are." I'd taken mine off at the entrance.

We descended a few steps from the dining table into the living room. I particularly liked the layering of the space. The sunken living room was what really attracted me to the house. It was just so different.

"You throw parties often?" she asked.

"Not at all."

"Oh, I assumed... because of all this space."

"I grew up in a huge house, but with so many other siblings, even that sometimes felt cramped. So, after college, I decided that I was going to buy the biggest house I could find on the market."

Grace laughed. "Now, that's a statement."

"Kidding. I didn't actually buy the biggest one. But obviously I have more space than I need. When I bought it, I figured maybe my family would drop by from time to time, but we mostly gather at the mansion. It's most comfortable for our grandparents, and for our parents too."

I sat next to her at an angle that allowed me to make eye contact and drink her in.

"What? Do I have something?" she asked, moving her lips. I realized I'd been staring at her mouth. She touched the corners with her fingers and then looked down at herself. "Did I spill bourbon on myself or something?"

"No, Grace. I just can't stop looking at you because you're fucking beautiful."

She drew in a sharp breath, looking up. "Zachary, this entire week, I swear to God, I was looking forward to our texting more than anything else."

I decided to lay out all my cards. "So was I."

"It was like... I don't know, stoking a fire inside me. I was smiling every time my phone buzzed, thinking maybe it was a message from you."

Hell yes. I put my drink on the small wooden table in front of the couch and moved even closer to her, touching her jaw. "Grace, I know what we discussed at the ranch."

"I'm not sure I handled that well," she whispered. "I just didn't know what else to say. I have no experience with..."

I frowned. "What?"

"Spending the night with someone I'm not dating. I mean, I've never done one-night stands."

I laughed. "That's a very polite way to put it."

She rotated her glass in her hands, glancing down at it for a split second before making eye contact again. She shook her head and licked her lips. And then I captured her mouth. Fuck, how I'd missed it. Her lips, her taste. I could taste her even with the bourbon and the Pimm's she'd had.

I lost myself in that kiss faster than I thought possible, deepening it more and more, following her cues. When she sighed, I pushed her farther onto the couch. I heard liquid sloshing and then felt Grace move her arm. I opened one eye and noticed that she'd put the glass on the table. I'd completely lost control.

All I could think about since having Grace was having her again. My entire body was vibrating with that desperate need. I drew one hand up her thigh, but not under her dress, not yet. I just touched her from her knees to where the fabric started. She moaned again, and I felt the skin on her legs turn into goose bumps. So I moved one hand onto the inner thigh.

"Grace, I want you. But I want you to feel at ease, not forced in any way." Knowing a bit more about her marriage now, I wanted to be careful.

"Oh, Zachary. Just your concern makes me feel good."

That was all I needed.

She pressed her chest against me. As I went farther up her inner thigh, I moved my thumb under her dress, drawing circles. A split second later, I realized Grace was shaking slightly in my arms. I inched my hand farther up, and she clenched her thighs together, trapping my hand between them, humming. She parted them the next second. I went even farther up, dragging my hand over her panties. Fuck, they were already soaked.

I pushed the fabric aside and slid three fingers into her. This time her moan was unmistakable; it shook her entire body. That turned me on to no end. I moved two fingers up and down that slip of fabric. I wasn't in a hurry. I wanted to turn her on so badly that she'd beg for my cock.

I needed to hear her, but I wanted to explore her as well, so I paused the kiss and took my hand from under her dress. She gasped, but then I immediately yanked the dress over her head.

"You're so sexy," I murmured. This woman was perfection.

She was wearing white lace lingerie that left absolutely nothing to the imagination. Because it was transparent, I could see her nipples and her pussy. I threw the dress behind me and nearly toppled the glass of bourbon. That gave me an idea. I grabbed it and held it between us. Grace looked at me through hooded eyelids, her chest quickly rising and falling. I liked how open she was for me already. Tilting the glass, I poured the bourbon over her, starting from under her bra. I caught the liquid with my mouth before it reached her navel.

She gasped, rocking her hips upward. "Zachary!" Her breath hitched.

I did it again, pouring just slightly next to the place where I'd done it before, where her skin was still warm.

"Oh my God!"

Then I poured under her navel and lowered her panties until I'd almost uncovered her clit. This time, I caught the liquid before it reached the fabric. She bucked off the couch so violently that her pussy nearly collided with my face. I wouldn't mind her sitting on my face, but I had other plans for now. I needed to get her panties out of the way. I yanked them down quickly past her knees and then her ankles, and she spread her thighs wide before I even got to ask for it. She was so ready for me, her pussy plump and wet.

I traced two fingers from her clit to her opening, keeping them there before moving them in a large circular motion.

"Zachary!" Grace exclaimed.

Hearing her say my name sent me into overdrive. With my free hand, I undid my pants and put my hand inside, squeezing my cock and moving my hand up and down. Then I realized Grace was watching me. She tilted her head slightly so she had perfect view. Her eyelids were even more hooded than before.

She licked her lips and said, "I want to do that. I want to touch you. I want your cock in my mouth."

I nearly burst right then at her words. Rising to my feet, I pushed my pants out of the way, then put one foot on the couch and positioned myself so that my cock was right in front of Grace's mouth. She immediately licked the crown, and the sensation shot through me. This was going to be intense. She looked at me while I slowly pushed into her mouth. I watched her intently so I could tell how much she could take me in.

She moaned when I was halfway in. I pulled out before pushing into her mouth again. This was fucking good. She was the most beautiful woman in the world, and this was my very favorite view of her: spread open on my couch with my cock in her mouth.

"Touch yourself, Grace. I know you're dying to."

She nodded, her eyes almost pleading. I saw her shoulder move as she put her hand between her thighs, and then her mouth clamped tighter around me.

I could die a happy man right now. Taking off my shirt at quick speed because I didn't want any clothes in the way, I then pushed in and out, taking her cues very seriously. As she moved her hand faster, her body started to jerk, and I pulled out. Her eyes widened.

"Keep touching yourself. I want to see you come right in front of me."

She winced but didn't stop moving her hand. She was very, very close to the edge, and I knew what would send her over. I pushed the strap of her bra down on one shoulder, revealing one breast only, then took an ice cube from the glass and drew shapes with it on her sensitive skin. I pressed the flat of my tongue against her nipple, then pulled my head back and ran the ice cube over her hard nub.

"Oh my God!" Her voice shook. She was close.

I took the nipple in my mouth again, playing with the ice on her breast before letting it slide in a straight line from under her bra to her clit.

She came right away, and I pulled back because she didn't need my help at all to ride this wave of pleasure. I watched her succumb to it while she moved her hand frantically, her hips jerking off the couch. She jackknifed as she dropped her head back. It was beautiful to see Grace unleashed like this.

When her body finally started to calm down, I felt like I was going to explode. I needed to be inside her. I didn't bother sitting back on the couch; I wanted her in a different position. When she opened her eyes and drew in a deep breath, I leaned in and held my hand out for her. She immediately put one in mine. I moved her until she was up on her knees, then turned her around.

"Grab the headrest, Grace. You'll need it."

She leaned forward until she could reach it, and I kneeled on the couch to be at the same level with her. I didn't waste any more time. I slid in, and she pushed herself against me at the same time, taking me in to the hilt.

"Fuck, Grace."

I'd wanted to ease in. I thought she needed it, but clearly I'd been wrong, as she could take all of me at once. Her moan was guttural. She was so damn snug around me that I could barely breathe. I needed a few seconds to compose myself before slamming into her. I had an almost animalistic pace that Grace enjoyed; I could tell by the way her body moved against mine, as if seeking even more friction. Her cries filled my living room, echoing around us.

This was what life was all about: being here with Grace, buried balls deep inside her. I didn't need anything else in this moment, just to hear Grace cry out and feel her get even tighter around me.

"Gra—ce, fu—uck." My voice broke twice on the two syllables, but this was just too good. Too intense.

She leaned even farther forward, and I realized she'd put her forearms on the top of the couch. She needed more leverage. I moved us deeper onto the couch because I wanted to maintain the angle, then started moving even faster. She laid her head on top of her crossed hands and her hair moved to one side, completely baring the side of her neck. I leaned over, placing a wet kiss just beneath her jaw.

"This is so good," she panted. "I didn't even know it could feel like that."

I simply groaned in response; I was far too far gone to form sentences. Instead, I brought my hand to her clit. I only touched it twice, and Grace came. This woman was made for me. I could play with her body just the way I wanted to. The way she responded to my touch was insanely sexy.

Once more her entire body convulsed. She groaned loudly, calling my name. "Please don't stop."

I wasn't going to even though I was going so hard that I was half afraid I'd break her. But she needed it, and so did I.

Her orgasm triggered mine. She was still coming, and judging by the way she clamped around my cock, she wasn't done yet. Giving this woman pleasure was my life's mission from now on. Every orgasm had to be like this one: never-ending and so powerful that she was now incoherent as well. I only understood "Zachary" and "Oh God."

Her body started to relax and soften just as I rode out my own climax. I pushed in and out of her long after we were both done, until my dick started to relax too. Then I stilled but still didn't pull out of her. I grabbed the shirt I'd discarded and put it under us on the couch as I finally pulled out and rested us both in a sitting position.

Grace's face was completely flushed. She closed her eyes as if she was still processing everything. But as we sat next to each other, she opened them slowly and took a deep breath. Then she licked her lips. "I'm parched," she whispered.

I grabbed my glass of bourbon from the coffee table and held it out for her. She took a sip and then dropped her head back.

"I'll never be able to drink bourbon without remembering this evening," she murmured.

"Fucking perfect," I replied, realizing I wanted to give her as many memories as possible that she couldn't sweep away. I wanted to make a mark.

"Um," she whispered, looking down, "I think I should go clean up. Don't want to make a mess. Good thinking with the shirt."

"Let's go together."

She wrapped his shirt tightly around her lower body as we walked around the house. I had a small bathroom here that I rarely used, but it was the closest. She was covering her breasts with one hand.

"Grace, what are you doing?"

She licked her lips. "I don't know. It feels a bit weird to walk around naked in your house."

"We just had mind-blowing sex on the couch," I reminded her.

"That was different," she said in a low voice.

"Why are you whispering?" I asked on a laugh.

"I don't know."

I liked all facets of Grace, the shy one and the dirty talker from earlier. I kissed her forehead and pointed to the shower. "This is small. I've got a bigger one upstairs."

"This will do," she said quickly.

Five minutes later, Grace had wrapped herself like a burrito in towels. I'd put one around my waist, more for her benefit than anything. She seemed to feel uncomfortable watching me walk around naked.

"Do you want to go back to the living room?" I asked.

She turned around, looking up at me. "What's the alternative?"

"I can show you the upper level." I put my hands on her shoulders, drawing my thumbs over her clavicle. "My bedroom is there."

"I see. First you lure me to the house, then completely ravage me on the couch, and now you're trying to lure me to your bedroom."

I loved the playfulness in her voice. We'd come a long way, and I was honored that she trusted me, wanted me, and I wasn't going to spoil that.

This woman was mine.

"That was my intention from the start, but..." I chuckled, shaking my head.

"What?" Grace asked.

"I'm used to being in control, though for some reason, I lose it when I'm with you."

She licked her lips. "And you don't like that?"

"I actually fucking love it. I don't even know why."

She smiled brilliantly. Not her society smile but the real one.

"All right, then. Lead me to your bedroom before we defile some other place in this house."

I burst out laughing. "I like how you think, Grace, because that was on my mind as well."

Chapter Eighteen

Grace

Zachary's bed was the most comfortable place on the planet. When I woke up in the morning, I stretched my arms, shaking my ass against the mattress. It was fluffy but still firm. I'd had the best night's sleep in forever.

I looked sideways, expecting to find Zachary in a very deep sleep, but the man wasn't there at all. His blankets were all off the bed. But then again, my side was sheetless too.

It had gotten really hot in the evening, especially after our sexy activities, and we'd thrown the covers off. I sat up, glancing around with a grin. We'd pulled the sheet off at both corners. I smiled, thinking how at peace I felt. Completely the opposite to how I'd felt back at the ranch, when I'd been extremely nervous. I wondered why there was a difference. Was it because of the way he'd treated me back at the bar? He'd been so patient with me and seemed genuinely interested in knowing why I was uncomfortable.

Zachary was different from any man I'd ever dated. He wasn't controlling or trying to overpower me. He actually cared about me, and that meant so much to me that I couldn't even explain. Lais was right. I needed to get out more often, but she was right about Zachary too. He really was special.

Even though I loved the bed, I wanted to find out where he'd gone. I got up and grabbed the towel I'd laid out on the armchair in the corner after drying myself following my shower last night. It was still a bit damp, but it would do. I covered myself up.

I walked carefully down the steps, realizing music was blasting through the house. Zachary loved jazz—what a pleasant surprise. There were certain local things I loved to the moon and back, and jazz was one of them.

Downstairs, I spotted him leaning against the kitchen island. He was talking on the phone.

"Sure. Just let me know when you want to watch it, and we'll do it. Yeah. You know me, I'm at your service. Yes. Of course I'll bring beignets for my favorite girl."

My chest tightened. *Holy shit. My girl? No, no, no.* I put a hand on my throat, swallowing hard, but I was having a bit of trouble breathing. My next intake of breath was audible.

Zachary glanced at me. "I'll call you back later, okay?" As soon as he lowered his phone, he rushed to me.

"Grace, are you okay?" He tried to touch my arm, but I stepped back. He frowned. "What's wrong?"

"On the phone, who was that?" I knew I sounded accusing, but I couldn't help it. I was distraught thinking he had another woman.

"What?"

"Who were you talking to?" I wanted him to answer quickly so he wouldn't have time to make anything up.

"That was Bella. She finally got Chad to approve of her watching *Goblet of Fire* and is now trying to find a day for us to actually watch it before he changes his mind."

No one could come up with that on the spot. It was impossible. Finally I was able to breathe properly.

"Right!" My shoulders slumped. My whole body seemed to unwind and relax. When had all my muscles knotted up? Zachary owed me nothing. We weren't exclusive. My behavior wasn't warranted, and I started feeling embarrassed at my actions. "I'm so, so sorry."

He was still frowning. "What just happened?"

I shook my head. "Nothing. I just came in here and..."

"Heard me talking on the phone, and you assumed what?"

I closed my eyes for a beat and then opened them again. "I didn't think you were talking to your niece."

"You thought I'd be making plans with another woman while you're still in my house?"

"When you put it like that, it sounds callous."

"It *would* be callous," he said in a strong voice, "and not something I'd ever do."

"I know. Ignore me. You don't owe me anything, I'm not sure why I'm acting like this." *Oh God.* I was full-on embarrassed right now.

"Grace, don't. You jumped to conclusions for a reason, and I don't like it."

I crossed my arms over my chest. "It was the first thing that came to mind. I'm sorry. I didn't want to offend you, but I don't know you that well, do I?"

Zachary's frown melted. Instead, he flashed me a very seductive smile. "That's right, you don't. But we'll change that."

"How?"

"First things first, let's head out and grab breakfast."

I rubbed my eyes. "I'm not exactly dressed for breakfast. My dress is a dead giveaway that it's a... you know... morning-after kind of thing."

"So? I'll be right there with you. Everyone will know you've been with me." He came closer. "That you're mine. They won't know exactly what I did to you."

I blushed. "I hope not, but they'll imagine. Don't you have any breakfast food in the fridge?"

"I don't have anything in the fridge. Period."

That couldn't possibly be true. He had one of those double-door monsters.

"Really? You don't cook at all?"

"I *can* cook. I choose not to. I eat a lot of takeout. And I go down to LeBlanc & Broussard's fairly often when I'm at the office or have stuff sent up."

"You've just described my life for the past year. Although, I do enjoy cooking." My stomach took that exact moment to grumble. "Damn, I am hungry. I'll go put my clothes on. Have to say, that dress looks good, but it's not very comfortable."

"Then let's head to your place. You can change into something else, and then we can find somewhere to go on your side of town."

"Ooooh, there's a bakery with the best bagels next to my building," I told him.

"Perfect. Do you have other plans for today?"

"Yes. I'm going to drop by my parents' house later."

"Are they out of the city today?" he asked.

I shook my head. "Nope. They're in the Garden District, but I don't have a set hour when I'll stop by."

He grinned. "That means you're mine for the foreseeable future."

The drive from Lakeview to the Warehouse District didn't take long on a Saturday morning. Zachary came up with me to the apartment. I couldn't help remembering the last time he was here. God, I'd been such a mess. But looking back, it was also the moment when my feelings had changed. Possibly because I owed him my life.

I changed in record time, not wanting to waste a minute I had with Zachary. He was different in a good way, and I wanted to learn more about him.

"I'm ready," I exclaimed when I rejoined him in my living room, twirling around for him to get the full view.

"Fuck, you look so beautiful. It makes me want to just keep you here."

"Careful, or I'll think you have no intention of being with me in public," I teased.

He cleared his throat. His eyes were feral.

"I can pounce on you out there too." He wiggled his eyebrows, then gestured to the street. "If that's your thing."

I gasped. "It's definitely not."

He laughed, taking my hand as we left the apartment. My bagel place was just one block away, and as usual, it was crowded. During the week, it was packed at eight o'clock in the morning, but on a weekend, it was just as busy at ten.

"Is this place that good?" Zachary asked. "I see another bagel place up there."

"It's like drinking Sazerac anywhere but the Lucky Bar," I explained to him.

"Fair point."

"What are you doing today?" I asked.

The corners of his mouth twitched. "Watching *Goblet of Fire* with Bella and whoever else from the family she managed to coerce."

"What do you mean by 'coerce'? It's one of the best movies."

He whistled. "I'm glad you think so. I think *Order of the Phoenix* is my favorite one."

I laughed. "I can't believe we're two adults talking about Harry Potter."

Zachary shrugged. "Why not? We practically grew up with it."

"So, you're going to your brother's house?"

"Yeah, in the Marigny. That's where he lives with Bella, his fiancée Scarlett, and their baby Simone."

"Fiancée?" I asked as we finally stepped inside once a huge group had left after getting their bagels.

"He was married to Bella's mom, but they divorced years ago. He was single for a long while, but now he's very happy with Scarlett. But in those years when he was single, the family got to spend a lot of time with Bella. These days, we hang with Bella and Simone when he and Scarlett go out for a date night."

"I like that the whole family is involved," I said.

Our turn came quickly.

"We'll have the Three Favorites and two coffees," I said as I looked at Zachary. "Trust me."

"I do. Bagels are not my thing."

I gaped at him. "You've got to be kidding me."

"Nope. I take after Bella, or I guess Bella takes after me. I'm a beignet guy."

I wrinkled my nose. "Never really got the hype around beignets."

He cocked a brow. "Really?"

I shrugged. "Yep. Not my poison. Mine are these."

The vendor sliced each of the three bagels in half before putting them in the carton. We grabbed it and our coffees and walked out, making space for others waiting in line—which had gotten longer.

There were a few tables in front of the bakery. No one was really sitting down because this was more of a take-out type of place, but Zachary and I snagged a table.

"The difference is in the toppings," I explained. "Cocoa, walnut, and pistachio."

"Pistachio cream cheese? All right. Not my favorite."

"I thought so, too, but it's actually really good."

"Then I'll start with that one," Zachary said. "That's how much I trust you."

I handed him the one he'd requested, and he took a bite.

"Not bad," he said, but clearly he wasn't impressed.

I, on the other hand, savored mine in very small bites. I only drank my coffee after eating so as not to spoil the taste.

"My favorite treat," I murmured.

"I'll keep that in mind."

I glanced at the time on my phone. "Hmm, I wonder if Mom would like me to drop by for lunch."

He frowned. "I was banking on more time with you."

"Oh, okay." I smiled, but suddenly, I was feeling a bit nervous. Now that we didn't have any food to share, I wasn't sure what we wanted to do.

"What do you typically do on Saturdays?" I asked him.

"It depends. I sometimes go with my grandfathers out in the bayou to fish. Although, I've been skipping that lately, probably because my dad's been offering to go."

"Everyone in your family like to fish?"

"No, just the grandfathers. The rest of us take turns going so we can keep an eye on them. The conversation with them is always good. Other times, I just hook up with some friends and play tennis. But they didn't arrange anything for this weekend. Even the most expensive tennis courts are booked into the next century."

"Playing tennis in this heat," I said, shuddering.

Zachary touched my leg under the table. "Only very early in the mornings."

"Define very early."

"Seven o'clock."

I practically felt my jaw drop. "On a Saturday?"

"I know. I can sacrifice some sleep for tennis."

He shifted in his chair, and I didn't realize what he was doing until he moved next to me. Feeling the warmth of his body was enough to make me happy. How surreal was that?

"I only sacrifice sleep for work," I said.

"Tell me about it." He interlaced our fingers like it was nothing at all. I sighed at the gesture. "What made you choose that industry?"

"I've always been a cosmetics freak. These past few years, I started being more mindful about the ingredients. And when I couldn't find what I wanted, I started making some of my own. My husband used to make fun of me, that I have all that money and yet I'm wasting my time putting together creams like some simpleton."

Zachary groaned. "Fucking hell."

I looked up. "I'm sorry. I don't know why I keep bringing him up. I don't think about him that often, I promise. It's just..."

"You do what you need to, Grace. I'm not judging you. He sounds like an asshole."

Those simple words put me at ease. Why was I so used to everyone judging me? Maybe because whenever I brought Roger up around Lais, she insisted that I should just never mention him again. My parents kind of did the same. I knew everyone did it out of love and because they wanted to see me happy, but I appreciated Zachary allowing me leeway.

"Well, you're right about that. But I'd been toying with the idea of starting the business even during my marriage. The problem was, it caused a huge fight every time I brought it up."

"He wanted you barefoot and dependent on him. And let me guess, it pissed him off that you were independent because you had your own money."

"Yes, exactly. How can you tell? It took me so long to see it."

"I think," Zachary said, slowly caressing the back of my head with his thumb, "that it's sometimes easier to see things objectively when you're not in that situation."

I nodded. "You're right. I waited until the divorce was final, so it didn't get to be a part of our asset divisions. But once I was free, I put all my resources and time into it."

"You financed it yourself?"

"Part of it, but I also needed investments. Banks weren't keen on loans. I found some investors. It was hard work because the Deveraux name isn't really popular nowadays."

"I'd say I'm sorry, but your brothers deserved it."

I snorted. "No question about that. Honestly, not even my parents are holding a grudge against Xander. As far as we know, he's the one who did all the legwork."

"Yeah, he is."

"Dad says it's a good thing he ousted them or else my brothers would've probably sunk the company altogether. Can't believe they would just throw away our family's legacy like that."

He frowned. "But it made things difficult for you. *We* made things difficult for you."

I shook my head. "The way I see it, my brothers are the ones who made it more difficult. Anyway, I got all the investment I needed. I don't plan to expand for now, so I don't need more capital. My ambition was to turn a profit as soon as possible. I don't believe in endless expansion without seeing profit."

"That's smart."

I felt something bloom in my chest at his words and realized how starved I was for praise. It wasn't just that I wasn't used to it. I simply didn't expect it at all, especially from a man who I was dating. It seemed completely foreign to me compared to what I'd experienced.

"Thanks. And it took four months for us to break even."

"Grace, that's really impressive. I bet investors lined up at the door after that."

I nodded proudly. "They did. Even those who turned me away. They insisted that if I was ever looking to expand, they were open to negotiate with me. But for now, I keep working with those who invested from the beginning."

"I like your business savvy. You're known for it. One of my grandmothers, Isabeau, mentioned it once."

"Isabeau," I said slowly. "Why does that sound familiar?"

"I think every man and his dog in New Orleans knows Isabeau LeBlanc."

"Wait! I think she was the head of the cotillion the year I attended or something. She was on the committee at least."

"She's on a lot of committees, so that doesn't surprise me. And she was in even more back then."

"So, what did she say about me?"

"That she thinks you're a good person. And that she heard your father's company was growing profits by leaps and bounds when you were still involved in it."

I pushed my hair back, nodding. "Yes. We had a few years of very high profits. It was always a point of contention between my brothers and me."

"Why?"

"Because they wanted to take more money out of the company for, you know, personal reasons. But I was very strict with what had to be reinvested and so on. Because of those reinvestments, profits grew, and so did their frustration with me. They were so happy when I announced that I was leaving. A small part of me was relieved that I didn't have to work with them anymore. I'd done it for so long for my dad, but..."

"I understand what you're saying. I couldn't imagine being at odds with my brothers and still working together. Was your mom involved in the company?" he asked.

"No. She does charity work. Your mom?"

"She was never part of the conglomerate. She opened her own gallery when she was in her twenties."

"There's no gallery named LeBlanc-Broussard..."

He flashed me a smile. "Mom is a bit of a rebel. She wanted to do things under a completely different name so people wouldn't put two and two together."

I grinned. "I like her. She came from a well-known family and married someone who also came from a well-known family, then decided to go rogue."

"That's Mom to a T. Even now, she mostly does her own thing. My grand-mothers were involved in the company—they were chefs. Now they have a fragrance shop."

"That's so interesting. Where is it?"

"It's called Fragrant Delights, on Dumaine."

"Oh! I've passed it so many times. They make soaps and lotions too. I'll drop by sometime. We could collaborate."

"Just be careful," he growled.

"With what?"

"My grandmothers, they... Well, they're special."

"In what way?"

He opened his mouth and closed it again. "That's a conversation for another day."

Then it dawned on me. "I wouldn't tell them anything about this."

"Grace!" Zachary leaned closer to me, raising our interlaced hands and kissing the back of mine. "If I know anything about my grandmothers, it's that they'll find out before I tell them. They always do. And I don't mind. I want the whole world to know that we're together."

"Oh, okay." I was melting inside. No man had ever cared about me in this way, and I loved it.

"I fucking love being seen out and about with you." He lowered our hands before kissing me. It was slow but deep, and I was a goner. Goodness, I could kiss this man all day.

He kissed me until I shuddered, and then pulled back. I winced when my phone beeped.

"Let me check that. I think it might be my mom." I glanced at the screen. "Yep, it is."

Mom: I've got your favorite for lunch in case you can make it.

"She's bribing me with lunch." I glanced at the clock on the phone. "Oh my God. We've been here for more than an hour already."

"And I enjoyed every second of it," Zachary said.

"Me too."

"I'll drive you to your parents' house."

"I can take my own car... unless you're going in that same direction."

"I am."

"Great. I'll Uber back. No sense in driving separately."

We headed back to his car, holding hands the whole way.

Half an hour later, we pulled in front of my parents' house. Zachary came over to my side even though I'd already started to open the door. He pulled it open even wider as I stepped out. Then he closed it, looking down at me.

"I want to see you again, Grace."

"I want to see you again as well," I whispered.

"Good. Then that's settled. Now, as to when—"

"Hi, Grace."

"Oh!" *Oh crap.* My parents were on the porch. I hadn't seen them.

Zachary stepped to one side. Mom and Dad were coming toward us. I instantly felt sixteen again.

"Hi, Mom. Hi, Dad."

"And who are you?" Dad asked Zachary without even as much as a hello.

"I'm Zachary LeBlanc, Mr. Deveraux."

"LeBlanc." Mom looked surprised. "Were you two at the ranch?"

Oh, that would be a good explanation… except it wasn't true.

I cleared my throat. "No, we had breakfast."

"For goodness' sake," Dad exclaimed. "This man was all over her, disrespecting her right in front of our house."

I stared down at my feet, now feeling even younger.

"Clayton, you don't have to be so explicit about things," Mom admonished. "Let the kids do what they want."

Dad cleared his throat. "No, I'm the head of this family."

I snapped my head up, needed to quell this before it got out of hand. "Dad, that won't work. I'm not sixteen. Zachary and I are dating. Please don't make a big deal about it, and don't embarrass me."

I didn't like to be short with my parents, especially not in front of others, but it had to be done.

Dad looked at me intently for a few seconds and then nodded. "Okay, but one of these days, you and I will have a chat," he informed Zachary, who nodded right back.

"Sure. I can give you my number. You can call me and ask anything you want, sir."

Dad just narrowed his eyes, which meant Zachary wasn't in the clear. Then again, I considered it a victory that he'd stopped his tirade.

Zachary turned to me. "Grace, have a great weekend."

"You too. Enjoy the movie."

He winked at me before getting in the car. "Will do. It was great meeting you, Mr. and Mrs. Deveraux."

"Likewise," Mom said, then turned to me the second he closed the door. "Oh, he's a looker."

I grinned. "I know."

Dad hmphed.

I rolled my eyes. "Oh, Dad, stop being such a grump. Come on. Let's all go inside."

I interlaced my arms with both of theirs, and the three of us walked up the front porch and into the house. It smelled of jambalaya.

I inhaled deeply. "Oh, this brings back memories of when I was a kid."

"Yes, I should tell Anne to make it more often," Mom said.

"Grace, I'm sorry," Dad apologized. "I didn't want to put you on the spot in front of him. You know I don't like to get involved in what you're doing."

"I know, Dad."

"I just worry about you, baby girl, after your marriage. Roger turned out to be such a bastard."

"He did. But Zachary is nothing like that."

As we all went to the living room and sat down at the mahogany dining table, Dad asked, "What do you know about him? Last time we talked, you were telling us that he's not a good person."

I cleared my throat. "Yeah, I was wrong about that."

He raised an eyebrow. "I find it hard to believe that you changed your mind so fast. Did he coerce you into something?"

"Do you have to believe the worst of everyone?" Mom asked.

"Darling, you know I like to give people the benefit of the doubt, but when it comes to our daughter's happiness, I'm not taking any more chances."

I loved my parents to the moon and back, but sometimes Dad could be overprotective.

"I misjudged him in the beginning. And, based on my past experience with men, I jumped to conclusions. But he's a really good person. He's good to me," I emphasized, and that seemed to take the wind out of Dad's sails.

"One more question."

"Clayton, really?" Mom chastised.

"Just one. You sure this isn't some LeBlanc vendetta against us Deveraux-es?"

That took me by surprise. "Dad, of course not. You said it yourself, you don't hold a grudge over them."

"I know, but it's a bit weird that Xander LeBlanc exposed your brothers, and now you're dating this Zachary."

I liked how he said "this Zachary," like he still hadn't decided whether to like him or not.

"The two things aren't related. If anything, Zachary was very cautious with me in the beginning precisely because of my brothers and everything that's happened."

"All right. Well"—he looked at Mom, and I could practically see him softening under her gaze—"if you think it's the right thing, then of course we're happy for you. So, are things moving forward with the horse ranch in any way?"

I shook my head. "I haven't heard from the owners since I went there last week."

"Honey, are you sure you want to do it at all? I mean, you really do work a lot," Mom said as Anna brought three portions of jambalaya.

I grinned. "Thanks, Anna. It smells delicious as usual."

"Of course. I knew you were coming today, so I asked your mom if I could make your favorite," she said.

I pressed my lips together so as not to laugh. I had been surprised when Mom said she'd made my favorite, just because it wasn't the type of thing she remembered. But of course, Anna had actually remembered it. Mom was very blasé about Anna blowing her cover.

"Thank you. That's very kind of you."

Anna scurried back out of the room. Even though my parents had asked her time and again to sit with us and eat, she said she didn't like to interrupt our family time.

I turned my attention to my parents. "I wouldn't have to do a lot," I admitted, "because the owners are very hands-on. It's something dear to my heart. Animal therapy helped me a lot when I went through the divorce. That's why I'd like to invest in something that I know would help others."

Mom looked at me with soft eyes. "You've always had a great heart."

"By the way," I said, "do you know Isabeau of the LeBlanc-Broussard clan?"

Dad looked up. "Of course. Everyone knows her. And Celine, too, though Isabeau is always a bit…"

"Harder to overlook," Mom said. "Why?"

"I heard they have a store in the Quarter with natural handmade fragrances and soaps, creams, and so on. I was thinking about maybe paying them a visit, see if there's a way we could work together."

"That would be a smart way to restore a bit of credibility to the Deveraux name in the Quarter," Dad said.

"That didn't occur to me." It was the first time I realized how important this was for him. He wanted to fix the family name in any way he could, and this collaboration would help a great deal.

"Darling," Mom cut in, "it's not Grace's responsibility to repair what our sons did wrong."

"No, no, of course not," Dad said. "It was just a thought."

I decided to change the subject. "So, tell me what you two have been up to."

My parents had an amazing social life. Even though they didn't attend as many events as they used to, they filled their time with a lot of activities such as visiting art museums and so on. I wanted to know every detail, and they were more than happy to oblige.

Chapter Nineteen

Zachary

"This is my absolute favorite one," Bella said, jumping off the couch the second the credits rolled on *Goblet of Fire*.

I was at Chad's home, and we were all in the living room. He was sitting between us, looking like he'd just spent the most boring two hours of his life staring at the TV screen. Scarlett had put Simone down for a sleep and was in full Potterhead mode. She'd been commentating on the movie with me and Bella the entire time. I bet one of the reasons Bella loved her so much was because she was a fan of Harry Potter.

Beckett had joined us. Bailey was here, too, because she was also a fan. She hadn't brought Xander over, though. Our brother had excused himself, saying that he needed to check some reports. I knew that was code for "you won't catch me dead there." He usually indulged Bella, but he probably figured that since so many of us were here anyway, it made no sense this time.

"You know what?" I said. "It's my favorite, too, butting heads with *Order of the Phoenix*."

Chad glared at me. What did I do wrong?

It hit me the next second when Bella said, "Dad, can we watch that one too?"

Oh fuck. I should've said that this one is my favorite.

"I misspoke. *Goblet of Fire* is my favorite of them all."

Bella narrowed her eyes. "Don't lie, Uncle Zachary. You said it's never good to lie."

"True." I knew I had to be careful with what I told her or I'd eat my words.

Bella jumped into her dad's lap, and I knew she was getting into full-on sales mode. "Look, you already agreed to let me watch *Goblet of Fire*. *Order of the Phoenix* can't be much darker than that, is it? I'm not scared at all."

Chad looked at me. "Is it darker?"

"Yes," I said without hesitation.

Bella glared at me. "Uncle Zachary."

"What? No lying, remember?"

She looked down at her hands.

"I, for one, feel like it was always amazing to wait for the next movie," I went on. "The first ones came out once a year, but the next ones we had to wait two whole years."

Bella looked at Scarlett. "But that means you were ancient when all of them came out."

It took all I had not to burst out laughing. *The things kids say.*

"I have an idea," Scarlett said. "Why don't you and I go upstairs and discuss the movie? There are some points that they left out, and I can tell you all about them."

Bella looked at Scarlett as if she hung the moon. I was beyond happy that my brother had decided to give his relationship with Scarlett a real try. It turned out to be exactly what he and Bella needed. After his divorce, he'd intended to stay celibate. He'd even managed for a few years—God knew how—until he met Scarlett.

The second Bella went upstairs, we all rose from the couch. I noticed Beckett was looking at me with a smug smile.

"I'm surprised you made it," he told me.

I narrowed my eyes. "Why wouldn't I make it?"

"Considering last night—"

"Beckett," I said in a warning tone.

"I thought you'd still be asleep," he finished.

"You were out until late last night?" Chad asked.

"I have no idea," Beckett replied. Now his smile wasn't just smug, it was downright malicious. "Zachary here ran into Grace Deveraux. He played the role of knight in shining armor very well, scaring off some dude who was hitting on her and being a jackass. Then I don't know what happened. Anthony and I went to Julian's bar with Grace's friend. She seemed very adamant that the two of them needed time alone."

There was a bit of silence in the room, and then Chad said, "Beckett, this is none of your business."

I turned to look at my older brother, a bit surprised. Then again, Chad had never been one to pry. I appreciated that.

A second later, he raised a brow at me. "But Grace Deveraux, really? Weren't you telling us that you two aren't on good terms?"

"Things change," I said.

"Ha!" Beckett exclaimed. "Damn. We tried to get Lais to tell us all the details, but my initial assumption that she was going to spill the beans was completely wrong. She didn't say one word."

"I bet that frustrated you to no end." That thought gave me much satisfaction.

"Well, I, for one think Zachary's business is his own," Bailey cut in.

"Bailey, you're a good soul," I said, "but half the family never got that memo."

She laughed. "That's true. Anyway, I've got to go. I promised Xander that I'd meet him for coffee in the Quarter later on."

Chad scoffed. "I knew it! He just blew off Bella."

"Come on, give the man credit where credit is due," Beckett said. "He does a lot for Bella, but he probably figured..."

"He wasn't needed here," I finished.

Chad seemed to consider this, then nodded. "Yeah, you're right. It was torture for me. I can't imagine how it would be for Xander."

Bailey bristled. "I can't believe you two. How can you be such grumps when it comes to Harry Potter?"

Chad stared at her. Bailey was feisty, but Chad hadn't had as much contact with her as the rest of us. She was a perfect match for Xander, the very
opposite of him. She was always happy, always looking at the bright side of
things, determined to live life to the fullest. Xander was... well, as she put it,
a grump. But they worked well together.

"I'll let you debate who's the grumpiest," I said. "I need to get going. I
promised our grandmothers I would stop by the store today."

Beckett whistled. "That's brave of you."

I turned to my younger brother. "Why?"

"They'll sniff you out until you give them the scoop on Grace."

I rubbed my eyes and then shrugged. "So what? I don't mind."

Beckett's eyes bulged. "What if they threaten you with the lilac again?
Grandmother said she was making a batch of cologne *for men*!"

Funnily enough, it didn't seem like such a threat. Not that I believed in it.
But at this stage, I didn't think anything could make me care for Grace more
than I already did.

"I know how to steer them away from that topic." I wanted to mention
Grace's idea of meeting with them to chat about a possible collaboration.
And yes, I was fully aware I was making myself an easy target by walking in
there. *Whatever.*

Usually, I kept my personal life as separate as possible from the family.
Part of it was because when I went on dates, they were more like hookups,
and that was it. But what Grace and I had was different. I just didn't like to
be put on the spot the way Beckett had done to me just now, and I was sure
the grandmothers would do the same as soon as I walked in. I was enjoying
his stunned expression, though. He clearly didn't see this coming.

"Bye, everyone. I'll see you when I see you," I said. There was no shortage
of get-togethers in the LeBlanc-Broussard clan. I'd lost track of when we
were meeting next, but I was certain that someone would remind me shortly
beforehand.

After I stepped out of the house. I called Isabeau to make sure they didn't
have their hands full.

"Hey, Isabeau, we just finished watching Harry Potter. I'll need maybe twenty minutes to get to your place. Is the timing good?"

"Of course. There's no bad time for our grandson to visit us."

"Want me to bring anything? Coffee? Beignets?"

"No, we're all set. Bailey brought us some pralines, so we're good." Another plus point for Bailey—she always looked out for our grandmothers.

I arrived at their store faster than anticipated. There were no customers inside, which was a surprise because they were usually swamped on weekends. When I stepped in, they were both hunched over a notebook.

They looked up at the same time. "Boy, you were quick!" Isabeau exclaimed.

"I was lucky."

They closed the notebook quickly and exchanged a glance that I could only describe as conspiratorial.

"What brings you here today?"

I looked around their store. Every time I came here, it dawned on me what a great job they'd done designing and decorating this place. It made you want to buy things even if you hadn't planned to.

"I want to talk to you about something."

"All right, we're all ears." Isabeau stood up straighter. Celine put the notebook in a drawer under the counter.

"So, remember that Grace is running her own business."

"Yes, of course," Isabeau said.

"You know she makes fragrances and creams."

Celine nodded. "We've even bought some of her creams. She's doing a fantastic job. We especially like that it's all handmade with natural ingredients in New Orleans."

"Grace mentioned that she'd like to stop by your store and talk to you about a possible collaboration," I said in a nonchalant tone.

Isabeau instantly smiled. Celine looked at her. "That girl's a genius. She's welcome anytime. We would love to help her out. Especially with our special ingredient."

Here comes the hard part.

"Celine, Isabeau," I said in a respectful tone. They bristled a little. "Don't start with any of that lilac story."

"Mind your own business, young man," Isabeau said, and they started to laugh.

Celine shook her head. "When are your boys going to learn you can't tell us what to do?"

"I know we can't. It's not my intention. But this thing you're doing is—" I searched for the right word, but couldn't come up with a softer one. "—intrusive."

Isabeau narrowed her eyes. "Let me get this straight. Do you believe that lilac has powers or not?"

"No," I said without hesitation, then realized I'd made a mistake. Both of them smiled triumphantly.

"Then what harm will it do if we give her a perfume with lilac? Poor girl truly does need some help in that department."

Celine tapped her temple. She reminded me a lot of Mom when she did that. "You know what? Maybe we should add something for just all-around good luck as well, or something to repel assholes."

I laughed even harder. My grandmothers rarely acted their age, and I hoped I was that way when I got older.

"There's no talking you out of it, is there?" I asked.

"No, not at all," Celine assured me.

"I do wonder what she has in mind for a collaboration," Isabeau added. "But we're open to anything. We have a wide range of products, but people always keep asking about more sophisticated things that we don't make."

"I already know a few products from Grace's line that would sell like hotcakes in our store," Celine said.

I was grateful that the two of them were so open to this.

"And besides," Isabeau said, "maybe associating with LeBlanc-Broussard will do her some good."

I narrowed my eyes slightly. "What do you mean?"

"After the whole debacle with her brothers, the family name has gotten a tad tarnished. We feel guilty about it, although we shouldn't. Those boys weren't good people, and it was high time everyone knew it," Celine explained.

"So, tell us a bit more about Grace." Isabeau took a few bottles from the shelf behind her and started mixing things.

"What do you want to know?" I asked.

"Whatever you want to tell us," Celine said.

It was hard to believe the two of them were so at odds at one point that they almost sabotaged my parents getting married. Now they were inseparable.

"She's a very hard worker. She's honest. She's been through a lot, and she's fantastic."

Isabeau smiled at me. "What an excellent recommendation. Now, since you're here, would you like to replenish your stock of soap and shower gel?"

"After you've explicitly told me that you're putting God knows what in them?"

Isabeau winked. "What harm did we do, really?"

Oh, Isabeau. I loved my grandmothers dearly, but they'd gotten a bit eccentric in their old age. Back when they were working as chefs, I didn't remember them ever talking about such nonsense like plants having powers. Or maybe they did and I just zoned it out. Who knew?

I nodded. "Sure. I'll take the lot."

"Perfect." She beamed.

The two of them exchanged another glance, but I let it drop. If this made them happy, I wasn't going to interfere.

Isabeau packed up my products, and we said our goodbyes. As soon as I got out of the store, I called Grace. This morning with her had been fucking fantastic. I didn't want our breakfast together to end. I'd been very close to convincing her to bail on her parents, but I'd promised Bella I'd watch the movie, and I didn't like to disappoint her.

Grace answered quickly. "Hey," she said.

"Are you still at your parents'?"

"No, I just left. I'm meeting Lais."

"Listen, I was at my grandmothers' store just now and told them about your idea. You're welcome to stop by at any time."

"Wow. Thanks. I didn't realize you were going to talk to them about it already."

"Why not? I wanted to get the ball rolling."

"Did they say when?"

"No, but they're always at the store."

"Oh, they're hard workers," Grace said with admiration in her tone.

"Yep. They've always been like that. Isabeau usually jokes that what they do now doesn't even require the stamina that being a chef had. Says managing a shop is so easy that she could do night shifts too."

She chuckled. "Being a chef is definitely not for the faint of heart. I'll give her that."

"What are you and Lais doing?" I asked.

"We didn't make specific plans. We'll probably have a coffee and..."

"Spill the beans?" I finished for her.

There was a short pause. I could already imagine her blushing and, if she was sitting, maybe pressing her thighs together.

Grace cleared her throat. "Yes, I will. All the spicy ones."

Now it was my turn to pause. I hadn't expected the return.

"What was your favorite one?" I asked as I headed toward my car. The Quarter was waking up from the afternoon lull and it was getting more crowded, preparing for yet another crazy night in town.

"Let me think. Probably the couch because it was unexpected."

So, she liked to be surprised. I was going to keep that in mind.

"What else?"

"The fact that you always listen without judging makes me feel safe."

That caught me completely off guard. I'd expected details about my prowess in bed, not something like this. Last night, it had taken a lot of effort to get her to tell me what was going on. That she trusted me enough to tell me only made me want to protect her all the more.

"You don't have to keep things from me, Grace. I promise I'll never judge or use what you say against you."

"I'm starting to understand that about you."

"Be sure to talk me up to Lais. It's always good if your best friend likes me," I teased to lighten things up a bit.

"True. And let me tell you, Lais doesn't like people very easily, but you're in luck. She seemed to like you even before meeting you."

"Even though you told her how infuriating I am?"

"Oh, yeah, I did that quite a few times," Grace said, and I could hear the smile in her voice.

I liked talking to her. This had never been my MO. In the past, it was dinner and then going home with them—mutually agreed upon, of course. But this felt natural and easy, and I wanted more of it.

"I do think you jumping in the Mississippi River earned you a lot of points."

"With you too," I pointed out.

"You know what I figured?"

"What?"

"That my lucky star is rising again."

"I'm not following," I said as walked toward the parking lot.

"I've always thought that each of us has a lucky star. I figured mine went into hiding for a while, but now I think things are finally turning around. I mean, things have been going super well for a while with the company and everything, but this feels different."

I nodded even though she couldn't see me. "You're going to get along excellently with Isabeau and Celine."

"What? Why?"

"Because they believe in esoteric stuff as well, like luck and plants having specific powers."

She laughed. "Zachary, we live in New Orleans. Don't tell me that you don't have some curiosity about the supernatural."

"I truly don't."

"That's a sacrilege!"

We both laughed at that.

"Hey, it would be boring if we were all the same, wouldn't it?" I asked.

"That's true. Now I'm looking forward to seeing your grandmothers even more."

"I'm looking forward to seeing *you*."

Yeah, Grace wasn't the only one laying all her cards on the table today.

"Me, too, but I'm not sure when."

"This week is going to be crazy again?" I guessed.

"Something like that, but every week is crazy, to be honest."

"We'll find time. Don't stress about it."

"How are you so relaxed about everything?"

"Why not? There's no rush to do anything. Summer evenings are endless, as are the weekends. The world is ours for the taking, Grace. No pressure."

"Every time we talk, I like you more."

"Are you sure it's just the talking that makes you like me?" I asked when I finally reached the car. "Not all those orgasms?"

I took immense pleasure in hearing her sharp intake of breath. I liked surprising her—switching from serious to flirty to dirty talking.

"Now that you bring it up, I do think you have a point."

"You think?"

"Want to drop by and prove it?" she challenged.

"Don't ask me twice, Grace. I'm already in my car."

"Oh, wow," she murmured.

"But I know you're spending the evening with Lais."

"Oh, that's right."

Had she forgotten already?

"But I promise we'll find the time soon enough," I added.

"I'm looking forward to that."

"So am I."

I decided that I was going to peel off all Grace's layers—one orgasm at a time.

Chapter Twenty

Grace

"Oh, the perks of being a business owner," I murmured on Tuesday evening when I was once again cooped up in my office all by myself. It was seven o'clock, and I still had quite a few tasks left. When my phone beeped, I thought it might be my assistant shooting me yet another to-do. But my entire body was immediately set aflame when I noticed the sender.

Zachary: Workday over?

Grace: I wish. Looks like this is going to be a dinner-at-the-office kind of week.

Zachary: What a coincidence. Same for me. It's another crisis week, but I don't mind. What are you having for dinner?

Grace: I haven't decided yet. Maybe some gumbo. It's my comfort dish.

Zachary: LeBlanc & Broussard has an excellent one. I can have it delivered to you.

My eyes bulged, and then a rush of warmth came over me. It was completely unexplainable.

Grace: I'd love that.

Zachary: Then consider it done.

Grace: How can I repay you?

Zachary: I have a few things in mind. I'll tell you when I see you in person.

I expected Zachary to text me back. When he didn't, I remembered that he'd said he had a lot to do as well. Yet he was taking the time to order me dinner. I was liking this man more and more every day.

As I opened up the spreadsheet I was currently working on, my phone lit up again and vibrated. I answered without checking the caller.

"Hey."

"Hi, Grace. Am I disturbing you?"

"Oh, hi, Gaston." I'd been certain it was Zachary. *Thank God I didn't answer in a flirty way.*

"Hi. Listen, I know I promised to call last week, but we've had a lot of work to do with Starlight."

"Is he okay?" My heart suddenly jumped into my throat. *How did I already get so attached to him?*

"Yes, but it turns out that he was obedient and quiet those first days because he was a bit shocked by the newness of it all. Then he started to show us how stubborn he can be."

"I see."

"But it's nothing we haven't seen before. So, listen, we wanted to ask if you were still interested in the ranch."

"What? Yes, of course." How could they doubt that? "I loved everything I saw."

"Right. Because we spoke to Zachary, and he requested to see some numbers." I felt uncomfortable knowing what they'd discussed with him, almost like it was too much information. "We'll send everything to you as well, and then it would help if you could make an offer when you can. There's no rush, of course. We're now dealing with Starlight and so on, but..."

"Yes, yes, of course. I won't leave you hanging, I promise."

"Perfect. Then I hope I can get you the numbers this week."

"There's no rush on that either, okay? Whenever you have time."

"I have to put them together first."

That didn't sound good. They hadn't already calculated everything? That could take a while, then, especially if they had to get builders quotes and so on. But I was in no rush. "Sure. Just keep me posted."

"Will do."

After hanging up, I debated if I should discuss this with Zachary, but it felt weird. And considering that Gaston didn't even have the numbers yet, this was going to take a while.

I returned to my to-do list. We were planning on partnering up with several physical businesses. We were doing great selling our products online, but I was a New Orleans girl at heart and wanted to see our products in stores, too, especially in the French Quarter. That was our gateway to the rest of the US because it was the biggest touristic spot in the city. I couldn't wait to visit Isabeau and Celine's store. I had a great feeling about that.

Half an hour later, my dinner arrived. I tipped the delivery boy very well and went to my desk. The gumbo smelled amazing; even without opening the lid, the aroma made my mouth water. They'd packed a plastic spoon and fork as well. I sent Zachary a picture and then dug in. He called me right away.

"Thanks so much. This is truly delicious."

"Good. I figured you'd like it. And I also figured this might be a good time to chat. How's your week been so far?"

"As busy as I thought. At least tonight, I'm getting this amazing dinner. Yesterday, I just had peanuts."

"For fuck's sake, Grace!" he growled.

"What? I sometimes forget to eat dinner. Then I get home and I'm starving, so I order some delivery. Seems like it's going to be that kind of week."

"I'll take care of you," he said easily, and I melted in my chair. "I'll send you dinner every evening."

"Zachary, you don't have to do that."

"Yes, I do. It'll be my pleasure."

I smiled as I ate another spoonful of gumbo. After swallowing, I asked, "Is this going to turn into a flirty phone call?"

"That's a definite possibility," he said in a very serious tone, as if we were talking about a business deal. "Just putting it out there, but I have nothing against that. I think late nights at the office are perfect for that."

"You're still at the office too?"

"Yeah, eating a steak. It's quite handy to work above LeBlanc-Broussard."

"I'd say." I laughed. "By the way, I'd love to drop by your grandmothers' store this week. Do they need a heads-up or something? Should I schedule?"

"No, they don't believe in schedules. The only risk you have is that the store will be too crowded and you might have to wait a bit, so maybe go at nine when they open or in the afternoon. There's always a lull in the Quarter at those times."

"Great, I'll do that."

Once again, I wondered if I should bring up my conversation with Gaston, but it felt weird. In that regard, we were still competing. They would probably just choose the better offer, which was fair. I'd do the same.

I decided on a more pleasant topic instead.

"So," I said, shifting a bit in my seat, "when do we start the flirty part?"

"You mean dirty talking?" Zachary said.

"Oh goodness." I cleared my throat. "Right. I don't think I can do this on the phone," I whispered, which made him laugh.

"There's no pressure, Grace. I promise there'll be plenty of opportunities in person. In fact, I'd prefer that."

"How come?"

"Because you turn me on faster than I thought was humanly possible. The last thing I want is to walk around my office with a hard-on."

My entire body was on edge right away. I cleared my throat, then choked on absolutely nothing and started to cough.

"Grace, are you okay?"

"Yeah, yeah. I just wasn't expecting that."

"It's the truth."

"Completely raw and unfiltered, huh?"

"That's the only way I know how to deliver it."

That was true. I enjoyed that about him.

"But for now," he went on, "I'll let you enjoy your dinner. Actually, you know what? Let me know what you want tomorrow, and I'll make it happen."

"Why don't you surprise me?"

"Will do."

After hanging up, I devoured the rest of my dinner. I feared that I'd go into a food coma after finishing it because the portion was quite large, but I'd been starving, so of course I ate it all. But I had a lot of energy, so I stayed at the office late into the evening.

The next morning, I decided to head down Dumaine to Fragrant Delights. I arrived in front of the shop at nine o'clock on the dot and glanced inside. Two elderly women were milling around. One was dressed in all black, and her hair fell right to her chin. The other one wore colorful clothes. Her hair was even longer.

I stepped inside. "Good morning."

Glancing around, I immediately felt at home. The floor-to-ceiling shelves were filled with bottles of all sizes as well as other paraphernalia. I loved the labels on the bottles—all handwritten, and of course bearing the LeBlanc-Broussard crest. Even though I knew the company was called the Orleans Conglomerate, they still used the family crest on several products, such as their famous pralines.

"Good morning," the woman dressed in black replied.

"I'm Grace Deveraux."

"Isabeau," she said.

I went toward the ladies to shake her hand.

"And I'm Celine," the other woman said, shaking my hand as well.

"It's nice to meet you both. I hope it's okay that I came by so early."

"Of course, of course," Celine exclaimed.

I felt instantly at ease with these two. So many people in the Quarter practically winced when they heard the name Deveraux, but not them.

"So, as you know, I'm in a similar business as you—"

"Only bigger and far more successful," Isabeau finished with a wink.

I smiled with my whole heart. I tried to gauge which one Zachary resembled most, but the truth was, neither of them reminded me of him.

"It's doing very well, thanks. But your shop is amazing."

"Oh, we do well. Then again, we only started this so our old bones wouldn't rot at home," Isabeau said. "We found out we quite like it."

"Right now, I'm only selling my merchandise online, but I'd like to put them it stores as well. I can send you a pitch to give you an idea of how it would benefit us both."

Isabeau waved her hand. "Darling girl, we've been in business far too long. We were chefs prior to this little operation and very much involved in strategic decisions regarding the restaurant. We don't need a pitch, just some prices so we can figure out what we need to order. But for now, tell us what you have in mind."

"I'd like to put my best-selling items in the store. They would complement your brand because I use natural products as well. I'm a firm believer in plants and their restorative powers."

Both women looked at each other and then back at me. "Go on," Celine encouraged.

"Some descriptions of the products take a bit of an esoteric angle. People seem to enjoy that."

"That fits right in with our philosophy," Isabeau said.

"I thought so too. You'd be the very first store in the Quarter to have my products."

Celine sighed. "Maybe it'll help a bit and make other stores trust the Deveraux name again if we merchandise a few of your items."

I stopped looking around the store. These two were so thoughtful, and I appreciated their support. "It probably would help. But if you find that it tarnishes your brand in any way, please don't hesitate to tell me, and I'll take them off your shelves, of course."

"Girl, we can handle anything that comes our way," Isabeau said, making me smile.

"You've had to deal with the fallout from your brothers' wrongdoings, and that's not fair. I have to admit that, for a while, I thought your father was in on it too," Celine said.

I bristled. "Oh no. My father is an honest man."

She nodded. "We know that now."

"May I ask what changed your minds?" I asked.

Celine laughed. Isabeau simply said, "We have our ways of finding out everything going on in the city."

"I don't doubt that," I said. "Do you have any questions? If you're open to it, I'm more than happy to include your products in our online shop. It's doing very well. We drive a lot of traffic to it daily."

Celine waved her hand. "We have enough on our hands with the demand we get from people who walk into our store. We couldn't keep up with more. We're happy with what we have."

"Well, if that changes, just let me know. I'll send you a spreadsheet with prices, and then just let me know what you need. Do you have an email address I should forward it to?"

"Of course. We're old, not decrepit," Isabeau replied, and I winced.

"Sorry, I didn't mean to offend you. My mom, for example, doesn't like emails at all."

"We do. Now, as a token of good faith, I would like to gift you one of our fragrances," Isabeau said.

I smiled, surprised by the gesture. "That's kind of you. I'd love one. I still can't believe that I've never been in here. How does it work? Do you need any information from me to make a custom one?"

"As it happens, we already made one," Celine said. Her voice was a bit different from before, but I couldn't tell why.

"Perfect."

"And do tell us if it doesn't work, okay? Then we'll call you back here and do some proper legwork."

"What do you mean, legwork?" I inquired.

Isabeau rolled her shoulders back and threw Celine a warning glance. I had a feeling that I was missing something.

"Just tell us if you like it," Isabeau said, but I was pretty sure that was not what Celine had meant.

Isabeau opened a drawer under the counter and picked up a small bottle. It was a delightful light pink, mimicking a crystal, and had a delicate, small golden cap.

"It's a perfume, not eau de cologne or eau de parfum, so it's very potent. You don't need to use more than a few drops."

I uncapped it carefully. "This is amazing. So many notes and..." My voice faded as I took in a deep breath. Since I worked with plants, I was good at distinguishing them. I could recognize the work of professionals. "Do I detect some star anise?"

"You've got an excellent nose!" Isabeau sounded proud.

"And lilac?"

Celine nodded. "Yes, yes. We love it."

"I love lilac too. Oh, this is thrilling. Do you have a body lotion that goes with it?"

"We'll make you one and send it to you."

"Perfect. Thank you. I insist on paying for both."

"We insist you pay for nothing," Isabeau replied. "That's no way of starting a partnership."

"Well, then," I said, taking out two creams I'd brought, "these two are for your personal use. It's our bestseller. I use it as well and love it." It was a rejuvenating face cream.

"We'll gladly accept," Celine replied.

Both women looked at me, smiling. This was going to be a success. I already knew it.

"Can you send us a batch quickly?" she continued. "We'll put it in our window display."

That was a pleasant surprise because they only had a small bottle of perfume in their display.

I nodded. "I'll send some today."

"Excellent. When people ask us about it, we'll tell them that we'll have the products in store soon."

I beamed at them. "I have a very good feeling about our partnership."

"So do we," Isabeau said, then changed the topic altogether. "We're hoping that Zachary is treating you all right."

I licked my lips. "He's a perfect gentleman. Although, we did have a rocky start."

"We heard about that."

"I think it's a nice sign that both of you are interested in the ranch," Celine said.

Isabeau turned to her, tilting her head, clearly trying to drive a point home.

"A sign?" I asked. My heart was beating fast.

Isabeau glanced at me. "We'll put our cards on the table before this becomes weird. We got wind that you two have gotten quite close."

I was so shocked that I was surprised my jaw didn't hit the floor. *Why didn't Zachary tell me this?*

"We don't need any details, but let's just say that we're thrilled about it," she continued.

"You are? How did you find out?"

Isabeau smirked. Not a smile. It was definitely a smirk.

"We can't divulge our sources, but word does travel in the French Quarter," Celine offered.

I only had vague memories of that because I'd been out of the Quarter, so to speak, for quite a while. It had been my brothers' domain.

I laughed nervously. "I'm not sure what to say."

"We didn't have to corner the poor girl," Celine said.

"We wouldn't have had to if you weren't so obvious," Isabeau chastised her.

Both turned to look at me.

"We apologize," Isabeau said. "I promise we didn't want to make you uncomfortable. All you have to know about it is that we're happy."

Despite their disclaimer, I was feeling awkward. As I opened my mouth, a group of about ten people walked in.

"Right. I'll send you all the financial information and some more samples," I said as I headed toward the door. "Have a great day."

"You, too, Grace," Isabeau said. She was smirking again.

Oh goodness. Zachary did say his grandmothers were forces to be reckoned with. I should've taken him more seriously.

***

The rest of the day was a whirlwind of to-dos and meetings, but I did manage to send a huge batch of samples to Isabeau and Celine. By the time the evening rolled around, I was exhausted. However, I was also looking forward to dinner. Zachary texted me earlier in the day to ask when I wanted my food delivered. I'd replied that 6:30 p.m. was okay.

At 6:20 p.m., I was already glancing at the door more often than necessary. At 6:27 p.m., there was a knock at the door. The building had someone at the reception desk, but once visitors were cleared downstairs, they could come right into my office.

"Come in."

The deliveryman entered and held up a take-out bag. "This is for you, miss."

"Thank you."

He put the bag on my desk, and I tipped him generously. I kept my composure until he left the room, then immediately dug into my bag of goodies.

"What did I get tonight?" I was excited. "Oh, jambalaya." That was yet another favorite of mine. I loved Southern comfort food. Might not be the best for the figure, but I loved it too much to think about that.

I opened the container, then snapped a photo and sent it to Zachary. He called before I even managed to take a bite.

"What's the verdict?" he asked as soon as I answered my phone.

"What are you talking about?" I asked nonchalantly.

"The jambalaya."

"I haven't tasted it yet."

"All right. Then I'll wait."

I felt extremely jittery, almost as if he was right here with me, eyes trained on me, waiting for my reaction. I swallowed a huge spoonful and went directly to heaven.

"I'm impressed. I thought I'd tasted all the jambalayas in the area, but this one is hands down the best."

"My grandmothers will be happy to know that. It's their original recipe, and they're convinced it's the best there is."

"As far as I'm concerned, it's true." I cleared my throat, took another spoonful, and swallowed it before saying, "By the way, speaking of your grandmothers..."

"Yeah?"

"I went by their store today."

"Did it go well?"

"Yes, they were very happy to collaborate. They even gave me a perfume."

Zachary groaned.

"What was that for?"

"Let me guess. It contains lilac?" he asked.

I frowned as I took a few more spoonfuls. "How would you know that?"

"Because it's a thing they do." He didn't elaborate.

"I'm going to need more details."

He sighed. "There's this story in my family that lilac sort of brings couples together."

I nearly choked on the jambalaya. "I'm sorry, what?"

He laughed. "Celine insists that it's because she gave my mom a perfume containing lilac that she met my dad, who turned out to be her soulmate.

They ended up together despite the fact that neither of the families wanted them to be."

"How come?"

"You don't know that the LeBlancs and Broussards were once competitors?"

"Oh, that's right. They had similar businesses. Honestly, it's been LeBlanc-Broussard my whole life. I've never paid much attention to the stories about what came before that."

"Anyway, the grandmothers gave a perfume containing lilac to each of my brothers' significant others. They insist it's the reason they're together."

I swallowed hard. "That's... I don't know how to describe it. Scary, maybe?"

"Nuts?" Zachary asked. "I mean, who actually thinks lilac has powers?"

"There are plants that do have powers," I began, "but I'm sensing that this isn't your type of conversation."

"No, it's not," he replied, making me laugh.

"Honestly, you were born and raised in New Orleans. You need to go with the flow when it comes to mystical things."

"I go with the flow with a lot of things, but not with nonsense."

I cleared my throat. "Anyway, they knew about us," I said quickly before stuffing my face full of jambalaya. That was a perfect excuse not to elaborate. A few seconds later, I realized Zachary wouldn't know why I wasn't answering.

"They told you that?" he asked.

"Mm-hmm," I mumbled, because I still hadn't finished chewing.

"How did they find out?"

I swallowed before saying, "Beats me. I figured you might know."

"No. Though, considering Beckett and his big mouth, I wouldn't put it past him to have mentioned it. My grandmothers are very resourceful."

"I bet they are. What are you having for dinner?" I asked.

"Jambalaya too. When I put the order in for you, I got in the mood as well. You're working late every day this week?"

I felt a pang of guilt in my chest. "Honestly, yes. Some weeks are like this."

"You don't have to explain anything to me, Grace, but I do have a proposition for you."

"I'm all ears."

"What about brunch at Commander's Palace on Saturday?"

"Yes! I used to go with my parents years ago when I was a kid. Last time I was there, I wasn't old enough to drink their cocktails."

"We can hit the bar this time. I'll make reservations. Do you have anything else going on Saturday?"

"No."

"Good, because I'd like to spend the whole day with you. On Sunday too."

This was a very good opportunity to try out my teasing skills. "You're so sure you're getting laid, huh?"

"Never. But I'm going to do my very best."

God, it was so easy to talk to this man. I could do it for hours.

"Tell me about your week. You said it's going to be crazy too."

He sighed. "Yeah. This is a busy season for the shipping business."

"Oh, I would've thought Christmas was peak."

"It is for land transportation, but not for the water. In my area, everything happens way before Christmas."

"Right. That makes sense."

"Now I'm dealing with several delays, and we're trying to find ways to solve that. But it'll all work out."

"I'll drink to that on Saturday."

"I can't wait, Grace."

"I can't either."

CHAPTER TWENTY-ONE

ZACHARY

"What do you mean, you can't join us anymore?" Anthony asked on Thursday evening. He, Beckett, and I were at the Lucky Bar, and I'd told them I couldn't make it fishing with the grandfathers this weekend. Beckett was looking at me like I'd informed him I was resigning from the family.

"I've made other plans," I said.

"What plans?"

Our youngest brothers were the most curious out of everyone in the family, but I didn't mind.

"I'm spending the weekend with Grace."

Anthony whistled. Beckett nodded appreciatively. "All right, so this is happening."

"It's happening," I confirmed, sipping my Sazerac.

The two of them exchanged a glance.

"What?" I asked.

"Nothing. We're just starting to wonder if there's some truth to the grandmothers' lilac story after all," Beckett offered as if he was commenting on the weather.

I rolled my eyes. "Let's not open up that can of worms. I have a hard enough time keeping a straight face when they mention it. But Grace is buying that story."

Anthony cocked a brow. "And you don't mind? Zachary, what gives?"

"What do you mean?" I asked.

"We went from every guy in the family—except Chad—doing what we do," Beckett said, referring to their single status, "to wanting to settle down."

I pointed my glass at them. "I never mentioned I was settling down."

"That's better, then," Anthony said. "I was starting to worry."

"And yet you *are* spending an entire weekend with her," Beckett pointed out.

"So? What's the problem with that?" I asked.

"Yeah, dude," Anthony said. "Two days of getting laid versus going fishing with us and the grandfathers? I'd take it too."

Beckett opened his mouth but then shook his head. Clearly he'd wanted to disagree but didn't.

The truth was that this meant far more than getting laid, but there was no way I could explain it to these two.

"So, what's new with you guys?" I asked.

"Same old, same old," Anthony replied. "Business is doing well. So is my personal life." He winked.

"Same for me," Beckett said. "Can't complain."

"What's the plan for Sunday?" I inquired.

"We're hoping to convince the grandfathers to change their spot on the bayou."

"Why?"

"Because I think they like to live dangerously in their old age," Beckett said through gritted teeth. "Their new favorite spot is in the sun."

"That's not so bad. The new boat definitely has a lot of shade."

"It gets very hot. If you would come more often, you'd know." Anthony said.

I cleared my throat. "Look, fishing's never been my thing, okay? I went out more often when they had that godforsaken wreck of a boat because I literally felt it would tip over and they'd become alligator food. But this one is solid."

"Yeah, but they might still become alligator food," Anthony pointed out, "because they like to fish in an area that's very popular with gators."

I nearly spit my drink out. "What? Why?"

"Apparently that's where the best fish are!" Beckett sounded exasperated, which was funny because my younger brothers very rarely got angry. They were like me in that regard.

"Fucking hell," I exclaimed.

"Yep, but don't worry. We'll keep them from becoming gator food while you get laid," Anthony said.

"Excellent plan," I replied smugly.

On Saturday morning, I picked Grace up at ten. Like her, I used to go to brunches at Commander's Palace as a kid with my parents, but I hadn't gone in a very long time. I knew many families in New Orleans went on a regular basis.

Grace came out of the building with a huge smile. She also had a big hat and sunglasses. I got out of the car and went around the corner, opening the door for her.

"You look fucking adorable with this huge hat."

She grinned. "I actually got lazy with putting on sunscreen this past week and got a bit of a sunburn." She took off her glasses, and I could see it better now as she tipped her head up. Her nose was completely red. "I look ridiculous."

"No, you look fucking adorable," I said. I kissed her right there against the car for the whole street to see.

This was addictive. *She* was addictive. I'd been starved for her this past week. Texts and calls weren't enough. I needed her close—in my arms, at my mercy.

She kissed me back just as intensely. I plastered her against the car, deepening the kiss, touching her waist before rubbing my thumb against the side of her left breast.

A thump interrupted us, and I pulled back, opening my eyes. Her hat had fallen to the ground. Clearing my throat, I took a step back. Grabbing it, I handed it to her before she got in the car.

Once she was settled, she said, "I'm ready to start our date. But don't kiss me again."

I jerked my head back. "Why not?"

"Because," she whispered, "there are kids around."

I looked up and down the street. True, there were, but I didn't see what one thing had to do with the other. Then again, I didn't want to make her uncomfortable.

I stepped closer, leaning slightly over her. "Just a quick one."

"Okay." She batted her eyelashes and gave me a quick peck. It wasn't what I had in mind, but clearly she wasn't ready for more.

"You smell amazing. You've changed your perfume."

"Yes. I'm wearing the one from your grandmothers."

And in that precise moment, I knew I was screwed. I couldn't tell how I knew it, or what exactly I meant by that. I just knew I was.

We arrived in the Garden District a short while later and parked close to Commander's Palace.

"I can't believe I haven't been here in years," Grace said. "I love everything about it. The vibrant blue facade, the Victorian architecture, and the food, of course."

It had Creole and Cajun specialties. It was widely considered to be one of the best in the South. Even my grandmothers respected the establishment. The place was already full of guests when we arrived. We were shown to our table in one of their outdoor spaces.

"It's a good thing we're sitting outside," Grace said. "It was a bit stuffy in there, wasn't it?"

I agreed. The weather was already hot and humid, but at least out here, there was a nice breeze. Jazz music played all around, and people were milling in and out with food.

Grace was glancing at everyone's drinks.

"What are you doing?" I asked.

"When I was a kid, I always hoped my parents would get distracted so I could sneak around and grab a cocktail."

"Full disclosure: last time I came, I was also not of drinking age. Let's hit the bar."

"Life with you is always an adventure, isn't it?" she asked.

I pulled her close, kissing her forehead, drawing in a deep breath. Her perfume filled my nostrils. I felt this unquenchable need to hold her tight.

She glanced up at me and smiled. "What's going through your mind, Zachary?"

"You don't want to know."

"All right, keep your secrets. I have mine," she said before moving back and walking inside.

I fell in step with her. "What secrets? I want to know everything."

"You can't because it's a two-way street," she teased.

"Challenge accepted. We'll circle back to that later," I said as we went straight to the bar. You ordered your own drinks at the bar, and there was a buffet as well, so no sitting down and ordering.

"What can I get you?" the bartender asked.

"I want the house specialty," Grace replied.

"Same for me." I had no idea what the specialty was, but it had to be good. I only intended to take a sip, since I was driving.

Grace looked stunning. The dress code for Commander's Palace was slightly elegant, and she was pulling that off effortlessly. She was wearing a long red dress with a black belt around her waist. It hid her figure because the dress didn't mold to her body, but my imagination still ran wild because I'd memorized every curve, every inch of her. I knew exactly what was hidden underneath.

"This weekend's specialty is a Grasshopper," the bartender said, putting two martini glasses in front of us filled with a green cocktail.

"Thank you," Grace replied. We each grabbed a glass and then moved farther away from the counter. As we clinked them, she added, "Oh, today's starting so well. A Grasshopper before it's even eleven o'clock."

"My thoughts exactly. But why the hell not? We have the entire weekend to do whatever we want." I looked intently into her eyes. "No rules, Grace."

She sucked in a breath and nodded. "No rules."

She downed the cocktail fast, but I only took a mouthful. It was insanely good. "I've got to tell Julian to stop by here more often, steal a recipe or two. This is good, and I'm not usually a Grasshopper kind of guy."

"I agree. That was good. I need some food, though. I just had a light breakfast when I got up today."

"Then let's get you some food. Can't let you starve." I felt the insane desire to take care of every single one of her needs.

Over the next hour, we tasted everything that looked good. from the usual suspects like gumbo, jambalaya, and po' boys to fried seafood.

She sat back and blew out a heavy breath. "I'm about to explode, and yet I want to somehow keep eating and drinking."

"Let's grab another cocktail," I suggested.

As we rose from the table, two men approached us. Did I know them? Because they seemed very intent on us.

"We never expected to see you around," one of the men said.

Both of them looked straight at Grace, who rolled her shoulders. "I'm sorry. Do I know you?"

"No, but we know you, Grace Deveraux. Or at least we know your brothers. I can't believe you've got the nerve to show your face at Commander's Palace. At least your parents are staying out of the public eye."

Grace cleared her throat, crossing her arms over her chest.

"Fuck off!" I said.

She shook her head almost imperceptibly, and I instantly knew what she meant: she wanted to deal with this by herself. And I respected that.

"My brothers' actions have nothing to do with me. Or my parents for that matter. I wasn't part of the company at that time, nor for years before they did what they did."

"That doesn't absolve you, and—"

"Yes, it really does," she replied. I'd never heard her sound so confident and self-assured, and I liked it. Damn, she had my admiration. She hadn't raised her voice, but even so, her delivery was strong and cutting. "Because I never would've approved of what they did. But that's beside the point. You don't get to come here when I'm enjoying brunch and belittle me because you did a bad business deal with my brothers. If you have a bone to pick, I suggest you pick it with them."

"We would if we could, but we don't know where they are."

"Well, neither do I," Grace said. "And now I suggest you stop interrupting my lunch."

"You listen to me—"

I couldn't believe they were pursuing this with her, so I stepped in with a very warning tone. "No." They both looked at me, clearly surprised, so I added, "You heard her. Fuck off."

"And who are you?" the second man asked.

"Zachary LeBlanc."

Both their faces changed. Clearly they recognized the name. "A LeBlanc and a Deveraux," the first one said. "That's unexpected."

"You're welcome to fuck off and be shocked by it somewhere else. You're done here," I said.

"That is no way to treat anyone—"

"Fucking go!" I raised my voice but not loudly enough to cause attention.

The second guy looked at Grace but had the good sense not to say anything else. She was holding her chin high, arms still crossed over her chest. She maintained her composure even after the two of them turned their backs and left our table.

Then she took a deep breath and whispered, "Wow, I didn't see that coming."

"Are you okay?" I asked, putting a hand on her upper back. "Want me to have them thrown out?"

She laughed, glancing at me. "No, Zachary. I think I dealt with it quite well."

"You did. You were fucking amazing." I brought my mouth to her ear. "So amazing, in fact, that it's a turn-on."

She gasped. "How can you do that?"

"What?" I asked.

"Switch between having a normal conversation and being all flirty." She said the word *flirty* as if she meant *dirty*.

"I just live in the moment, Grace. But seriously, how are you feeling?"

"Kind of took the wind out of my sails. That was a first, to be honest." She shrugged as we sat back down. "Someone just walking up to me and insulting me because of my brothers." She grabbed the fork, turning it around on her empty plate. "I've only encountered antagonism when I was talking to investors, but even they weren't so in-your-face."

"They were way out of line. Everyone knows that neither you nor your father were part of the company when they ran their Ponzi scheme."

Grace shook her head. "Dad assured me he actually reimbursed everyone once he took over. That's why the company's cash reserves are low. So I don't understand why those guys even felt the need to come up to me."

"Because some people just get off on conflicts and fighting. You handled that brilliantly."

She smiled. "It felt good to stand up for myself. When the news first broke, I felt responsible. Then I realized it wasn't my fault at all. I even tried to tell Dad not to empty the company's coffers because of my brothers, but he said it wasn't fair to everyone else, and I guess he was right."

"Your father is a good man. I didn't know about the reimbursement."

"He didn't want to make a big deal of it."

"Want me to bring you another cocktail? Surprise you?"

She sighed. "Honestly, I've lost my appetite."

"That encounter definitely soured the mood. Want us to leave?"

"I can't believe I'm saying this, but yes. Do you mind?"

I shook my head. "Not at all. Today is all about having fun and a good time, Grace. If this place doesn't check those marks, then it's time we hightail it out of here."

Her expression transformed from serious to happy almost instantly. I interlaced our hands as we walked through the restaurant, which had gotten fuller since we first went to the bar.

"Oh, crap," she exclaimed once we were outside.

"What's the matter?" I asked.

"The strap of my sandal. The buckle fell off." She looked around. "I can't see it."

I glanced at the concrete floor too. "Grace, there's zero chance of finding it."

"I agree. Do you mind if we go to my place real quick so I can change shoes?"

"Not at all. I told you this weekend is just about having fun, so there's no reason to stress about anything."

During the drive, I tried to gauge if Grace was still thinking about the incident, but she was talking about how much she enjoyed the summer in New Orleans, so I assumed she'd moved on. After parking the car, I went up with her into her apartment and waited in the living room.

"Damn. None of the shoes I own actually go with this dress," she said. She was standing in front of a closet full of shoes.

I stared at her. "Is that a trick statement?"

She looked at me. "What? No, never mind. It's a woman thing. I'll change my dress real quick, too, okay?"

"Sure."

As she went into her bedroom, I tried very hard not to think about the fact that she was going to take off her dress. I could visualize her naked body in my mind's eye. I was on the verge of bursting in on her already.

Fucking hell, Zachary.

"Oh, shoot," I heard her say through the door.

"Grace?" I asked.

"I just got caught in my dress. Damn it."

"Need help?" I jumped to my feet. I wasn't going to barge in, but if she needed assistance, that was an entirely different thing.

"Um, yes, please. I don't think I can do it on my own without ripping off my dress."

I went into her bedroom before she'd even finished the sentence. And what a damn sight.

She had her dress over her head, both arms stuck. Her legs and ass were on full display. Her lingerie was once again lace, covering only the upper part of her buttocks.

"I don't understand what happened. Must have caught on my bra."

"I'll check."

Indeed, it had caught on the back of her bra. I unclasped it, and then she tugged at the dress, pulling it over her head. She turned around, grinning up at me.

"Whoops. Sorry about that."

Her hair was wild around her head from the dress. I liked her like this, all messed up.

Then she gasped slightly. "Oh, you undid my bra."

"Yeah. It was the only way to..."

Her straps fell off her shoulders, and then the bra slipped down to her waist. I had a full view of her breasts.

"Fuck, Grace."

Chapter Twenty-Two

Zachary

I'd managed to keep myself under control until now, but having this woman bared in front of me, wearing only her lace panties...

I was a red-blooded man; I wasn't made out of stone. Without any warning, I kissed her the way I'd wanted to since I picked her up that morning—wet and deep. I cupped one breast, teasing her nipple with my thumb. It went taut beneath my touch almost immediately. Her gorgeous body was made for me and only me. I refused to believe it ever responded to anyone else the way it did to me. I ran my other hand down her back and then cupped her buttocks. She rose onto her toes, putting both arms around my neck.

Yes. Oh fuck, yes.

I kissed her until I was so hard that I had to stop touching her long enough to get rid of my pants. It wasn't enough to simply lower the zipper and open the button to release the pressure. I wanted them out of the way. Looking her straight in the eyes, I pushed my pants down, then my underwear too.

"Your mouth is red," I told her. "I fucking love it."

She covered it slowly, then looked down at herself and back up at me.

"Always surprising me," she said with a grin. "Then again, I did kind of cause this by getting lost in my dress."

I groaned. "I was on the verge of coming in here even before that just thinking that you were taking your clothes off."

"I want to do this." She put her hands on the lowest button on my shirt and worked her way up. "You look so sexy with this shirt and these cuff links.

I can't believe I didn't see them until now. They suit you. You should wear them more often."

I tilted my head. "I'm not a cuff link type of man, but for you, I'll wear them."

Her eyes lit up as she pushed the shirt down my arms. I took off the undershirt myself, and she sighed.

"Oh, you know, this past week, I've been wondering if these were real or I was hyping them up in my imagination." She trailed her fingers down my abs, then moved her mouth in a straight line from my stomach down to my navel. My cock rubbed against her neck. The contact was enough to make me groan. I was so damn hard already. "And I," she said, sitting on her bed, which put her face-to-face with my cock, "also wondered if this was as amazing as I remembered. And what do you know? It is."

She licked slowly from the base up to the tip. Pleasure rushed through me. Being with this woman heightened everything.

"No," I said, taking a step back. "Right now, I want to bury my face in your pussy, Grace."

She gasped, pressing her thighs together and looking downward. She always said that I surprised her because I moved from flirty to serious, but she kept me on my toes too. I never knew when dirty talking would elicit this reaction, or when she'd get shy. But I loved both responses. I realized I simply liked every facet of Grace.

"Zachary," she murmured.

I inspected her bed. It wasn't high enough, so I lifted her off it and put her on the desk in the corner.

"This is better." I sat down on the chair at the desk, spreading her thighs wide. "Put your feet here." I patted my thighs.

She did just that, and I pulled her ass to the very edge of her desk. She moaned even before I put my mouth on her. She was already wet. Instead of starting with her clit, I dipped my tongue inside her, curling it once, twice, three times. Grace's body undulated beneath me. Then her shoulders turned forward and backward. She grabbed the edge of the desk with one hand and my hair with the other. My woman wanted to ride my face, and I loved it.

I kept moving my tongue inside her, applying pressure on her clit—first with the tip of my nose and then with my thumb—until I felt her clench around my tongue. Making this woman come was one of my pleasures in life. In fact, it was at the very top of my favorite things to do.

From this position, I had a view of her gorgeous breasts, but I couldn't see her face. That was fine. This wasn't the only orgasm I planned to give her today.

With my tongue buried inside her, I was aware of every single reaction to everything I did to her. When she came, I knew she needed space to move, so I pulled my head back, but I kept my thumb on her clit. Her ass came off the desk as she planted her feet deep on my thighs.

"Zacharyyyyyyyyyyyyyyy!" Her orgasm was beautiful. The skin on her entire torso turned pink. She squeezed her breasts with both hands as she put her ass back on the desk. I rose to my feet and entered her in one swift thrust.

"Grace!" I groaned.

Pleasure unlike anything I'd experienced filled me—and torture, too, of course, because I was desperate to come already. Feeling her wrapped around me like this was enough to satisfy me for a split second.

"Zachary, here?"

"Yes. I'll fuck you right here on this desk, Grace. Do you have anything against that?"

"No," she whispered as I pulled back and slammed in once more. I lifted her knees, keeping my hands under them. That changed the angle and made her roll a bit back.

"Oh my God, that's even deeper," she murmured.

I threw my head back, giving in to all of my instincts and needs. I wanted her to know exactly how badly I needed her. There was no reason to hide or pretend.

I knew I could go in deeper, but not on this desk. I took Grace in my arms and put her at the edge of the bed in a similar position as before. Only now she could comfortably lean backward, which she did without my even needing to say a word. That was how in sync we were, and it was fucking amazing. I slammed in balls deep this time.

"Fuck, Grace," I exclaimed. "This is so good."

She started to cry out my name, but she couldn't even manage that before I slammed back in again. She rewarded me with a moan.

I forced myself to stand up straight so I could look down at her. Watching her enjoy it was just as much part of the pleasure as driving my cock inside her was. When she came close, I changed tactics, pulling out and rubbing the length of my cock over her clit.

"Oh God. Oh God. Zachary, what are you doing?" Her voice shook. Hell, even her breath seemed to shake.

"I'm working you up, beautiful. I want to see you come."

"But I want—"

"Oh, I promise I'll drive inside you the second you do. I will. I wouldn't miss feeling your pussy tighten around my cock for any reason. The world could be ending and I'd be right here with you. Nothing could stop me from making you come."

She moaned again and then fell completely onto the bed with her arms spread wide at her sides. Then she grabbed both breasts. I knew she was about to come before she even cried out my name, so I slid back inside her, far slower than before. She was already pulsing like mad, getting tighter and tighter. With every inch I managed to push in, I lost sense of control over myself even more.

I was right there with her as my own release caught up with me, and I didn't hold back one bit. Not my groans, not the way my body moved. I was at her mercy now, just as much as she was at mine. And I wouldn't have it any other way.

After I'd cleaned myself up and dressed, I waited in her living room while she finished doing the same. A few minutes later, she peeked out from the bedroom.

"You're awfully silent." She wiggled her eyebrows. "Want to come in and help me put on my dress?"

I groaned. "Grace, why are you tempting me like this?"

"Because it's so much fun. What do you want to do today?"

"I haven't planned anything." Once she disappeared into the room once more, I added, "All I care is that we do something together."

"Did you know that the wine and food festival is taking place this weekend?"

"I didn't." I was certain that at least part of my family was attending. My grandmothers went religiously every year, and usually so did Chad, since he ran a restaurant.

Grace came out wearing a casual white dress. It was very long, almost brushing the floor. She looked amazing in it.

"It could be fun." She wrinkled her nose, jutting a hip to one side. "Although... what if I run into other unpleasant people?"

I immediately rose to my feet, heading to her. "I'll put them in their place."

She licked her lips, smiling. She was so relaxed around me, always smiling. "You would, wouldn't you? I liked how you told them to fuck off."

"And I liked how fierce and strong you were."

Emotions swirled in her eyes. "You think I'm strong?"

"Hell yes. You ended a shit marriage at the same time that your family was involved in that scandal. Yet you came out on the other side as a winner."

"I wouldn't say that," she murmured.

"You're a fighter. That makes you a winner in my book."

"That's an interesting way of looking at things."

I kissed her forehead and then her temple. "You're very strong, Grace, and I admire that about you. But we don't have to go out to the festival if you don't want to."

"No! I refuse to cower and not do the things I enjoy just because someone could decide to walk up to me and be rude. I can handle anyone." Her shoulders slumped. "I wish my parents would understand that as well. They keep to themselves."

I frowned. "But you said your father reimbursed people."

"He did. I thought that once that happened, the family would be in the clear. If not forgiven, at least no longer shunned. But I think some people just feel angry because they were fooled by my brothers."

"Then let's not waste any more time talking about that. I think it's just going to take some time until wounds heal in the city, Grace. That's all."

I admired this woman with every fiber of my being: her fight, her optimism. Everything about her simply mesmerized me.

Since I never went to the festival, I didn't know where it was, but Grace knew where everything was throughout the city.

"I actually found out because I saw some posters about it right here in the warehouse district," she said. "Why don't we just stay in the area?"

"Whatever makes you happy, Grace."

Her eyes widened. "You really mean that?"

"Fuck yes. Of course I mean that. If staying in the area makes you happy, then that's what we'll do. If you want us to head to one of the other locations, then we can."

She stepped in front of me, putting her arms on my shoulders. "You're charming me more every day."

"That's exactly my plan," I whispered in her ear.

She shuddered. "Oh, it's an actual plan, huh?"

"Not really. And if we don't get going, it's going to end up with us in bed again."

Grace laughed, but then we did leave her apartment. Two blocks away from her building, there was an entire street closed off to traffic for the day. It was filled with all sorts of stands that sold cheese and wine mostly, but there was plenty of other food, too—specifically seafood.

She was grinning, glancing around at every stand.

"I like how happy this place makes you."

She looked over her shoulder. "I missed these kinds of events when I was married. My ex absolutely abhorred everything that was public. He thought it was beneath him. Then again, so did my brothers and a lot of people I went to school with."

"Most of the people I went to school with had that exact same attitude to festivals."

I liked that we were both different from the people we grew up with. Both our families were. Being affluent financially didn't mean you had to be an asshole.

"All right. Well, I'm actually still full of food," Grace said, and she actually sounded regretful.

I started to laugh.

She raised a brow. "You're mocking me?"

"No, you're adorable," I told her and meant it.

"I would like to try some of that wine." She pointed to a selection of reds at the cart in front of us.

"Want us to work our way from the lightest to the strongest one?"

She nodded. "What an excellent idea."

I took her hand and walked with her up to the cart. I looked at the menu he was offering.

"We'll take the Expert Tasting," I said. It was the most comprehensive option.

Next to me, Grace giggled. I kissed the side of her head again. I couldn't stop touching and kissing her. I could practically feel her joy vibrate through her.

"Do you promise to not let me get drunk?" Grace asked, serious all of a sudden.

I narrowed my eyes. "You want me to promise that after I just asked for the expert option?"

"You're right. Then promise you'll take care of me if I get too drunk."

"You can count on that, Grace. I'll always take care of you."

She grinned. "Then let's do it. Let's get good and drunk."

"I wonder if we're going to run into my family," I said, looking up and down the street.

"Oh, they like to attend festivals?"

"Half my family comes to this one every year, but there's no telling at which location." I paused, then asked, "By the way, how would you feel about having brunch with my family next Saturday?"

Her eyes widened. "Wow. I mean, sure, I'd love it. Are you sure it's okay with... I don't know, me being a Deveraux and all that?"

"I think we're way past that, Grace. Besides, my grandmothers are big fans of yours already. That translates into the whole family liking you."

"Even though they haven't met me?"

"The LeBlancs and Broussards work in strange ways."

She smiled. "Then I can't wait to meet them."

CHAPTER TWENTY-THREE

GRACE

As the next week started, I could still pinch myself just thinking about the weekend. It had been exactly what I'd needed, and I hadn't even been aware of it. But Zachary had a way of simply guessing what I needed, as if somehow he knew me even better than I knew myself.

Even though Mondays were usually difficult and I had a million to-dos, I was ecstatic today... until the afternoon. My phone beeped with an incoming call from someone I'd hoped to never hear from again: Roger, my ex-husband. My first instinct was to not answer. We'd finished everything between us a long time ago. Why would he even want to talk to me?

But I was no chicken, and there had to be a reason he was contacting me. Ignoring it would only postpone the issue, make me obsess about it. I got up from behind my desk and went to close the door; I didn't want anyone to witness this. Then I answered the phone as I leaned against the door.

"Grace," he said instead of hello.

My entire body stiffened. "Why are you calling me?"

"Such a friendly reply."

"There is no reason for me to be friendly. So, get to the point or I'll end this conversation right now."

"You're dating Zachary LeBlanc," Roger stated.

His words felt like an electric shock, though I wasn't sure why.

"Yes." I cleared my throat and balled my free hand into a fist. "Do you have a problem with that? Is that why you're calling?"

"Fuck yes, that's what I'm calling about."

I unhitched myself from the doorframe of my office.

"How the fuck could you even think about dating a LeBlanc?"

"How is it any of your concern?"

"I bet your family is ashamed of you."

Now the anger was threatening to spill out of me. "Don't you dare talk about my family. You know nothing about them. You never bothered to get to know my parents at all."

"I know your brothers well enough."

"Because you're just like them. I wouldn't brag about that if I were you."

"Your brothers are on the run because of those damn LeBlancs, and you're dating one of them. That's rich, Grace."

I laughed, but there was no humor. I was seething as I went back to my desk but decided to lean against it instead of sitting in my chair. I was too agitated. "My brothers are on the run because they're thieves and have no scruples or morals, much like you."

"Family is family."

Once again, I wanted to yell at him, but I'd promised myself a long time ago that I wouldn't give him that power over me. Nothing he said or did could hurt me, not anymore. He was trying to get a rise out of me, and I wasn't going to allow it.

"It only applies to my parents in my case." It wasn't as if my brothers ever lived by that credo. They were more than happy to let me know that they didn't want me back in their company once I decided to leave.

"Grace, you can't be serious. You can date anyone you fucking want in New Orleans, but not a LeBlanc."

I smiled. Now I was starting to feel a little smug. "Why? You're pissed off that I found someone who is vastly superior to you?"

He made a sound as if he was drowning in his own words. Hitting his ego was a low blow, but I didn't really care at this point. I had this innate desire to hurt him as much he'd hurt me. That wasn't really possible, though, because I didn't have it in me. But this gave me enough satisfaction.

"If that's what you need to tell yourself."

Talking to him now made me wonder what in the ever-loving fuck I ever saw in him.

"I don't need to tell myself anything," I replied coolly. "Is there any other reason you're calling?"

"No, you need to—"

I hung up before he could finish his sentence.

Motherfucker!

I was so pissed, I couldn't even believe it. I rose from my desk and paced my office once again. I was mad at him, but mostly at myself.

Oh, come on, Grace. You've done therapy. You've gotten so much better at not letting his words hurt you. Why do you care what he says?

I didn't, but for some insane reason, I still couldn't cool off. I bit the inside of my cheek, putting my hands on my hips as I glanced at my computer screen from afar. No, work wasn't going to cut it. I needed something else to take my mind off this.

And I knew exactly what that was.

On a whim, I called Felicia, keeping my fingers crossed. She answered quickly.

"Hi, Grace, darling." I loved her voice. It was always warm—just like her.

"Hey, Felicia. I was wondering if you'd mind if I dropped by the ranch this afternoon."

"Sure, sure. We'd love to see you."

"I just want to hang out with the horses for a while," I said because I couldn't think of a single other reason. Why pretend? And I didn't want to put any pressure on them about the ranch.

"That's what they're here for, whenever anyone needs them. And I'll prep you a good hearty dinner."

"There's no need," I replied, feeling guilty already.

"Nonsense, darling. I cook for myself and Gaston anyway. We don't mind sharing and would love the conversation."

"If it's not too much trouble." It was two o'clock now. "I should be there around five thirty or so."

"That's perfect! We can have dinner around six thirty or seven, then," she said.

I smiled to myself, already feeling calmer. Felicia had that effect on me. "Thanks. See you in a bit."

After hanging up, I immediately left the office so I wouldn't change my mind. My team was a bit surprised that I took off in the middle of the day without much of an explanation, but they didn't prod, and I was grateful for that.

I thought I might cool off on the way, but no such thing happened. In fact, I only seemed to truly calm down once I was in the stable with Starlight. I liked the other horses, too, but he and I had a special bond, so I decided to take him out for a walk.

"Oh, Starlight. You're the only one I can talk to," I said once we returned to the stable. I'd talked the poor horse's ear off, but I was feeling far more relaxed now as I started to brush his mane. His breathing was steady, and it was soothing me. Why couldn't I shake off my ex's words? Who cared what he thought?

But as I took out the last knot in Starlight's mane, it finally dawned on me. Roger's comment about my parents was rubbing me the wrong way. They certainly didn't seem to mind who I was dating, but what if they really did and never told me?

As I stared at Starlight's mane, I decided to call my parents. They'd never be coy with me if I outright asked them something.

I pressed my mom's number, but she didn't answer, which was par for the course. My mom always forgot her phone somewhere around the house. Then I tried Dad. As he picked up, I turned on FaceTime.

"Grace, where are you?" He frowned. This probably looked weird to him. There was a feeding station behind me, indicating I was in a barn.

"I'm at a ranch, in the stables."

"Oh, right. Okay. So, is there anything we can help you with?" He may have realized this wasn't just a checkup call, since we usually did those when I was relaxing at home.

"Um, is Mom around?"

"No, she's out with a friend and forgot her phone at home."

I laughed. "Of course."

"There's something on your mind," Dad stated.

I nodded, leaning against the wall of the stall. "Yes. So, you know I've been dating Zachary."

"Is he treating you right?" His voice was harsh.

"Yes. He's wonderful, actually."

My dad smiled from ear to ear. "Really?"

I nodded. "We've never openly discussed this, but do you mind that I'm dating a LeBlanc?"

He frowned. "You know, several of our friends have actually asked us this."

"Dad! You didn't say—"

"I told them that I don't care who my daughter dates as long as she's happy." His eyes turned even softer. "And by the looks of you, you are."

"I am."

"And I also told everyone that I have no beef with the LeBlancs. My sons brought this upon themselves with their own criminal actions. The LeBlancs merely brought it all to light. If Xander hadn't, it would've been much worse for us all. The legal ramifications would've been never-ending."

I swallowed hard. "That's exactly how I see it. I just didn't know how you truly felt. You'd tell me if something was weighing on you, right?" I asked.

"Of course. I made myself a promise after your divorce that I'd never hold back my opinion. Listen, if I'd caught my sons with what they were doing, I would've given them the boot myself."

His words chilled me. I knew they were 100 percent true.

"I would've handled everything behind closed doors," he continued, "then made them make amends with everyone they swindled. Again, I bear no resentment toward the LeBlancs, and I'm more than happy that things are going well between you and Zachary."

"Thanks, Dad. That means the world to me." I checked the clock and gasped. "Oh, goodness, I have to go." Felicia said dinner would be ready at six thirty, and it was twenty after already. I didn't like to be late.

"Of course."

"Thanks a lot, Dad."

"Always, my girl. I'm here for you, no matter what you need."

During my marriage, I'd grown a bit distant from my parents. I didn't want them to have a front-row seat for the shit show that was my life. Even during the divorce, I sort of kept them at arm's length. But I was feeling closer to them than ever right now.

After wrapping up, I patted Starlight again before hurrying to the main house. I felt as if a weight had dropped from my shoulders, and I was smiling from ear to ear when I joined Felicia and Gaston in the kitchen. She'd made coq au vin, by the smell of it. It was my favorite type of stew, typically made with chicken.

"You truly are a whiz in the kitchen," I told Felicia.

"Oh, that's what all our guests say."

She and Gaston exchanged glances, and then he looked at me.

"We meant to ask you, did you reconsider the idea of going into this together with Zachary?"

My heart somersaulted at his question. Did they discuss this with him?

I bit the inside of my cheek. *Had* I reconsidered it? I mean, things between Zachary and me were wonderful, but it was one thing to spend time together and have fun and something else entirely to go into business together. What if things fell apart between us further down the road?

Gaston and Felicia must have interpreted my silence as a negative because Gaston said, "Forget we asked. This isn't about business. You came here today because you needed the ranch."

"I did," I replied, thankful they weren't prodding more. I truly didn't have an answer for them. This was something I'd discuss with Zachary first before telling them.

But the idea was taking root in my mind. So much so that, as I said my goodbyes later that evening, I wondered if I should bring it up to Zachary. I took out my phone, then decided that I couldn't just corner him with this on a call.

However, I did want to check on my man. Holy shit, I was already thinking of him as my man. But it didn't scare me.

Climbing into the car, I set my purse down and then texted him.

Grace: How did your week start?

I grinned when the little dots appeared, showing he was typing. I truly loved that he didn't make me wait—unless he was busy, of course. But other than that, he wasn't playing hard to get.

Zachary: After the weekend I had, fucking fantastic. Nothing could bring me down. Yours?

I grinned even wider as I replied.

Grace: The same. I'm over the moon.

Zachary: That's exactly what I wanted to hear. I'm patting myself on the back right now.

I laughed.

Grace: You should.

Zachary: By the way, I can't wait for you to meet my family.

While I'd been a bit worried when he first told me about it, now I was looking forward to it.

I decided to send him one last text before starting the drive back to the city.

Grace: I can't wait to meet them either. If they're anything like your grandmothers, I know I'll love them.

Zachary: No one can top my grandmothers, but I will say that they're a likable bunch. Can I call you?

I sighed.

Grace: Actually, I'm heading back from the ranch. I went to check on Starlight. I'd better focus on the road.

Zachary: SO YOU'RE TEXTING INSTEAD? Do not text me back.

I was tempted to message one last time, just so I could see his reaction, but then decided to text someone else entirely before starting the engine.

My ex.

Grace: Don't you ever dare contact me again! I'm blocking your number.

The second I sent the message, I went ahead and did it. Why hadn't I blocked him in the first place? Probably because our last interactions had been through lawyers, so he hadn't called me in a long time.

I felt a cathartic release in that moment. Hell yes. This chapter in my life was more than closed. I wasn't going to let the cloud of my failed marriage hang over me, not anymore. I had a bright future ahead of me.

And I was certain that Zachary LeBlanc was going to be part of it.

Chapter Twenty-Four
Zachary

The next week, I finally got some financials from Felicia and Gaston: the current profit and loss sheet as well as what they estimated they needed for the renovations. I liked the numbers. My initial intention had been to ask Xander to take a look at them, but that wasn't necessary. It was very straightforward.

I replied to Gaston's email almost within the hour of getting the documents to make an offer. Then I put the whole issue at the back of my mind because I was swamped with shipping delays, and I was in crisis management mode. The one other priority I had was to give my family a heads-up that I wanted to introduce Grace to them.

It might be a surprise for Mom and Dad, since our grandmothers had put two and two together. I bet our grandfathers already knew as well. And my brothers were in the loop. But Mom and Dad usually kept themselves out of the LeBlanc-Broussard gossip line. That's why I called Mom on Tuesday, around lunchtime. I knew she had the afternoon off on Tuesdays because she always hosted an evening event at the gallery.

"Hi, son," she answered. "How come you're calling?"

I didn't call very often. It just wasn't my MO. I usually texted.

"How are you, Mom?"

"Busy, but good busy. I did hear through the grapevine, though, that it's a shipping hell week."

I laughed because that was exactly how I'd dubbed this time of year last year.

"Yes, but it's nothing I can't handle."

"I never worry about you," she said. "So, to what do I owe the pleasure?"

"On Saturday, I'd like to bring someone to brunch," I said bluntly.

"Would that someone happen to be Grace Deveraux?"

My eyes widened in surprise. "Yes, but how do you know?"

"Everyone in the family talks. I heard a whisper here, a word there, and I started to wonder if there was something happening between the two of you."

I took everything back that I'd thought about Mom and Dad. Clearly they were just as involved in gossip as everyone else.

"Yes, I'd like Grace to officially meet our family. She's already met Anthony and Beckett, plus the grandmothers."

"So, you're serious about her," Mom concluded.

I cleared my throat. "I like her a lot."

"Oh, I'm always so thrilled when one of you finds happiness. It's all I want for my sons. Having a partner is one of the greatest joys in life. I'll tell everyone you're bringing her to brunch," Mom said.

"Thanks. How did you know I was going to ask that?"

"Because I have a sixth sense. I know when my boys need something from me. Not that you do very often. You're all very independent—maybe a bit too much so."

"Thanks, Mom."

"You're welcome. Now, I have to go because I want to explore this very unusual new shop that opened next to the gallery. I've been meaning to check it out for a while."

"Sure. Have fun." I laughed as I hung up. My family was definitely a strange bunch.

I felt good about bringing Grace. Sure, it could be overwhelming, but at least she'd already met some of the clan. I couldn't wait for Saturday.

As the day passed, though, I realized I didn't want to wait that long to see her. So, at five o'clock that afternoon, I texted her.

Zachary: Workday over?

Grace: No chance in hell. It's going to be another dinner-at-the-office kind of week.

Zachary: I'll take care of you.

I was about to instruct LeBlanc & Broussard to send her dinner when I got a better idea. I was going to deliver it to her myself. That way, I could also see her.

I'd never felt the impulse to be close to a woman. To seek her presence so often. But things were changing. I took everything with ease my whole life, and I never questioned why I did something. I simply followed my instinct.

Forty minutes later, I entered the lobby of Grace's building with two portions of jambalaya. Since it was comfort food for both of us, why not share it? I walked straight to the reception desk. A tall brunette looked up at me.

"Delivery from LeBlanc & Broussard?" she asked.

I nodded. "Exactly."

"I will have to ask for ID, just because you're a different guy than last time."

"Sure."

I took out my wallet and showed her my ID.

She jerked her head back. "Zachary *LeBlanc*. All right. Fourth floor, Unit B."

"Thank you."

The building was still teeming with people coming in and out. The atmosphere was much less casual than in the Quarter. There were plenty of offices there, too, but you wouldn't know judging by how people dressed. But almost everyone I met in this lobby was wearing a suit or something similar and seemed very businesslike.

I went straight to Grace's floor and was surprised by the complete silence. There was a light at the end of the corridor on the right. I assumed that's where her office was. I didn't want to call out and give myself away.

Was she the last one working?

Then again, it would fit Grace to a T. She demanded more of herself than of the people surrounding her.

"I'm in my office," she called loudly. "Just like last time."

I walked there with quick steps, then stopped in the doorway.

"Just a... Oh, Zachary?" she asked, noticing me as I stepped in. "Did you tell me you were coming?"

"No, I figured I'd surprise you."

She grinned and pushed her laptop to one side. Then, as if she'd thought better of it, she rose to her feet, coming around to the other side of the desk.

"What goodies did you bring?" she asked.

I walked to the desk, putting the bag down. "Jambalaya. But first, I demand a kiss."

"Oh, so you're not doing this out of the goodness of your heart, huh?" she murmured. "You expect payback?"

"Lots of payback."

I kissed her so damn hard that I pushed her against the desk. Then I deepened it even more. I couldn't stop exploring her. I sat her on the desk, and she groaned as I put my hands between her knees, trying to push them open so I could step between them.

Grace put a hand on my chest, pulling her head back.

"Zachary," she whispered. "This skirt is too tight. You'll rip it."

"Then take it off," I growled.

"Oh, you bad man. You want me to take off my clothes right here in the middle of my office?"

I took a deep breath and moved back. "Fuck, you're right. I don't even think I remembered we were here."

She threw her head back, laughing. I leaned in, kissing her neck, then immediately nuzzled down to her collarbone. Her tank top had a V-neckline that very much appealed to me. Before I knew it, I kissed right down to the hem of the fabric. Grace gasped again, and I straightened up.

Fuck, this was a bad idea. "I don't understand why I can't keep myself in check."

"I have a thought," she said. "Walk back a few steps."

I did what she said as she rounded her desk, sitting back in her chair.

"How about that, huh?" she asked. "Now we have the desk between us."

Yeah, that wasn't going to work, but I didn't say anything.

"Now, let's eat."

I was glad for the distraction. We ate straight out of the carton with the forks I'd brought.

"I don't think I will ever tire of this jambalaya."

"You can mention that to the grandmothers on Saturday. They'll love you even more."

"How did your family react?" Grace asked, looking up from her food.

"I told Mom and asked her to spread the word."

She narrowed her eyes. "Interesting tactic."

"I figured Mom and Dad would be the only ones who wouldn't know about us. I decided to inform her. But she'd already figured it out."

Grace's mouth fell open. "Are you serious?"

"Yeah. That's just how things work in the family."

"I'm starting to get a bit jittery," she said.

"There's absolutely no reason to be, Grace."

I thought I'd be happy just being here with her, but now I simply wanted to touch her more and more.

"It might be a bit overwhelming, but you'll get used to it fast enough," I added.

"I mean, I already know some of your family," she said.

"Exactly."

I didn't say anything else as we continued to eat.

I finished first, and Grace ate two more spoonfuls before declaring, "Oh, I'm so full."

To my astonishment, she pushed her chair back and rose to her feet.

"What are you doing?" I asked.

"Well, you behaved during dinner." She went to the door, closing it. "So now I guess you more than deserve your reward."

My cock twitched. "And what is that?"

"Since you were so keen on taking off my skirt, why don't I start with that?"

This evening was shaping up to be so much better than I'd envisioned this morning. I kept racking my brain, knowing I had something else to discuss with Grace tonight.

Then it dawned on me. I'd wanted to talk to her about Gaston and Felicia, but this didn't seem like a good time.

For now, I was simply going to focus on pleasing this gorgeous woman.

Chapter Twenty-Five

Zachary

"Grace, I have to say, you win a hundred points," Beckett said on Saturday, putting an arm around her shoulders, "for facing a LeBlanc-Broussard brunch."

She laughed, and I had to give it to my brother—he could put anyone at ease.

Grace and I had arrived an hour ago. After the initial introductions, I quickly realized that she was starting to get overwhelmed. And yet my younger brother had made her feel comfortable.

"Well, why not? I've heard so much about all of you," Grace said as she loaded more food onto her plate.

I thought we were going to have an easygoing brunch as usual, but my grandmothers had gone all out. They'd cooked seven different dishes and three desserts. They hadn't put the sweets on the table yet, but they announced what they were serving beforehand, so we'd all save enough room.

I swatted my brother's arm. "Take your hands off my woman."

He started to laugh. There were several other snickers around the table as well.

Fucking hell, I hadn't meant to sound so serious. It had been a tease, but still, seeing him so close to Grace triggered something inside me.

She cocked her head in my direction, smiling. Her eyes were just as full of joy as they'd been when I took her to that festival. Being with me made her happy.

"Someone's territorial," Anthony replied.

"Hell yes," I said, loud enough for everyone to hear. The whole table started to laugh.

"But all the LeBlancs are like that," Georgie commented.

"How would you know?" Beckett asked in fascination.

"Just by observing. Obviously, I don't have enough information on you two." She pointed to Anthony and Beckett. "But I think it's safe to say you're the same. After all, Julian was territorial even before we were actually together. When..."

She stopped talking, looking at Grace with a quick glance.

"It's about my brother, isn't it?" Grace asked, wincing.

"Sorry, I didn't mean to bring it up like that. But you know what? I actually owe it to him that this one started to play a knight in shining armor and pretended to be my boyfriend. Gave me a smoking-hot kiss right in front of Kyle."

"Oh, I bet he was seething. Serves him right." Then Grace sighed. "On behalf of my brothers, I am sorry for all the ruckus they've caused."

"Oh, nonsense, girl," Isabeau said. "You do not apologize for the sins of others."

"I quite agree with that statement." I pulled Grace closer to me and kissed her shoulder.

"So, I just wanted to say with everyone here," Celine started, "that I think the match between our perfumes and lotions and your creams is made in heaven, Grace. People are truly enjoying them. We've even had some of the neighboring shops ask if we could put them in touch with you so they can carry them too."

My grandmothers truly were saints. I smiled at them.

"Sure. You can give my email to everyone. I'll respond personally," Grace said.

"We'll do that."

"And if I don't reply to them within a few days, they can also call me. Some of my emails do land in spam, especially from unknown senders."

"We'll relay the information," Isabeau said.

I was surprised at the affection in her tone. The two of them clearly had a soft spot for Grace. It made me happy, but I just didn't expect it. Celine and especially Isabeau were notoriously suspicious of strangers. Winning them over wasn't very easy, though they'd softened over the years.

But her mentioning emails made me think about Gaston's again. He hadn't even replied to my offer. I was of two minds to discuss it with Grace, see if she'd changed her mind about us both going into business together. But there was no point in bringing it up right now. Gaston would eventually answer, and then we could both sit together and have a good talk.

"I'd love to carry your products too," Georgie said. "They don't fit with the whole Books & Beads vibe, but I carry miscellaneous products from time to time."

"That would be amazing. I'll send you a kit of my most popular items."

"Great, I'm happy to display them for you." Georgie beamed

The fact that even my brother's fiancée was embracing Grace like this made me a thousand times more grateful for my family than I'd ever been. I knew for a fact that not everyone's family was like that. Growing up, going to the schools I did, I realized most people's families were simply interested in appearances.

"Now we have another question," Isabeau said. "Which of the dishes is your favorite?"

"That's a trick question, so be careful," Anthony said.

"Nah, dude. That's fine. If anything, I think Isabeau is starting to like Grace more than us. She hasn't even asked us which one's our favorite," Beckett replied.

Isabeau looked at my brothers in exasperation. "That's because I already know which one it is. Hasn't changed over the past thirty years. I don't expect it to change for the foreseeable future."

"Right. That does make sense," Anthony conceded.

Grace grinned from ear to ear. "I'm biased because I've always been a fan of gumbo, but it's the gumbo. I think it's the best I've ever had, just as the jambalaya from LeBlanc & Broussard is."

Scarlett beamed at her, hoisting Simone higher up on her hip. "I'd take credit for the compliment, but I'm just following the recipe that Isabeau and Celine left at the restaurant."

Both my grandmothers were about to burst with pride. Yeah, they were looking at Grace as if she was practically a LeBlanc already.

I swallowed hard. Damn, how did my mind go there so easily? And yet now that it had, I couldn't help but linger on the thought. Damn it, this woman was turning everything I knew about myself on its head. I never truly set out to be a bachelor forever; I simply took things as they came. Yet now that I was thirty, I'd never even seriously considered taking the next step with a woman, let alone how her name would sound with my last name. I wasn't going to question things too closely now either. I was happy with Grace. That was all that mattered.

Once we all finished eating, our grandmothers had us move to the sitting area so we could eat dessert.

"Should I come to the kitchen and help?" Grace asked.

"We're going to need everyone's help," Isabeau said. "It's a lot of plates for the two of us to bring."

"That's just going to transform into eating dessert in the kitchen again," Anthony said.

Isabeau laughed. "I have nothing against that."

"Then come on, clan. Let's all move to the kitchen."

Bella had been pretty quiet the whole day before she suddenly came up to me. She, Grace, and I were at the very back of the group as we headed to the kitchen.

"Uncle Zachary?" she asked, looking at Grace shyly. "Can I ask you something?"

"Yeah, sure."

"Would you like me to give you privacy?" Grace asked her.

Bella hesitated for a brief second before saying, "No. Maybe it's better to have someone else's opinion who's not part of the family too."

I blinked rapidly. Jesus, she truly sounded like an adult when she spoke like that. Well, at least a teenager, which she was on her way to becoming.

"Do you want to give me your opinion, Grace?" she asked.

"Sure." Grace sounded completely taken aback.

"Okay. So, I asked Uncle Zachary a while ago if I have to be friends with the popular girls in school even though I don't really like them and they want me to drop my friends. And he told me that I don't have to, that I can stick with my friends."

"Your uncle is right. No one can pressure you into not spending time with your friends."

"Well, now I have another issue. The mean girls are spreading lies about *me* behind my back. And I'm not sure what to do."

Fuck.

"Oh, I do know, actually," Grace said. "Whenever someone comes up to you with those lies, you just stand your ground and tell them the truth. You don't even have to tell them who spread the lies. You can just tell them that it's not true."

"And that will work?" Bella asked skeptically.

"For some it will. For those that it doesn't, they're not worth your time anyway."

I nodded. "I quite agree with her."

She grinned. "Thanks, Grace. Thanks, Uncle Zachary. You two are the best. Now I'm going to ask everyone else in the family what their opinion is too."

"Why?" I inquired.

"So I can see which one is the most popular."

I started to laugh as Bella darted away, and then Grace said, "Oh God, she's so adorable. And you're adorable with her."

"I love her. We all do. Do you like kids?" I asked. Then I remembered what she'd told me what felt like months ago, that she and her husband had been trying to have children.

"Yes, I do," she said, beaming from ear to ear. "Growing up, I always dreamed of having a girl and a boy. Or two girls. I always felt a bit like the odd one out having two brothers, you know?"

"I have five, so I don't even know how to answer that."

Grace laughed. "I really like your family."

"Small secret—they like you too. And another piece of advice: don't say you have a favorite dessert."

"Why not?" she asked, looking at me strangely.

"Because my grandmothers are testing new recipes, and although they say they want feedback, they actually want praise. To their credit, though, their desserts are very good."

"Navigating LeBlanc-Broussard politics isn't for the faint of heart, is it?"

I chuckled. "You've got that right."

Chapter Twenty-Six

Zachary

The shipping crisis lasted longer than I'd anticipated, but it seemed to finally settle down a bit two weeks later when the final order was confirmed.

"Hell yes," I exclaimed, jumping up from behind my desk.

I looked from the window down to the courtyard of LeBlanc & Broussard, feeling like a haze had lifted. I might be good with challenges and maintaining a cool head, but that didn't mean they didn't exhaust me. In fact, if it weren't for Grace these past few weeks, I would've lost my cool more often than not. But being with her balanced me. She was exactly what I needed, and I couldn't wait to see her later this evening.

I really needed to stretch my legs. As I was preparing to go downstairs for a coffee break, I heard the phone buzz on my desk. I had a cardinal rule: I never took it with me on breaks because it defeated the whole purpose. I'd gone against the grain the past two weeks because it was a difficult time, but now I'd fully intended to leave the thing behind.

"Fuck," I said, going back to my desk. If anyone reported any other delays...

But the name on the screen made me relax. *Gaston.* I immediately put it to my ear.

"Hello," I said.

"Hey, Zachary."

"I haven't heard from you in a while."

"Listen, we'd be more than happy to work with you. Your offer is fantastic, and I'm sure we'll be able to collaborate well."

"That's great," I said. "I'll get everything approved by our legal department and will send the money maybe as early as next week. Just one question. How about Grace?"

We hadn't talked about this at all. Partly because we'd both been extremely busy at work, and partly because there hadn't been much to talk about since I hadn't heard from Gaston and Felicia much lately.

"She's not in the running anymore."

I frowned as I decided to head downstairs while talking on the phone even if it meant I'd keep it with me during my break.

I was very surprised and wondered what made her change her mind. I planned to ask her that tonight, because I would've been willing to walk away if it meant she got it. But maybe she decided that she had already her hands full with growing her company. After the grandmothers collaborated with her, it was like the whole city wanted to do business with Grace too.

"So, listen, Felicia and I were wondering if you could drop by the ranch with all the contracts and everything else that's needed. It's a difficult time for us to make a day trip to New Orleans."

"Sure, don't worry. I'll go there. But first I need to draw up all the paperwork."

"Yeah, yeah," Gaston said distractedly.

"All right, then. I won't keep you any longer."

Admittedly, I was distracted as well, thinking about Grace. She'd seemed very adamant about investing in the beginning, so it was strange that she'd no longer be interested. I wondered what her reasoning was to pull back. Was she overwhelmed at work? Because I could help out there as well.

I needed to get to the bottom of this, and I'd do just that during our date tonight.

———

Grace

I sighed as I sniffed the new samples of creams. I loved them. A large segment of the market was looking for fragrance-free creams because they figured it meant they were more natural. But since we worked with all-natural products, I was proudly boasting how nice ours smelled. This particular one had lilac. Yeah, Isabeau and Celine inspired me. I loved the scent, but it didn't add any benefits to the cream itself, like rejuvenating or calming properties. But it was divine.

I closed my eyes, and for some reason, it made me think of Zachary. The man had taken over my life, and I was enjoying it. I had never imagined this, just as I never imagined that his family was going to embrace me so openly, especially after the debacle with my brothers. I really couldn't believe the way Kyle had treated Georgie. She was an amazing woman and certainly didn't deserve that. My brother was a lot like my ex—an asshole through and through.

Opening my eyes, I put down the jar of cream and emailed my team to send this sample to Isabeau and Celine's store too.

They'd sent me updated sales numbers last week. It wasn't going to be a big stream of income, but it was a good start. I liked the idea of seeing my products in shops around the Quarter.

Just as I sent the email, my phone beeped, and I smiled when I saw the screen. It was Gaston. *Finally!* I'd been waiting for his call. It made me antsy that he hadn't said a peep.

I immediately tapped the speakerphone, setting the phone on my couch because I still had cream on my hands and didn't want to smear my screen.

"Hello, Grace."

"Hi, Gaston. Haven't heard from you in a while."

"I know, I know. I promise I wasn't stringing you along. So, listen, I don't want to waste your time any longer."

My throat closed up. "Oh?"

"We've decided to take Zachary's offer."

I swallowed hard, feeling as if he was pressing on my neck, obstructing the influx of air.

"Right, right." I cleared my throat. "Is it a matter of money? Or do you think he's a better collaboration partner? Because if it's money, I can improve my offer."

"Zachary told us that he can outbid whatever you offer."

"I see." I couldn't help but feel betrayed.

"We're really sorry. Felicia and I like you a lot, and you bonded with the horses beautifully, but this is a business decision after all."

"Yes, of course. I understand."

"And you did say you don't want the two of you to invest together."

I swallowed hard. That's right, I'd told him that.

"But you're welcome to come out here to the ranch and spend time with the horses whenever you want."

I smiled. "Thank you, Gaston. That's very considerate of you." I was feeling very off-kilter.

"All right, then. Have a great rest of the week."

"Sure. You too."

I wanted to ask a bit more about Starlight, but I couldn't bring myself to. I was so disappointed.

As I hung up, I rubbed my hands together until the cream set in. I needed to get out of my apartment. This place was chock-full of samples, and right now it felt claustrophobic. I took the phone carefully between two fingers, opened the door with an elbow, and then headed straight downstairs.

Zachary had told him that he could always outbid me. It was smart to let him know that from the get-go, but I couldn't shake off that feeling of betrayal. I couldn't help thinking about my ex, who always wanted to one-up me no matter what. But this wasn't the same thing.

I was headed straight toward the bagels and donut shop.

Oh God, I didn't want to lose out on the ranch. I'd already gotten attached to Starlight even though we'd only spent a few hours together. But I'd always been very quick to bond with animals. Once upon a time, I'd been quick to attach to people too. My ex-husband changed that. Zachary had helped me rediscover my old self. Now I was wondering if I'd made a mistake. My heart was growing heavier by the second.

Why didn't he tell me he planned to outbid me? Of course Gaston and Felicia would go with whoever offered more. If I was faced with two investors and one would give me more money, I'd take it too. Unless they were an asshole, which Zachary wasn't. He was a smart businessman and was going to be an asset to the ranch.

I didn't understand why he hadn't said a word, though. I'd been getting my hopes up for no reason. I would've preferred to know if I'd been out of the running all along.

There was quite a line in front of the bakery, so I had far too much time to fret over everything until my turn came.

"What can we get you today, Grace?"

"Something extra sweet."

"That kind of day, huh? You do like chocolate and pistachio, so how about I give you one of these?" She pointed to two donuts that were beautifully glazed with both pistachio and chocolate.

"Perfect. You're right, it *is* a double-glazed kind of day."

"And double-treat kind of day," she added on a wink, and I nodded.

That was certainly true. I was going to eat them right away, but I still let her pack them in a nice paper bag. I only resisted opening it until I stepped outside. Then I immediately dug my hand into the bag, retrieving the first donut and biting into it. Sugar usually improved my mood from the very first bite, but this time it didn't quite work. I was still mulling over these past few weeks and all that had taken place.

Had Zachary mentioned the ranch and I missed it somehow? I did have a history of overlooking details to pretend that everything was okay. But I was certain this wasn't the case. Things with Zachary had been different compared to my marriage. Utterly and completely different.

When my phone beeped with a message, I went straight to the nearest bench and sat down. I didn't want to multitask and risk dropping my remaining donut. Checking the screen, I saw it was Zachary.

Zachary: What time do you want me to pick you up?

Oh, that's right. We have a date tonight. My stomach somersaulted. I'd been looking forward to it this whole week, but now I truly wasn't in the mood anymore.

I put a hand on my chest. Yep, that was betrayal I felt right there. No reason to pretend. I didn't want to leave him hanging, so I typed back quickly.

Grace: I'm not in the mood for going out tonight. I heard from Gaston. Congrats.

Then I quickly sent another message.

Grace: I hope you understand.

He replied immediately.

Zachary: Sure, no worries. We'll go out another time. I'll go with Anthony and Beckett.

I put the phone down, biting into my second donut. After finishing it, I went back inside the bakery. I needed an additional treat, and I wasn't even sorry about it.

Chapter Twenty-Seven

Zachary

Since Grace didn't have time to go out tonight, I texted Anthony and Beckett. They'd asked me to join them at a bar this evening, but I'd flat-out refused because I had plans. I had half a mind to insist Grace go out tonight because I wanted to celebrate with *her* and find out why she wasn't interested in the ranch anymore. But she was having a busy week, so I didn't press. I had plenty of time to pamper her and talk to her this weekend.

After leaving my office, I went directly to Bourbon Street. Julian had snapped up this location after Kyle skipped town. I was glad he did. Love it or hate it, Bourbon was the place to be in the French Quarter.

It wasn't my favorite type of hangout. It was more of a club than a bar, but it was convenient and the closest to LeBlanc & Broussard. Anthony and Beckett were already sitting on one of the half-moon couches in one corner. Anthony waved at me. As I sat down, I realized they had three drinks.

"Bold of you to already order for me."

"They're testing some new drinks, and I volunteered us as guinea pigs," Anthony explained.

"Good thinking. If not us, then who? What am I drinking, by the way?"

"I forgot the name. Just keep in mind if you like it or not."

I glanced at their glasses. I had something different.

"So?" Anthony asked as I took a sip.

"It's good," I replied.

"So, why are you hanging out with our sorry asses? Did Grace ditch you?"

I shrugged. "Maybe I just decided that I want to hang out with my brothers."

Anthony tilted his head. "No, that's not it. You were very quick to turn us down because you had plans with Grace."

"She's busy tonight and isn't in the mood for going out, and I wanted to celebrate, so I figured why not call you?"

"That way of talking makes us feel really special," Beckett said. "So, what are we celebrating?"

"The owners of the ranch called me today. They want me to be the sole investor."

"That's great news. I know you really wanted that."

I nodded. "I do."

"So, how about Grace?" Anthony asked.

"Gaston said she isn't in the running."

"Right," Beckett replied, then held up his glass. "Okay, let's clink even though we're all drunk."

"Wait a second," Anthony said. "What do you mean, she's not in the running?"

I looked straight at him. "She probably decided not to go forward with it."

"She told you that?" he asked.

"No." I waved my hand. "We never talked about it. We always had better things to do. And honestly, Gaston took so long to reach out that I assumed he'd changed his mind about taking on an investor at all."

Anthony looked at Beckett.

"What?" Beckett raised a brow at him.

"I'm thinking," Anthony replied. He turned to look at me again, frowning. I wasn't used to seeing my younger brother frowning.

"What's bothering you?" I asked.

"The question is, why isn't anything bothering you?"

I jerked my head back. "Sorry?"

"So, you were supposed to go with Grace tonight?"

"Yeah," I replied, wondering why we were back to that.

"And then you talked to this owner of the ranch who told you that he's moving forward with you."

"Exactly."

"And then Grace ditched you?"

I rolled my eyes. "She didn't ditch me. She just said that she's not in the mood to go out tonight and congratulated me on the investment. Then 'I hope you understand.'"

Both of my brothers groaned.

"What?" I asked.

"Dude, come on," Anthony said.

I replayed the messages in my mind, a visual reel of each text.

"Fuck," I exclaimed. "I assumed that 'I hope you understand' just meant that she hoped I didn't get mad for her bailing on our date."

"No, I think your woman might be upset," Beckett said. "But don't quote me on it in case I'm wrong. Definitely not my area of expertise, knowing how women think or understanding what they want."

"Shit." I took out my phone and looked at her messages again. I blinked. "Fuck! You're right."

How the hell did I misinterpret this? True, I'd been running on adrenaline for the past few weeks, but it was right there in black-and-white.

I ran a hand through my hair, looking up at my brothers. "I need to leave."

Beckett laughed. "Making us feel even more special."

"Dude, I screwed up. I need to fix it."

"You know," Anthony said, "this is the first time I've seen you lose your cool... Well, maybe that's not the right way to say it." He took another sip, tilting his head like he was having a lot of fun. "But you're usually so in control of yourself, so sure that you can solve any situation or challenge. Now you're fretting over some messages."

I stood up, pointing at him. "It's not just a few messages. You know that. Stop making fun of me."

"No chance," Anthony replied.

Beckett laughed again. "Dude, sorry to break it to you, but you can't boss us around. But it's fun when you try. So, by all means, continue entertaining us."

"Another time. I need to go see Grace."

"Where is she?" Anthony asked.

I considered this for a second. "She told me her schedule for today..."

Why wasn't I remembering it? My neurons were more fried than I thought.

Then it hit me. "She worked from home today. That's right. I was supposed to pick her up from home."

"Dude, you really are fucking exhausted," Beckett said in a serious tone.

"As I said, it's been a rough few weeks."

Anthony straightened up at the table. "You know you can always count on us to pick up some slack whenever you have an emergency, right? We know you're the fixer and all that, but we're here to help."

"Thanks. I'll keep that in mind for the future. Right now, I need to find my woman and apologize."

"No way we can help there," Beckett said.

Anthony nodded. "We would probably just make it worse."

"I didn't ask the two of you to help," I pointed out.

"I will say, though," Beckett replied, "that we already did by pointing out that you can't read, I guess."

I shook my head. "Stop giving me a hard time."

"There you go again, trying to tell us what to do. It's not working," Anthony argued.

"Okay, I'm leaving now. I have to get to Grace."

I hurried out of the bar, pulling my keys out of my pocket as I practically jogged to the parking lot behind LeBlanc & Broussard. I wanted to see Grace right now. The more I thought about our messages, the more callous my replies seemed. Like I was rubbing it in her face.

I should've discussed this with her earlier, but with everything we both had going on, it slid to the back burner. I didn't even give much thought to what would happen when Gaston finally contacted us again. I just assumed we'd work it out.

When I arrived in Grace's neighborhood, I parked right in front of her building. As I stepped out of the car, I checked her window. The lights were on—she was home. I didn't want to call and check beforehand because this apology was a face-to-face kind of thing. I was lucky that her favorite bakery was open until late into the evening and on the same block as her building.

I stepped inside and looked at the display case. They were almost sold out.

"Good evening. How can I help you?" the sales assistant said.

"I'll have all your remaining donuts with... Is that pistachio?"

"Yes. And before you say that no one likes it—"

"My girlfriend does."

Her eyes lit up. "Oh, you're dating Grace, right?"

"Exactly," I said.

"I thought you looked familiar. She loves them. She was in here earlier today—twice, actually. She looked pretty down, too, so I'm sure these are going to cheer her up."

Fucking hell. She'd already been here twice?

"Please add those cupcakes also." I pointed behind her. One was pink, the other blue.

"On it." She smiled. "You're bringing out the big guns."

Nah. These were far from being the big guns. They were just damage control.

As soon as I paid and she packed everything up, I headed to Grace's building. I was about to buzz the intercom when I realized the door was open. The doorman signaled with his head that I could come in.

"Good evening." He didn't ask for my ID. Then again, I'd been here often over the past few weeks, so he knew who I was.

I went straight to the elevator but didn't have any patience to actually wait for it, so I jogged up the stairs. Usually, when I encountered a difficult situation, I liked to prepare beforehand if possible. But right now, my mind was completely blank. The only thing I knew for certain was that I needed to see her and make things right.

Once I reached her door, I knocked, but nothing happened. I knocked again, louder. Was she not home? Maybe she'd forgotten the lights were on.

I rang the bell next, and then I finally heard footsteps. Grace opened the door a moment later.

"Hi, Zachary. Did you text that you were coming?"

She stood back and then swallowed hard. She was wearing a delicious nightgown—black silk that barely covered her pussy. Her nipples were peeking out.

Jesus, Zachary. Grovel first, seduce later.

"No." I held up both bags. "I come with goodies."

"Sure."

She opened the door wider, and I stepped inside. As far as her enthusiasm at seeing me, I had hoped for much better. But then again, what did I expect?

"Listen. Tonight... Well, today, actually, when you texted," I said, giving her the bag with the pistachio and chocolate donuts, "I didn't realize what your messages meant."

She opened the bag, then stopped in the act of reaching inside. "What do you mean?" She took out one donut and bit into it immediately. "Oh, I love these, though I already had a few today."

I was wondering if she was talking about the donuts because she didn't know what else to say.

"Grace..." I stepped closer, pushing a strand of hair behind her ear. A few stray ones caught at the edge of her mouth, which was now sticky from the sugar. I disentangled them slowly. "I didn't realize you didn't want to go out because of what went down with Gaston."

She frowned, swallowing hard. "I'm not even sure what to say."

"Let's talk about it."

The noise in the background was incessant. I kept looking over my shoulder. "What are you watching?"

She grinned sheepishly. "Yet another Hugh Grant rom-com."

"There's more than one?" I asked, stunned.

"Oh, Zachary. Yes, there are many. How can...? Never mind." She lowered her eyes to the donut.

"Listen, we should talk about the ranch. I didn't bring it up because..." I ran a head through my hair. "It didn't seem to be going anywhere considering Gaston didn't contact either of us. I figured we'd talk when he got in touch."

Grace nodded. "Look, I'm not even sure why I'm upset."

Fucking hell, she's upset? I'd thought she might be confused at best, not upset.

"But you outbid me, so it's fair that he chose you as an investor," she continued.

"Wait a second. What do you mean, I outbid you? I asked Gaston today about you, and he just said you're not in the running."

"Yes... *because* you outbid me."

I just stared at her.

"Let me pause this," she said, walking into the living room.

I took off my shoes and followed her. Something wasn't right here.

"I don't even know what your bid was, so how could I outbid you?"

After pausing, Grace glanced at me sideways. "You told Gaston that no matter what I offered, you'd outbid me. Which is fair, but—" She sighed. "I wish you'd told me sooner. Then I wouldn't have gotten my hopes up."

I blinked rapidly. "Grace, I told him that a million years ago when I first talked to him. I completely forgot. I wouldn't just outright ask him now how much you're bidding so I could purposefully offer more—not without talking to you, anyway."

"Oh." She'd taken out the second donut but put it back down and placed the bag on her coffee table. "Right. Okay. Sorry. I assumed... Well, never mind."

"Tell me what you assumed." I was panicking now. I wanted to make this right.

I cupped her face with both hands, and something changed in her body language. She seemed less closed off than when I'd first stepped in.

"I jumped to conclusions." She winced and added, "I felt betrayed."

"And I didn't even pick up on that. I truly am running on too little sleep! But that's no excuse. I wouldn't do something to one-up you. Why would you think that?"

She broke eye contact, looking down at her hands. She seemed to shrink in front of me.

"Because of him?" I asked softly.

Grace shook her head, looking back up. "No, I think it's time I stopped blaming everything on him. I'm obviously not healed even though I've tried hard. Apparently not hard enough." She frowned, closing her eyes. She seemed to be having this conversation more with herself. "I can't believe I didn't just ask you what was going on. I preferred to hole up in here by myself."

"Grace, you don't have to be so hard on yourself. Babe..." I caressed her cheeks in small strokes, and she opened her eyes again.

"I'm sorry," she whispered.

"For what?"

"Today."

"Grace, listen to me. We all interpret things incorrectly or misconstrue them. Just know I would never do anything to hurt you."

"But this is different, and you know it. I carry more baggage than I thought."

"So? Who cares? I love you, Grace. We're on this journey together."

Her eyes instantly softened. I felt the tension in her entire body ease even though I was only touching her face. I wanted to look down and double-check if her hands were relaxed by her side, but I didn't trust myself to glance downward. Even in the midst of a serious conversation, Grace's gorgeous body could totally throw me off my game.

"You love me?" she whispered, like that was an outrageous thing to say.

"Yes, Grace. How can you doubt it? You mean so much to me, babe."

To my astonishment, she became teary-eyed. "I figured I'd have to heal completely to deserve to be loved."

"You deserve everything, and I want to be the one to give it to you. I wouldn't change a thing about you, Grace."

"I love you so much, Zachary. I can hardly believe the things you're saying."

I stepped even closer, kissing one corner of her mouth and then the other one. I could feel the adrenaline leaving my body. I'd been so on edge since reading her second text. Only now was I starting to relax.

"We're in this together, Grace. Everything is a journey. And I'll say it again—a million times if needed. You don't need to have it all together or anything to be worthy of love. I love you. I love you more than I thought I could be capable of. You don't have to do anything to earn it."

She looked up at me from beneath her eyelashes. Her mouth curled up in a small, shy smile, but then it grew in size. Then she put her hands on my shoulders. I knew what would follow even before her feet left the floor. I braced myself just before Grace jumped into my arms, my hands immediately going to her ass cheeks to hold her up—and she was fucking commando.

Chapter Twenty-Eight

Zachary

I groaned, but she sealed her mouth over her mind as I held her tightly. Her ass was damn near perfection. *She* was perfect. Why didn't she see it? But it didn't matter. I was going to be there at her side every day to make her see how perfect she was.

I kissed her hard, and she whimpered slightly as I walked with her through the living room. I liked holding her up, but I could kiss her even better if I could prop her against something. The kitchen island would do. I set her ass on it and rested my hands on her thighs, deepening the kiss.

I was dying to have her. But for now, I wanted to explore her mouth. I wanted this intimacy, so I slowed down, enjoying tasting pistachio and chocolate on her tongue. I fucking loved the sounds she made—small whimpers at first, then outright moans. I pulled her ass closer to the edge of the counter, spreading her thighs so I could comfortably step between them, then clasped her ankles with both hands, keeping them in place the way I wanted them. Her whimpers and moans became even more pronounced. She moved her hands from my shoulders to my chest, tugging at my collar.

I pulled back with a smirk. "You always want my shirt out of the way."

"Of course."

Her mouth was already red. I kept her legs in place as her fingers worked on my buttons, then moved my hands farther up her calves until I reached her knees. After she finished with my shirt, she pushed it off my shoulders.

"Fuck, Grace."

I captured her lips again. Her mouth was addictive—today even more so than usual. Maybe because we'd both admitted how deeply we felt for the other. Maybe because Grace was finally accepting that she was mine.

Wanting to kiss the rest of her body, too, I pulled back, looking down into her cleavage. "I deserve a prize," I murmured.

"For what?"

"For not jumping your bones the second you opened the door. You look so damn sexy in this nightgown. It might be my favorite." I touched one of her breasts over the fabric, and she instantly arched her back. "But now I want to take it off."

She grinned. "Hmm, I didn't see that coming at all."

She shifted on the counter until her nightgown was past her ass, and then I tugged it over her head. I always liked how messy her hair got after I undressed her.

"You're so fucking gorgeous. I'll worship you every single day."

I changed my mind. This counter might not be good for fucking because she was much higher than my dick. But I could do other things in the meantime.

I lowered my mouth to her breasts, and she propped herself up with her palms behind her. She was leaning back at the perfect angle so that I could explore her breasts. She raised one leg, planting her foot on the counter.

Deciding that I wanted her in the bed after all, before we got too caught up in ourselves, I straightened and lifted her into my arms, carrying her to her bedroom.

She giggled. "Someone remembered to find the bed first this time."

"What an exception, right?" I said before lowering her onto the bed and getting rid of the rest of my clothes.

She looked at me hungrily, especially at my cock. It was already hard.

"How long has it been like that?" she asked, rising to her knees and wrapping her hand around my cock.

"Honestly? Since I walked inside and saw you in that nightgown. I could barely string two words together."

She looked fucking beautiful with her lips just inches away from my crown.

"Those were good words for someone whose mind was somewhere else entirely." Then she swept her tongue over my crown.

I didn't have any words left at all, just a guttural groan. She pulled back and fisted my cock. I instinctively pushed my hips forward, but I wanted to do things differently even though having her mouth on me was filling me with fucking life. It was everything I needed to be happy. And her pussy. I always needed her pussy, which was why I pulled back completely.

"I wasn't done," she protested.

"I know, beautiful. But I've got other plans for us right now. Or more specifically, for you." I tilted my head. "Lie on your back and spread your thighs wide."

She licked her lips and her eyes widened, but then she sat back down and opened her legs before lying back. Her pussy was perfect, pink and wet already. I put one knee on the bed and pushed one finger inside her.

"Oh..." she moaned.

Then I pushed the second one in. *Hell yeah.* I stretched her lightly. She was so damn tight.

"You need an orgasm before you can take my cock, beautiful," I warned her.

Her breath hitched. "Zachary," she panted between moans.

I curled my fingers inside her, reaching her G-spot. I wasn't touching her clit yet; I needed to open her up first, and then I'd work her up all in good time.

From up here, I could see her entirely. Her face, the way her mouth scrunched up with every sound of pleasure. Her eyes were already unfocused, and her cheeks were tinted red, as was her pussy. Her nipples were even harder. Her chest was moving rapidly. She was even curling her toes and fingers. *Fuck yes!* She was getting closer and closer. I could feel her inner muscles working hard.

I took out my fingers and brushed her clit with both of them.

"Oooooooh," she exclaimed.

Then I changed my position without taking my hand off her clit so I could easily slide into her. Putting both her feet on my chest so her ass was hanging off the bed somewhat, I kept working her clit as I pushed my cock inside. She cried out beautifully and then came that very second, before I'd even managed to push inside her all the way.

I stopped as she clenched tight around me, not wanting to risk hurting her. I was looking at her, positively transfixed. I'd never tire of watching her come and succumb to me like this. She writhed on the bed, tossing and turning wildly, tugging at her own hair, her breasts, and then at the blanket.

The second her inner muscles relaxed, giving in just a bit, I pushed all the way in.

I groaned. "Fuck, being inside you is the best feeling in the world."

I turned my head sideways, kissing her ankle. She pressed her arm against my chest, lifting her ass slightly. I realized what she was doing. She wanted to move too. My woman was ready for fucking, and I didn't hold back for even one second. I pushed in and out, and her moans of pleasure turned into cries of agony again.

We both moved frantically. Even though she'd already come, I felt the tension build inside her again. Her body was so easy to read for me; I knew what every sharp intake of breath meant, what every cry signaled. I tilted slightly forward and moved her feet off my chest so they were hanging sideways. This angle was so much more delicious, and I could hit her G-spot too.

"Zachary!" Her eyes flew wide open, as if she was shocked by the sensations overwhelming her.

"Fucking hell, Grace. I love you, woman. This is real."

Being entwined like this with her felt incredible. I propped my hands next to her on the bed so I could lean down and lick one nipple, all the while thrusting inside her. She put her heels on the bed as well. She could slam against me even better now.

"Zachary, I can't believe it, but I'm going to..."

"I know, babe. Just let it happen. Enjoy it. Come all over my cock."

She closed her eyes again, and I saw her mouth open as if in slow motion before the cry tore out of her. Looking between us, I noticed that she was touching her clit. The sight, combined with her cries of pleasure, was too much. I came hard too. So damn hard, in fact, that my thighs nearly gave in.

I lowered myself over her completely, putting my hands between her buttocks and the mattress, just driving in like a madman while she was still coming. I was determined to give her every drop of my climax too.

Then I stilled and pulled my hands from under her ass, planting them at her sides once more. I was completely out of breath. I was dripping with sweat, and Grace was too. I pushed myself up onto my elbows, enough that I could watch her. Her eyes were closed, her lips curled up in a smile. I kissed her chin and then one corner of her mouth.

She opened her eyes. "You're watching me," she murmured.

"You're so damn beautiful, Grace. And you're all mine. Only mine."

She nodded and moved her palms up my biceps, resting them on my shoulders for a few seconds before putting them at the sides of my neck. Then she nodded. "Only yours. I love you. And it's bigger than me."

I'd never heard her sound so raw.

I pressed my forehead against hers. "It's the same for me," I assured her.

"You have such a way with words. I don't, but I know exactly how I can prove just how deeply I feel for you."

"And what is that?"

"I'm going to share the remaining donut with you instead of eating it all by myself."

I burst out laughing, straightening up. "You truly do love me more than I imagined."

CHAPTER TWENTY-NINE

GRACE

One year later

"God, I love this place so much," I said.

I looked around the fully renovated ranch. The first batch of campers was arriving tomorrow. Zachary and I came so we could help Gaston and Felicia with last-minute preparations. In the end, we invested together, and I was ecstatic about it. I never would've thought that I'd trust anyone enough to intertwine my life with theirs. But with Zachary, I was ready for anything.

My business had been doing incredibly well over the past year. More and more stores in the Quarter had started to carry our products. I still made the most money still through the online shop, but that was okay. After all, I'd never assumed that I would make a lot selling in physical stores. But having more shops sign up for our products meant that the Deveraux name was in the clear.

My parents were ecstatic. They'd started to attend more events throughout town and were more at ease when going to the theater or other public places. They were good people and deserved to enjoy their retirement without wondering what people were whispering behind their backs.

We hadn't heard from my brothers, but we also weren't really expecting them to be in contact. They'd never done well with defeat. The way I looked at it, time healed all wounds, and maybe sometime in the future they'd make their way back. I just hoped they learned their lesson before they did.

"Are you already done?" Zachary asked, coming up behind me.

Felicia said they didn't need much help with anything except preparing gumbo, and we'd both been cooped up in the kitchen until now. Then she remembered that she still had some flowers to water, and I'd volunteered to do that.

I showed him the empty sprinkler. "Yep, all done. Should we get out of Gaston and Felicia's hair?"

"Want to go by the stables first? You didn't get to comb Starlight today."

I smiled sheepishly. "You caught on to that, huh?"

He chuckled. "Babe, it's what you do whenever you come here. You find one excuse or another. The last one was particularly hilarious."

"What? It was honest."

"Really? 'The wind blew too hard and now his hair is tangled up'?"

"But it was."

"He's a horse."

I pushed his shoulder playfully. "Hey, don't let him hear you. I'm convinced that he might believe he's human."

Zachary laughed and tilted forward, kissing my forehead. "You're so damn lovable, I swear."

I'd never tire of hearing him say such incredible things.

His phone beeped, and he glanced at it, then groaned.

"What's wrong?" I asked.

"Yet another one of Anthony's secretaries quit."

"Oh. He's having trouble keeping them?"

He sighed. "You could say that. No one lasts more than a few months. I believe one or two described him as an arrogant asshole before leaving."

My eyes bulged. "That doesn't seem like Anthony at all. He's so friendly."

"He is. Except with his assistants."

"Why?"

"There's a story behind that, but I'll tell it to you another time."

Hmm... Suddenly I wondered if Isabeau and Celine could have something to cure that. Possibly even lilac.

Oh, damn. I was spending way too much time with those two.

Another crack of thunder rumbled across the sky, and we both looked up.

"Let's head to the stables and then go back to the city. Gaston kept saying that today's storm will be sizable," I murmured. Looking at the sky, I was certain that he was quite right.

The second we entered the stable, Starlight neighed. I swear he sensed my presence even before he could see me. Zachary and I walked to him together, passing the other occupied stalls along the way. The ranch acquired more horses in the past year. After much debating, we'd decided to ask Gaston and Felicia if they'd like to add more cabins, not just renovate the existing ones. They'd been ecstatic about it, so that's what we did. With the increased capacity, they'd needed more horses.

"Hello, pretty boy," I said, stopping in front of him. "What do you say about getting your hair done?"

Zachary grinned and pointed to a gorgeous silvery box at the side of Starlight's stall.

"What is that?" I asked.

"I figured it was time Starlight got a new combing set."

I melted. "You're spoiling my boy. And me."

I picked up the box, turning it around. It was by a very well-known comb-maker for horses.

I loved Zachary to the moon at back for doing this. He knew how much Starlight meant to me.

I opened the box and took out the comb. Then I noticed there was a second box inside that looked quite different. It was velvet.

I furrowed my brow. "Do they make accessories for horses now?"

"I don't know," Zachary replied. His tone was playful but also tense.

I immediately took out the velvet box and put down the bigger one because I needed both hands to open it. I gasped as I did so. This was an accessory, all right, but it wasn't what I'd thought.

I looked up at Zachary. He was smiling from ear to ear as he took the box from me and got down on one knee.

"Grace Deveraux, I've waited for this day for months."

Warmth enveloped me as if he was giving me a hug. "Months?" I whispered.

"Yes. I wanted to do this on a day that meant something to us. Inaugurating the opening of our first project together is the perfect moment. I know that when we first met here at this ranch, things looked bleak. I never would've thought that one year later, we'd be standing here together. Although, I will admit that I thought you were smoking hot."

I started to laugh and put both hands on my cheeks because my eyes were burning. In case I teared up, I wanted to brush them out of the way before Zachary could see them.

"Grace, I love you. And I'd love nothing more than for us to be husband and wife. Our lives are already intertwined, but this would make me the happiest man on earth."

He cleared his throat, and I figured he was going to add something more, but he didn't. He simply swallowed hard, and I realized that my gorgeous, amazing man who always had the right words for everything was now too emotional to speak. So I decided to speak up instead.

"Yes. God, yes, I'd love to marry you."

My heart gave a double beat. I was on pins and needles, but for all the good reasons. I never imagined saying yes to anyone ever again. But with Zachary, it felt right. It felt perfect, like I was doing exactly what I was supposed to do.

"I want to be your wife. I want us to be together, as you said so beautifully last year, and be each other's companion on this journey. You're the best man I've ever met, Zachary. I thought all the wrong things about you in the beginning. I was certain I'd seen right through you. But in my defense, you thought the worst of me too."

He laughed. "Not the worst, just didn't have the greatest impression. But discovering who you truly are, Grace, has been the privilege of my life because you're incredible," he said as he put the ring on my finger.

It was a huge diamond, princess cut. It had to be at least five or six carats, and I knew it would steal the show no matter where I went.

Suddenly, I realized this was perfect because I wanted that. I wanted everyone to know I'd soon be Mrs. LeBlanc.

"I love you," Zachary said and slowly rose to his feet.

I was still transfixed by the ring. It had tiny round diamonds in the band as well. They were so finely crafted that I could feel them by running my finger on the band.

"This is the most beautiful ring I've ever seen. God, I love you so much!"

"I'm glad you like it," Zachary said. The emotion in his voice mirrored mine.

He cupped my waist and pulled me close. Then he kissed me slow and hot, and I couldn't get enough.

I wrapped my right arm around his neck but kept my other hand in the air, afraid that I could damage my ring, as I kissed him right back. I could stay like this with him forever. I didn't want this moment to end. It was magic, us out here on the bayou in this place that first brought us together as, well, enemies. And now we planned to become husband and wife.

The sound of thunder startled us apart. I lowered the arm I'd been holding up in the air, and Zachary grinned at me.

"What?" I said defensively, bringing my left hand close to my chest. "I didn't want to risk losing the ring in my hair or something like that." I was being ridiculous, of course, because it fit perfectly. It couldn't just fall off.

The unmistakable sound of raindrops on the roof filled the air.

"Oh no. We should make a run for it to the main house." I looked at Starlight. "Sorry, baby boy. You're going to get your hair done another time, okay?" I put my forehead on his muzzle so he knew that I loved him. It was just perfect that he'd gotten to witness this magical moment.

Zachary closed the box of Starlight's new combing set, and then we both stepped out. As we reached the door of the stable and he pushed it open, I grinned. It was already a downpour.

"Gaston was right. This will be a storm."

Zachary smiled at me. "We've got plenty of experience with that too."

I tilted my head and wiggled my eyebrows. "Are you insinuating what I think you are?"

"Hell yes. Storm gets too bad, I have no problem locking us up in one of the cabins now that they all have AC and actual nice beds."

I grinned. "Neither do I."

Printed in Great Britain
by Amazon

63080827R00137